This is a work of fiction. Similarities to real people, places, or events are entirely coincidental.

FORTUNE'S HAND

First edition. February 29, 2016.

Copyright © 2016 Tyrel Viner.

ISBN: 978-1530902484

Written by Tyrel Viner.

Fortune's Hand
Sorcerer's Diary Series: Book 1

By: Tyrel Viner

To: My Beloved Katey,
Happy Birthday Princess!
Thank you for being wonderful

— Tyrel Viner

Copyright © 2016 by Tyrel Viner
All rights reserved. This book or any portion thereof may not be reproduced or used in any manner whatsoever without the express written permission of the author except for the use of brief quotations in a book review.
Printed in the United States of America
First Printing, 2016
<u>Cover art by:</u> John O'Seadna

Excerpt

"...I closed my eyes and tried to let the night carry my anxiety away. The skin crawling sensation of someone watching was less severe than it had been down in the village, but it still tickled at the back of my mind. I sucked in a breath and stalked toward the far point of the bluff. There was an old worn trail up there that swept down the front of the cliff and ended in a small ledge of rock overlooking the town.

I rounded the corner onto the ledge and stopped short. My breath caught in my throat. A man stood on the ledge in front of me, nearly invisible in his dark cloak. One of his feet rested on a large rock near the cliff's edge, his face lit only by the glowing embers of his pipe. He turned to stare at me and I recognized the seemingly lifeless eyes of the caravan's belligerent leader.

We stared at each other wordlessly for several long seconds. I could feel the hatred rising from him like a foul stink and saw a dozen signal lamps resting against the rock face behind him.

The sensation of his presence wormed its way over my skin and tugged my gaze back down toward the valley where he had been watching. Even through thee gathering mist, moonlight glinted across the valley floor. It reflected from dozens of exposed sword edges or glittering off pieces of polished black armor. Flickering torchlight from the town outlined an army of people crawling across the open ground. On the ledge in front of me, the man's hand drifted across his waist toward his sword hilt. Somewhere on the ground below, the army surrounding my town disturbed a sleeping bird which screamed against the hills. I turned and ran..."

1.

My horse was in her normal spot, a rotted out half-shell of a stable stall. No other horse would have stayed, but Varya was different. When I'd found her, the son of the local Lord had been about to kill her. Most people considered her rust colored hide and jet black mane and tail a terrible omen. Village wisdom said anyone who rode a horse with such an ill-fated color combination was doomed to hard roads and long rides, but I'd loved her from the start. She had cost me everything I had, and a trade I preferred not to think about, but she had been worth both.

The stable boy stood beside the stall, shifting his weight from foot to foot and chewing his bottom lip. "You shouldn't do this, Cary. Master Owen is going to be really mad."

I yanked my saddle out of its hiding place and swatted it clean with an oil rag before settling it onto Varya's back. "I don't care if Master Owen gets mad at me. If one more of those dirty caravan guards tries to pull me into his lap, I swear to the new gods I will stab someone. Then where will we be?"

Kevin bit his lip even harder than he had been and twice turned as if to run back to the inn and tell Master Owen where I was, but he stayed where he stood and watched me finish saddling my horse. "I don't want to get in trouble," he whined.

"I'll be back before dawn. If anyone asks where I am just lie and say you haven't seen me."

"I can't lie! It's a sin!"

"Keep your mouth shut and I'll give you a copper penny."

Kevin's eyes grew thoughtful. "Two?"

I laughed. "If you steal a bag of that rich feed the caravan horses are getting and hide it in Varya's stall I'll make it three."

"Done." Kevin beamed.

I swung into Varya's saddle and rode out the stable's rear door, pointing her nose out of town and letting her choose her own speed. The mid-summer heat of the day had broken shortly after sunset and a cool breeze made the wheat fields on the Western edge of town dance in the moonlight.

Voices I didn't recognize drifted across the field toward me and I eased Varya to a stop. I'd had enough of strangers for the night. I peered into the night, trying to figure out if the voices were moving or if I could simply go around. Finally, a match flared. The flame pulsed up and down over the bowl of a pipe and I groaned inwardly. It was another pair of caravan guards on watch duty.

This merchant train was the most heavily guarded caravan I'd ever seen. It was guarded by a full score of armed men, all of them wearing the same black uniform below a coat of mail. It had been impressive at first, but they'd treated everyone in town like complete jackasses for two whole days now. No one knew what was in the caravan or where it was heading, and we were all starting to not care. We just wanted them to leave.

I shifted in the saddle and turned Varya, guiding her down the edge of the field to hide the sound of her hooves. We eased out onto a winding farm path that cut between farms and led out of town. I tried to relax and enjoy the cool breeze, but the night felt heavy and oppressive again. The guards were everywhere. They were watching the roads and the inn and now they were stationed in the fields? What was so valuable that they were guarding the entire town? I could feel my skin start to crawl like I was being watched and I kicked Varya a little faster. There was a mist rising already and now I wanted to get out of town more than ever.

We rode through fields and along farm paths until the lights of town began to fade behind us. There was no longer any doubt in my mind about the feeling. Someone was watching me, but I couldn't tell who or where they were. Finally, I turned Varya toward the mountains and let her pick her way up the rough trail toward Haftan's pass. No one from the town would be up there tonight. I could finally get a chance to relax.

Haftan's pass was the main reason our village existed. The main road led straight down it into town, but I was coming at it from the side, climbing an old cart path up toward the higher bluffs alongside the pass that overlooked the town.

Nearly an hour later, we neared the top of the bluff I'd been aiming for. The light from the moon was good and I let Varya choose her own pace and footing on the uneven ground. I watched the sides of the trail, studying the plants and bushes, hoping to find some of the rarer night blooming flowers from the area. Most people in town didn't climb these mountains after dark and I could sell the blooms to any of the town's herb collectors or midwives.

I pulled Varya to a stop near the top and slid from the saddle to lead her toward the clearing on the bluff top. Originally, it had been a well-used and patrolled campsite, but since the town had grown at the bottom of the pass and the larger caravans took the newer road, the clearing had largely been left to the use of the romantic or the restless. The romantic just wanted to be left alone, and the restless usually left you alone if you knew what you were doing.

The clearing was empty and I let the reins fall from my hand. Varya snuffled my arm affectionately and moved away to search for some of the wild carrots that grew nearby. I wasn't worried about her getting too far away. She knew enough to stay close.

I closed my eyes and tried to let the night carry my anxiety away. The skin crawling sensation of someone watching was less severe than it had been down in the village, but it still tickled at the back of my mind. I sucked in a breath and stalked toward the far point of the bluff. There was an old worn trail up there that swept down the front of the cliff and ended in a small ledge of rock overlooking the town.

I rounded the corner onto the ledge and stopped short. My breath caught in my throat. A man stood on the ledge in front of me, nearly invisible in his dark cloak. One of his feet rested on a large rock near the cliff's edge, his face lit only by the glowing embers of his pipe. He turned to stare at me and I recognized the seemingly lifeless eyes of the caravan's belligerent leader.

We stared at each other wordlessly for several long seconds. I could feel the hatred rising from him like a foul stink and saw a dozen signal lamps resting against the rock face behind him.

The sensation of his presence wormed its way over my skin, tugging my gaze down to what he'd been watching on the valley floor. Even through the gathering mist, moonlight glinted from dozens of exposed sword edges or glittered off pieces of polished black armor. Flickering torchlight from the town outlined an army of people crawling across the open ground. On the ledge in front of me, the man's hand drifted across his waist toward his sword hilt. Somewhere on the ground below, the army surrounding my town disturbed a sleeping bird which screamed against the hills. I turned and ran.

I felt the swift rush of air behind me and the jagged tip of the man's sword tore a ragged gash through my cloak. I threw myself up the path, scrambling with hands and feet to gain speed. The man's heavy boots clattered on the loose rock as he tried to gain purchase and handle his sword at the same time. It slowed him enough that I gained the clearing several steps ahead of him.

My feet flew through the long grasses as I raced toward the outline of Varya's distant form. She whinnied and reared as I watched, striking out with her front hooves. I gulped air, trying to get enough breath scream. I never got the chance. The shadows shifted in front of me and moonlight glinted from the cracked enamel of a black gauntlet a second before it slammed into my nose.

I crashed to the ground, too stunned to move. My nose was splayed sideways across my face and blood ran down my chin. The man who hit me gave me a leering smile and hauled me to my feet by the front of my dress. The world swam in my vision and I emptied my stomach, vomiting down the front of the man's armor. His smile vanished with a growl and he knocked me sprawling to the ground.

He dragged me through the clearing by my hair, aiming for a stand of nearby trees. I kicked at the ground and clawed at his hand, but my fingers slid uselessly off his hard gauntlet.

He threw me to the ground at the base of the trees. I landed head first, slamming my broken nose against an exposed root. The world dimmed at the edges of my vision and pain roared through me. I curled onto my side, covering my face with my hands. The man stood over me, fumbling at the clasps of his vomit smeared breastplate. The heavy metal plate clanged to the ground near me. His hands dropped to his pants and his face opened in wide, a gap-toothed smile. He planted his booted foot in my stomach, driving the air from my body and kicking me onto my stomach.

I clawed at the ground with weak fingers and tried to crawl forward. He caught at my leg and hauled me back toward him, flipping my dress above my waist with his other hand. I jammed my hands against the ground with the last of my strength and mule-kicked backward as hard as I could. The hard-heel of my riding boot found the manhood he'd been reaching for and the man crumbled around his pain. I lunged to my feet, scrambling blindly into the forest.

My heart pounded in my ears and my breath rasped in my throat. The forest around me was thick and dark. Only the occasional splash of moonlight filtered through the leaves and I was already half blind with nausea and pain. A heavy hand landed hard on my shoulder and spun me sideways into a massive tree. I dropped to the ground, choking down my screams of pain and kicked at the hand grabbing my leg. My dress tore beneath the jagged gauntlet and I was free again. I lunged to my feet and ran on instinct. Somewhere in front of me was help. I didn't know how I knew, but I was sure I'd be safe if I could only find it.

The guard on my heels hit me with a frantic lunge and knocked me sideways. I fell screaming into a massive pile of deadfall and the world seemed to dim around me. My screams bounced from tree to tree as rough hands grabbed my legs and began dragging me backward. Three men held me and another two looked on with wicked smiles. I kept screaming, emptying my lungs as loud as I could, again and again, praying someone would hear me.

Silver light suddenly ripped the night apart. I cringed, blinking away at the blindness. More than a dozen silhouetted forms shimmered into existence, rising out of the ground or simply sparking into the air. The restless had come!

My blood ran cold. I had never seen so many restless in one place. Old spirits of men and women who had died while lost in the mountain mists and were cursed to wander until their bodies were found.

If you knew what you were doing, and knew the paths to avoid, the restless were relatively harmless, but to the ignorant or the lost they could be deadly. Their dim lights and bleak wordless calls could lead people astray deep into the forest or off the same mist laden cliffs they'd fallen from themselves. Alone, they were deadly to the unwary. In groups their powers grew. When enough of them gathered, they could leave the misty paths of the mountains and walk the streets of town. They could draw the breath from someone's body, killing the person and giving the restless an empty vessel to inhabit for a time. The possessed body immediately became frantic, speaking gibberish and lashing out at anyone near. No one understood what made them this way. We only knew they grew stronger in groups. And there were more restless surrounding me than I had ever seen before.

I screamed in complete terror and twisted back the way I had come, desperately reaching toward the rapists and monsters behind me. It would be an easier fate than dying to become an empty vessel stolen by hungry ghosts.

Blades whistled through the air behind me. Rage and panic warred on the faces of the men behind me, but it was useless. Steel can't hurt ghosts. Their screams grew desperate as the silver bodies of the restless pressed against them. One of the men fell, clawing at his eyes. Another sank to his knees almost gracefully as a glimmering silver form poured itself inside him.

Silence wrapped around me even though I knew I was still screaming. No sound reached my ears not even when one of the soldiers was borne to the ground beside me by the press of the empty dead. I looked down. Thick fingers of cold mist wrapped across my body and wound slowly up my legs. I gasped for breath, suffocating as my vision faded.

2.

The blazing light of day beat against my eyes. My throat was so raw I could barely breathe, but I managed to twist my head enough to block some of the light. Pain seared through me and wracking coughs shook my body. I clenched my eyes tight and grit my teeth against the roaring pain in my head. When it finally started to fade, I lay quivering on the ground. My face was swollen and tight and I reached forward to gently touch my nose. The smashed bone sat sideways on my face, covered in dried blood. I grunted stupidly and grabbed hold with both hands, wrenching it forward with a sickening pop. I gasped in pain. My stomach wrenched. I vomited on the ground and passed back out.

Every inch of my body ached when I woke again. My head throbbed and every time I tried to take a deep breath I coughed dried blood. Every time I moved my head even slightly, the world threatened to spin out of control and drop me back into darkness. I clawed grime away from my eyes, trying not to think about what it was made of, and blinked until my vision started to clear.

I was in a dense thicket surrounded by heavy thorns and thick brush. My clothes were torn and most of my skin was covered in jagged scrapes and scratches. I didn't recognize anything. Even the mountains seemed to have changed. I worked my tongue around in my mouth until it was wet enough to let me swallow before turning my head slowly, searching for the fallen bodies of the soldiers. Nothing.

My heart started pounding. Had the restless carried the bodies off? Walked them off like possessed puppets to raise havoc among their army? Did that mean I was safe? What about the village? My heart skipped a beat. The Village!

Terror gnawed at me. Had anyone survived? Had the mists reached low enough out of the mountains before the attack? Were they all cursed? The endless questions wheeled through me. After a few moments, I pushed the panic away and drew in a ragged breath. I was alive. That was a start. The sun was warm and bright and I saw no trace of either ghosts or men as I turned slowly from side to side. On my left a rough trail had been broken through the heavy brush. My eyes locked on the path and held on.

The path was fresh and deep. The broken branches still gleamed wet in the sun and showed their green insides. Whoever had broken the path had done so recently. Deep gouges scored the ground, churning the dark soil and scattering old leaves. My eyes flicked toward my boots before I could stop them. The toes were mostly clean, but the heels were caked in fresh dirt that rode high up the back, like I'd been dragging them through the dirt.

I looked again at the path. It was rough and torn. It was also very low. Branches that crossed between the bushes more than waist high hung unbroken and unmolested. Loose leaves clung to the higher levels of thorny plants. A quick glance at my mud-stained cloak and boots confirmed that I had been lying on my back when I was dragged in here.

I swallowed hard. Any person dragging me into this thicket would have broken every branch on the way in. Or at least thrust them aside and knocked the leaves to the ground. That left two choices: a beast that must have wandered away before eating me or something that didn't have to move branches to get through...

A stick snapped behind me and I dove through the brush toward the path. Something caught my foot and I slammed, breathless, to the ground. I twisted to look, feeling the blood drain from my face. A skeletal hand protruded from the ground. Its bony fingers clenched around the tip of my boot. I finally released the scream I'd been holding and yanked my foot free. Ancient flesh tore away from the dried bones, scattering fragments of fingers through the air. I scrambled backward on hands and heels, wild-eyed, burying myself deep into the bushes of the thicket.

I skittered to a stop against the trunk of a massive thorn bush, whipping my head from side to side. There was no trace of anyone or anything nearby, but a second later I heard another stick pop. My eyes snapped toward the pile of torn brush where I'd woken. One of the branches had broken as I shifted and another had sprung free, righting itself now that I had moved.

My shoulders slumped beneath my cloak and I crawled forward again, tugging myself free of the massive thorns. My right hand landed on something small and rough as I crawled. It was a small bone. A piece of the dead fingers I'd scattered in my panic. I stared at it for a moment while cold fingers walked along my spine. In the corner of my eye I knew I could see something that hadn't been there before, had been seeing it since I stopped scrambling in fact, but I was too afraid to really look at it. My mouth went dry and I stared at the small bone in my hand for what felt like hours before raising my head to look at the torn dirt of the thicket floor.

Half of a skeleton was visible beneath the heavy growth of thorn bushes. The bones were ash white and dirt-stained. One long arm had come free when I'd yanked my boot out of it's grip and now lay apart from the twisted ribcage that was partly hidden among the thorns. My heart stopped beating. I froze, staring at the pile of ancient bone and praying it would not begin moving on it's own. I didn't know if it really could, but there were too many stories.

After a few seconds of stillness I crept forward, whispering prayer after prayer and collecting the scattered pieces of bone from the forest floor. Too many of my father's old stories crowded the back of my mind about the horror of ghosts and the torment of the unburied. He had originally taken us to the village at Haftan's pass to study the curse of the restless. We stayed long enough for him to die there and I hadn't been able to bring myself to move on since.

Freeing the skeleton from the tangled buses was slow work, but I couldn't leave the clearing until it was done. I'd disturbed a grave and broken someone's earthly remains. If I didn't make it right somehow I could be haunted or cursed. That thought terrified me more than moving the skeleton. The priests and storytellers all agreed; the magic of the forest was dark and dangerous. Too many people who tangled with it never came back the same.

I worked slowly, freeing the skeleton from the bushes and dragging into the small torn clearing. I whispered whatever prayers I could think of while I worked. Hoping they would give the dead man peace or give me peace of mind. Remnants of sturdy clothing still clung to the bones. The rusted metal buckles and tarnished buttons of a once wealthy man tore free and fell into the dirt and the rotted remains of a wide leather belt held both an old knife and a massive saber.

I hesitated for a moment before pulling the old knife free. I would not have done it, but I needed the knife to pry the rest of the body out of the heavy brush. My vision blurred around a stream of tears as something cold and terrifying ate its way up my spine. The blade of the heavy knife scraped against bone one final time as I tore away a pile of moss covered rotting leaves. Sunlight bathed the ancient skull and I suddenly felt like there was someone standing behind me.

My blood ran cold and I froze in place. My grip tightened on the handle of the knife as I turned sideways enough to peer over my shoulder. The air behind me shimmered and tongues of silver fire rippled away from the ghostly silhouette of one of the restless.

A shudder ran through me. I had never seen a restless in the daylight. As far as I knew, they weren't supposed to be able to come out in the daylight. I held the heavy knife in my hand. It was useless against a ghost, but I kept it close because it was all I had. I backed toward the wall of the thicket, watching the empty ghost.

It was a man, or at least used to be. I could see the hints of muscular arms and legs and the chest was too broad for a woman. His face held no real features, only the vague suggestions of eyes, nose, and mouth.

The featureless silver form stood tall and still, watching me without coming nearer. I held myself from screaming. It wouldn't do any good either. Instead, I kept my eyes glued to the silver form, waiting for something to happen. After a long moment, the strange face shifted to gaze downward at the skull near the base of the thorn bush.

My jaw dropped and my father's voice echoed in my ears. The restless were damned to wander for their time or until their bodies were found. Somehow, the ghost standing before me and the rotted skeleton at my feet were the same person. Somehow, one of the restless had dragged me away from the fight to where his body lay.

The featureless gaze shifted back to me, waiting. I gaped at it, clueless as to what it wanted. "I..." I stammered, searching for something to say. "I found your body. You...You're free now."

The spirit stood there without moving, waiting for something more. After a moment, the face turned, shifting toward the body on the ground. I swallowed, nodding. "I'll bury you properly and make sure your grave is marked. You can rest now."

The restless ghost threw his silver arms wide and burst into a shower of silver sparks that faded on the air. I threw myself away from the silver flames, but they vanished before they even came close, replaced by a soft breeze and an indescribable feeling of gratitude.

With the spirit gone the body seemed different. It was like a piece of crockery an old friend had left behind, nothing more. I looked it over carefully whenever I took a break from using the heavy knife to scrape out a grave in the thicket floor. Inside a still sturdy pouch I found a pair of dirty gold coins. My jaw dropped at the sight and I quickly slipped them inside the small pouch I wore around my neck. Two gold sovereigns was almost more money than I'd ever seen in a single place. The old sword was wired tight to the worn belt but I managed to work it free with the knife and placed it to the side to take with me. He wouldn't need any of it any more.

It took me the better part of an hour to carve out the grave in the middle of the thicket. When I finished I gently laid the bones into the new grave, covering it with loose dirt and several heavy branches I'd cut from the surrounding bushes. I didn't know the man's name or profession, but I whispered the old prayers I'd learned when I was younger, asking the New Gods to grant the dead man peace and entry into whatever realm would suit him best. I whispered my thanks a final time and crawled out of the deep thicket with the heavy saber.

Nothing looked familiar. The trees that filled the area were tall and thick and the soil I'd cut through in the thicket was deep and black. Most of the area near the village had been clear cut for lumber and to make way for farm fields, which meant I was most likely in the old growth forest on the far side of Haftan's pass.

I was at the bottom of a long, steep-sided gully that blocked the possibility of finding any familiar landmarks, but I needed to find something soon. My stomach was raw with hunger and my thirst was so great it was starting to make my head hurt again. My hands were raw and bloody and my fingers were already starting to swell, but the gully seemed to narrow to my left and with luck I'd be able to climb the sides to higher ground and get my bearings.

My mind was overrun with dark thoughts. With every step I took I could only wonder if I even had a home left to go back to. Thoughts of my friends, of Varya, of Master Owen, of all that I knew and found safe butchered or burnt swept through me until they drowned out everything else. I had to stop several times, forcing myself to breathe and push away the thoughts, focusing only on the ache in my body and the effort required to keep going.

I collapsed in a heap at the top of the gully. My legs and arms were shaking from exhaustion. My throat was raw with thirst. I could barely move at first, but after a while the shaking stopped, and a while after that I managed to claw myself up to standing with the help of a nearby tree. My shoulders slumped beneath my cloak. Nothing looked familiar. I swore under my breath and stomped along the ridgeline to higher ground. If I couldn't find anything familiar then I at least needed something that wasn't endless forest: a road, a river, anything.

The sun was already half set when I reached the point of the ridge. The long shadows of early twilight covered nearly everything in darkness, distorting shapes and distance. I spat weakly and turned away to ease myself back down the ridge and collapse near the base of an old tree. I wedged myself among the exposed roots, thankful that the nights were still warm.

My dreams were dark. Armies of skeletal soldiers chased each other through the forest, screaming unheard battle cries through useless mouths.

I woke sometimes after midnight, surrounded by mist. The moon was the only source of light that reached me. It turned the point of the ridge where I lay into an island of stability, surrounded by clouds. My skin tingled with pins and needles as I shifted in place, trying to get blood and warmth back into my fingers and toes. As I shifted, I noticed a shining light off to my left. I staggered to my feet to cry out, but my harsh cry stuck in my throat as I recognized the flickering silver light of one of the restless. I shuddered and sank back down, drawing my cloak tighter around me, praying I wouldn't join them.

Cold mist clung to everything in sight. It seeped through my cloak and stole the warmth from my body. I curled into a ball, wrapping my arms around my knees and shivering under my cloak. A shudder of cold fear shook me and something in my pocket rattled. I reached inside and scraped my fingers along ancient bone. I gasped in surprise and yanked the bones free, emptying my pocket into my palm. It was the remnants of the skeletal hand I'd scattered in my first panicked flight from the grave.

I stared down at the pile of bones in my hand. Had I forgotten to bury them? I shook my head. It didn't make sense. I'd spent all day walking and working. How I had not noticed them before? The cold, rough surface of the bones played against my skin and I suddenly realized I *had* noticed them before. I'd been noticing them all day. They'd been a soft and comforting weight in my pocket, reassuring and welcoming.

The memories were dreamlike. I could remember feeling the bulge throughout the day, touching it whenever I was tired or whenever I felt hopeless, but at the same time I hadn't noticed I was doing it until right then. The pile of small bones felt reassuring in my hand, but part of me was very afraid. Part of me wanted to throw the pile of bones away and run screaming in the other direction. The bones and memories both reeked of raw magic. They were a reminder of everything I wanted to forget. They were also my only source of comfort.

Holding the bones somehow felt like being near an old friend. They were warm to the touch and made me feel like I wasn't alone. Tears slipped down my cheeks. I didn't even know where I was. I didn't know if anyone was looking for me or even if they were alive. I was cold and hungry and scared. I looked down at the pile of soft bones in my hand and felt the panic ease away from my heart.

I cradled the bones in my hand and let their warmth seep into my palms. "You know," I whispered to the pile of broken bones in my hand. "My father loved to tell stories. They were always full of great deeds and battles. They were about heroes and challenges and I really used to love them. I didn't realize how horrible they were to live in."

The bones sat in my hand without responding, but I kept talking. "A lot of the stories were full of signs and portents, omens and harbingers. They were like little hints to show the hero which way to go." I smiled softly. My father's stories had always been able to make me smile. "I could really use something like that right now." I straightened and closed my eyes, smiling at the memories. I let the ancient bones trickle through my fingers to the ground. "Where do I go from here?"

The rattle and clack of falling bones faded echoed into the surrounding mist. I sighed and shook my head, laughing at my own silliness as I looked down. The bones lay on the ground, clumped into the three near-perfect branches of an arrow pointing away into the darkness.

The sight drove daggers of terror into my spine. It felt like fire burning into my mind. I skittered back into the recesses of the tree where I'd been sleeping. My heart pounded and I shook with fear, hugging my knees to my chest until darkness took me.

3.

I woke with the dawn, my eyes locking on the twisted skeletal arrow on the ground in front of me. I stared at it, unmoving, for several long minutes. The worn bones pulled at my vision, demanding I acknowledge their message. I swallowed hard and shook myself out of the tangle of tree roots. After another moment, I gathered the small pile of bone from the ground and slid them into the small pouch at my side. I needed more than just stories and nightmares.

My joints and muscles ached with every slow move back toward the point of the ridge. I was hoping that landmarks might be easier to find in the daylight. The day brightened quickly at the point of the ridge and the forest spread endlessly in all directions. Almost everything looked the same, except for a single large bluff far across the forest. It was the tallest hill I could see and was nearly bald rock on the top. It was a long walk, seven or eight leagues without food or water, but if I was lucky, it could be the bald top bluff that marked the northern span of Haftan's pass. If I was wrong it wouldn't get me any more lost than I already was. A shock ran through me. The bluff was in the same direction the arrow of bone had been pointing.

The sun rose through the day as I walked. I tried to keep my pace relaxed and even. Walking too fast would only tire me out and remind me of my need for water. Once I made it down to the forest floor I kept track of my goal through occasional breaks in the trees. The bald top made it easy to identify, which is why it made a good boundary to the pass. If that's what it was.

Twice along the way I found plants that I knew were edible and once I managed to scavenge a few handfuls of acorns from beneath a massive oak. Together they managed to quiet my stomach, but still left me raw with thirst.

By the time I stumbled to the base of the massive bluff, the sun was already setting. The last few miles of my journey had been at a snail's pace. My arms and legs shook with every staggering step and a growing numbness seemed to be growing through me. I found a level spot in some shade and slumped to the ground in a heap.

I didn't wake until well after sunrise the next morning. My heart beat too fast. I was light-headed and I could barely breathe. All I wanted was more sleep. I couldn't think about anything else except sleep and my need for water. I lay on my side for almost an hour, half awake, until I started to notice the pain in my side. I was laying on a rock. I groaned and shifted, but it didn't help. The rock was still there and the pain was growing. Finally, I heaved my side high enough to swat at the ground below me. There was no rock. It was the pouch of bones at my side.

I ripped the bag off my belt and tried to throw it away. The damn thing had led me here to die. The worn leather slapped against a tree less than an arm's length away and dumped the bones across the dirt. I slumped back down. Too tired to care.

My eyes stared blankly at the empty leather bag in front of me. One of the longer bones had landed near it, just on the other side from me. After a while my eyes started to focus, more from boredom than interest. Another piece of bone lay beyond the first, forming a straight line with the bag.

The panicked flapping of my heart stopped for the span of a breath and another spasm hit my body. I lurched up to prop myself on an elbow and cough until I could barely breathe. My vision faded out briefly before coming back in, blurred and unfocused. Almost nothing made any sense anymore. I coughed some more, straining my mind to try and figure out what was happening. The only thing I could see clearly was a line of small bone stretching away from me.

Before I knew what was happening, I had started crawling forward. Every joint and muscle complained and all I wanted was rest, but I kept crawling, gathering the bones as I passed them.

When I'd collected the last bone I stopped moving. There was nowhere else for me to go and I couldn't think of anything to do except settled back to the ground and enjoy the soft breeze. I only knew that I was grateful for the soft breeze. The wind was cool and musical. It sounded like soft wind chimes and smelled like water.

Water!

The word echoed through me and I crashed through the last few feet of brush to skitter to the ground near a small spring. It was small, barely more than a trickle leaking from the crack in a ledge of rock, but it was cool and wet and ended in a small pool about the width of my forearm. I crawled across the grass and thrust my face into the small muddy pool.

The water burned down my throat and made me sick almost as soon as it hit my stomach. I gagged, but managed to avoid throwing up the muddy water. I pulled away from the pool, splashing water on my face and trying to force myself to go slow. My skin seemed to suck up the water like a dry rag, but after a while I finally felt strong enough to try another drink. This one tasted like a muddy kind of heaven. I started to cry as tension eased from my shoulders, the desperate ache fading from my stomach.

It took more than an hour before I moved away from the muddy spring to search the area around the stream, hoping to find something edible. All I found were the empty branches of a blackberry bush that had been stripped bare. I thought about cursing and shrugged. It didn't really seem worth the trouble.

I sat near the small stream until midday, drinking my fill and repeatedly soaking my skin as much as I could. By the afternoon my strength had returned enough for me to start walking again. I took a last drink and started working my way up the hill. I tried to stick to game trails as much as I could, moving upward and around toward the face of the bluff, stopping often to search for food and to look for any sign of the worn road leading to Haftan's pass.

One of the game trails I stumbled on was fresh, scarcely more than a break in the bushes. It led me into the branches of a small blackberry bush heavy with fruit and I fell to my knees, hungry beyond belief. I tore the berries from the branches and shoved them into my mouth.. The juice ran freely down my throat, joyfully filling my belly. I ate until my stomach stopped aching and more, laughing at my good fortune and stuffing myself silly. I filled the pocket of my dress with the rest of the berries I could find and started back up the hill.

It was a long climb without civilized trails. I followed the game trails where I could, but often had to abandon them in favor of moving constantly upward and across. Hours after I left the stream I stumbled out of a stand of trees and onto a stolen point overlooking the worn caravan road leading through Haftan's pass.

Relief washed over me. I finally knew where I was. Whatever else was happening, I at least had a place to start. The pocket of my dress was empty again. I'd finished the last of my berries a while ago, but the creeping anxiety of being lost was finally gone. I turned away from the road, slipping down the side of the ridge and working my way up the caravan road as quickly and quietly as I could.

I hit the top of Haftan's pass and ran along the road, turning up the side path toward the clearing on top of the bluff, racing back toward the ledge overlooking the town. My thoughts pounded and all thoughts of caution fled. I actually laughed as I ran through the trees, wishing the past few days had been little more than a strange fever-dream brought on by the restless.

My feet flew over the ground of the clearing and I leapt up the last of the hill to the point overlooking town. The closer I got to the edge, the slower my feet moved. I dragged myself to a stop at the edge of the clearing, staring down into the valley. I couldn't speak. I couldn't move. It felt like my heart was dying.

My eyes swept over the ground, taking in the whole of the valley even though I was unable to process what I saw. Some of the buildings in town were still standing. They were a jarring normality amid the burnt out remains and piles of ash that remained of the rest of the town. Tears streamed down my face and I noticed with a wry shake of my head Master Owen's inn would need a new roof soon and someone had left the smithy door open again.

I focused on the details and forced out the rest. The early grain had been cut and the debris of ransacked houses and barns lay everywhere. Torn rags and bloody clothes were strewn across the ground. I closed my eyes and counted to twenty, breathing slowly before looking again. Scattered throughout the lawns and roads of my town, anywhere there had been open ground, were tall wooden lodge poles with a crossbar several feet off the ground. On each pole were two townspeople, crucified back to back.

I clutched the heavy saber to my chest and stood there, staring at the grave of my town. My feet seemed to move of their own accord, automatically picking out the path back toward the road and down into town.

Most of the girls and some of the boys had been strung up in the nude and their bodies bore the telltale signs of rape. I walked with my head up and forced myself to see everything. I walked through the entire expanse of town, trying to remember something nice about every person I passed.

Something was wrong. There were too few bodies. Over half of the town was missing. Even the remaining buildings were empty. All of the town's livestock was gone. Most of the kitchens and cellars had been emptied, and every scrap of rope or tack had been taken, but there were no extra bodies. Hundreds of people were missing, men, women, and children. Hope fluttered faintly in my breast. Maybe they had gotten away.

From the rear courtyard of the inn I took a ladder and small hatchet from the small utility cabinet and started working my way through town. I climbed each pole as I came to them and cut down the crucified bodies, dragging each of them into the nearest standing building. I laid each one on the floor or in the beds and prayed over each. Once I had placed several people in a building, I lit a fire in the hearth and spread it through the rooms.

I only paused once, long enough to step into the small outbuilding where I rented a room. I didn't own much, and much of what I had was missing, but beneath the bed I still had my traveling backpack. I took my best traveling dress from the wardrobe and packed it along with my sewing kit, hand mirror, and hair brush. All of which had been gifts. I slid the ancient heavy saber into the bag as well and left it on one of the smaller hills outside of town before heading back in to finish what I had to do.

By the time I was done, flames filled the night sky. The only building remaining was the smithy. The thick stone walls and slate roof were too tough to burn. The sky was filled with great plumes of black smoke that carried the sickly sweet smell of burning flesh. I sat on the small hill near my pack and watched the fire dance through town until I fell asleep, completely exhausted.

4.

The bed I woke up in was large, comfortable, and clearly not the hillside. My hands and feet were clean and well bandaged and I was warm and dry under a heavy blanket. It took me a while to recognize the smithy's cottage. I'd only been inside it once or twice, and never for very long. The house was long and warm. Large windows let in the light from outside and the rafters for the loft above were high over my head. There was a well-worn table and chairs, and a massive cauldron bubbled over the fire on the far side of the room. I was alone in the room, but outside the air rang with song.

It was sad and beautiful and somehow sounded old beyond measure. It was a song about life and love and the passing of time. It was a funeral dirge and it made me ache. The sound poured over me, washing me clean from the inside out. I buried my head in the nearest pillow and sobbed until the tears stopped coming. Eventually, I sat up, working my way to the side of the bed. It felt like years since I'd heard another person's voice. I needed to see who it belonged to.

I struggled to my feet even as my body protested. I was sore and aching, but the need to see other living people was too strong to resist. I staggered toward the front of the cabin and the song, gently opening the door so as not to disturb the singer.

Four people stood on the grass outside the cottage's front door. The three nearest to me stood quietly with heads bowed and hands clasped in front of them, but the fourth stood apart, his hands raised out from his body, his head thrown back in song. He wore a rich dark blue vest with the green embroidered vines of a holy acolyte. His hands were spread wide, like he was trying to gather the entire scene of ash and ruins in his embrace. I blinked away a new stream of tears and leaned against the frame of the door, watching the lean man sing.

After several minutes, when his song finally ended, the acolyte walked forward, disappearing from view behind the smoking ruins. I closed my eyes to savor my last view of him for a few seconds before looking again.

The three remaining people stood respectfully silent for a few more minutes before turning to face me. One of them, the taller of the two women, smiled at me and spoke softly to her companions. I couldn't hear what she said, but the two people nodded and walked away, looking to attend to some errand around the side of the house.

The tall woman smiled again, striding across the lawn toward me. I stood to meet her, studying her appearance as she got closer. She was tall, lean, and probably only a few years older than I was. She wore thick buckskin leggings and mid-length boots below a muslin tunic and green half-jacket that bore the heavy black insignia of the Royal Messengers. She wore her flame red hair in a long braid and carried a long curved knife on her belt. Her eyes glimmered in the daylight as she came closer, memorizing every aspect of my features.

Everything a messenger experienced, they remembered forever. Their senses and memories had been change by magic, heightened through a strange process of alchemy until they were far beyond a normal human. A royal Messenger could recall every detail of an event so clearly that a painter could reproduce it. They were magically enhanced mimics and could reproduce a sound or voice with perfect accuracy. Some of them, it was said, could even twist their bodies, mimicking people's faces or copying a person's natural smell with enough accuracy to bait dogs.

Most people thought magic was something that should be left to the New Gods, but this woman was steeped in it. She'd let magic change her very being. Most people I'd known in town wouldn't have even considered her human any longer. She approached me carefully, her nostrils flaring slightly as she caught the scent of my body on the wind and stored it for later use. She stopped just outside of arm's reach, studying me. "Are you okay?" she asked. "Can you tell me what happened here?"

Her boots and her outfit were worn well-travelled. The bone handle of the knife at her belt was sweat-stained from frequent use. She held out an easy hand. "My name is Tara. I'm one of the King's Messengers. Can you tell me your name?"

"I..." The question was so simple and seemed so irrelevant I wasn't even sure how to answer for a moment. "My name is Cary. Uhm... Carytas Empyrean. This is... This used to be my village. The night it was attacked I was out riding. I saw the people who did it, but that was three or four days ago. When I came back here yesterday..."

She looked at the smoking ruins and nodded. "It was on fire."

"N..No," I said. "I did that. The people were all dead. Crucified. I cut them down and took them into their homes before burning it down. It was the only thing I could think to do."

Her soft gaze fell to my bandaged hands. "Are you hungry?" she asked. "The food should be about done."

I led the way back inside and sat slowly into a chair by the massive table. Tara ladled a bowl of stew out of the cauldron and set the carved wooden bowl in front of me. The warm smell of meat and dumplings tickled my nose and my stomach twisted. I was instantly ravenous. I pulled the bowl to me and wolfed down the stew, finishing my bowl before Tara had even returned to the table with her own helping. The Messenger didn't even pause. She switched my empty bowl with her full one and returned to the pot without batting an eye. I relished the warmth in my stomach, the feeling of food and fullness.

"All of the people with me are Landsmen," she said, settling into the chair nearest me. "They're elite soldiers. We're tracking the people who did this."

I nodded and ate. This time I managed to taste the food before I swallowed. Tara sat calmly beside me. She seemed content to eat and let me take as much time as I needed, breaking her silence only to introduce me to her companions as they entered.

First through the door, almost before Tara had settled herself was a short, small built woman in a long dark greatcoat and knee high black boots. She carried a strange looking weapon almost carelessly in her right hand. It looked like an odd combination of half club and half blunt spear. She had silver hair pulled loosely behind her and long slender ears jutting upward beneath a strange, tri-cornered hat.

My spoon fell back in my bowl still laden with food and I stared in stunned silence. I couldn't fathom what horrible spell had cursed this otherwise beautiful woman with such a strange deformity. She strode easily across the room, spooning stew into a bowl before turning. Her rich blue eyes met mine and narrowed. She lowered the bowl to the table. "Is there a problem?" she asked in a truly dangerous tone.

My jaws clicked shut and I stammered, "Y...You have pointy ears!"

The woman jerked like I'd slapped her. "What of it?" she barked. "You have a crooked nose."

"I do not!" My hand rose to my face. "My nose is just f-"

My fingers touched my face and I froze. Tara burst into surprised laughter. I ran to the water bucket and stared at my reflection. I couldn't quite believe it. My nose slanted to one side, slightly crooked where it had broken. I must not have gotten it straight when I set it. I hung my head and muttered, slinking back toward the table in embarrassment.

The short woman with the blazing eyes still stood on the other side of the table. Her chin was raised in pride and even at her smaller stature she radiated confidence and power. I met her gaze and ignored Tara's continued laughter. My face flushed. "I'm sorry, my lady. It was wrong of me to judge you by your differences without knowing the full story. I've just never seen such a strange omen. Would it offend you if I asked how you came to be so strangely cursed?"

Her bowl of stew slipped from her limp fingers and clattered against the wooden table top. She looked at Tara with wide eyes and tried to speak, her mouth working soundlessly for several seconds. I could feel the blood draining from my face. I couldn't imagine what I'd done wrong. Tara's laughter choked to a halt. She stared at me, paling as she struggled to breathe past her laughter. "Great Gods Cary," she choked out, nearly falling out of her chair. "Haven't you ever seen an elf before?"

The small woman erupted in harsh, barking laughter and collapsed into a chair. I just stared. I'd only heard of elves in stories. They were from a continent far across the western ocean. I didn't know much more than that. No one I'd ever met had even seen one. My voice was very small. "I've heard of elves," I said. "But I...I didn't know they had pointy ears."

Tara laughed even harder, holding her stomach and slipping out of her chair onto the floor. The small woman stood and moved around the table. Her harsh barks of laughter faded to a warm smile. She put her hands on my shoulders and kissed me gently on the cheek. "My name is Serena Lightpull and my ears rise to points because I'm an elf." She took a step back. "Now, tell me your name."

"Cary."

"Okay, Cary." Her eyes gleamed. "What kind of curse ruined your nose?"

I laughed. "I know," I said. "It's horrible. I didn't get it straight when I set the bone."

"Setting your own nose is hard. It's always better if someone else helps."

"There wasn't anyone else there." I shrugged, suddenly very tired. "It's been a rough few days."

Her face softened as she watched me. "You should probably eat something."

I sat back at the table and ate for a while before two more people walked in the front door. Jason was a tall, lanky swordsman with powerful arms and a flat and handsome face split by a broad, confident smile. His clothes were worn and well-travelled, but his dark green surcoat and the long straight sword hanging from his hip glowed with quality and pride beneath the dirty black cloak over his shoulder. He smiled and bowed with easy grace. I liked him immediately.

I opened my mouth to say 'Hi' and froze. My chest tightened and my eyes widened. Walking in the door behind Jason was the man whose song had stolen my heart. He wore loose black leggings tucked into soft boots and a rich blue doublet covered his lean bodied frame. The skin I could see was tanned from long hours in the sun and the sleeves of his tunic were rolled and tied around strongly muscled upper arms. His face was older than I'd expected, but was unlined and lively. His salt and pepper hair hung long, framing his kind smile and sad eyes with natural perfection. When he took my hand and introduced himself as Thomas a long warm tingle ran the length of my body.

A booted foot kicked me beneath the table, shattering my reverie. I jumped slightly and spun in my chair to face the others. Jason stood by the fire, filling his bowl and talking to Serena, but Tara was grinning at me like a wild raccoon. I swallowed hard and turned back to my stew, silently aware of Thomas moving through the room and settling down to eat.

Thomas' presence drew my eyes like an anchor in my heart. I forced myself to breathe slowly and focus on my bowl of stew. The food was delicious and soon even Thomas couldn't drag my eye away. In back of the cottage the sound of grinding metal filled the air. I sighed softly. It was strangely comforting to hear someone working.

I turned to look around the room, my hand slipping to my belt. The ancient leather pouch still hung at my side. I rubbed it slowly, feeling the old bones through the worn pouch. Tara's impish voice broke the silence. "What are you looking for?"

I shook my head, snapping back to the table. "I was wondering what happened to my sword."

Tara gave and evil grin. "Friss found it."

"Who's Friss?"

Jason's voice held a combination of admiration and amusement. "SwordMaster Friss is Captain of the Landsmen and my instructor. He was utterly scandalized by the shape that sword was in."

"He's been out there almost since we found you," Tara added, laughing. "You're lucky you were unconscious or he might have taken a strap to you at the sight of it."

Jason gave her a look. "It wasn't that bad." He turned to me. "Where did you get it anyway? Was it an heirloom of some kind, or hanging on someone's wall?"

"No, it was lying in someone's grave." Jason's jaw dropped open in shock and I realized what I'd said. "I...I didn't steal it," I sputtered hastily. "His ghost gave it to me."

The room fell into instant silence. Every eye turned toward me. Serena raised an eyebrow and from the corner of my eye I saw Thomas slowly put his spoonful of stew back into his bowl. Tara looked at me through glittering eyes. "I think it's time you tell us what happened."

5.

The Landsmen listened without interrupting except when Tara asked an occasional question. Once I started, I couldn't stop. I told them everything: my run in with the restless, being given the sword, the bones, everything. The room was silent for a few moments when I finished until a deeply resonating voice sounded from the side of the room. "If his ghost gave this to you and I've gone to all the trouble to clean it, you should probably learn to use it."

I twisted toward the voice. The torso and head of a truly massive man leaned through the window at the rear of the house. He was shirtless. His tan skin gleamed with sweat. Even leaning through the open window, I could tell he was at least a full foot taller than I was. He was completely bald save for his eyebrows and great shaggy black sideburns that ran from his ears to the line of his chin. Dozens of old small, scars scored his chest and arms. On the left side of his chest were seven deep horizontal scars like a ladder. He stood with solid grace and radiated power. All of his body rippled with muscle. In one hand he held a long blanket wrapped bundle.

I'd seen dangerous men before. Guards on caravan trains or the King's patrol coming through the pass. They were men who looked like they could burst into a whirlwind of destruction at any moment. This was not one of them. He stood with a quiet softness that scared me more than any of the others could have. His movements wouldn't be chaos and carnage. They'd be a precise and relentless river of death.

His eyes took me in with a single glance. Just one movement down and back up, locking my eyes in place with his own dark centered orbs. "If you come with us, you'll begin at first light. Otherwise, find a teacher."

Friss held the blanketed bundle outward. I sprang to my feet like a child trying to avoid a scolding and took it from him. I could feel the already familiar heft of my sword hidden beneath the blanket. There was strength to it, a sort of warmth while it was in my arms. Everyone watched me. I felt their eyes boring into my back for a split second before turning to lay the sword gently on the bed. Friss watched me a moment longer before turning to walk out of sight. I turned to toward the others. "What did he mean, '*if* I come with you'?"

Tara looked around the table and shrugged, hooking her thumb at the door. Jason and Thomas both stood and slid their bowls toward the center of the table before leaving the room. Serena rose and gathered the dishes, heading for the wash basin.

I cocked an eyebrow at Tara. "Did you know that it's nearly impossible to lie to a Messenger?" she asked.

"No."

She nodded. "People's voices change when they lie and we can tell the difference. You haven't lied to us, not even about the more colorful aspects of your tale, but we have a job to do and we can't stop or slow down any more than we already have. The nearest town is three day's walk in the direction opposite of the one we're going and you shouldn't stay here. In two days' time this place will be crawling with every type of scavenger you can imagine. Two and four legged.

"The other option is an offer that hasn't been made yet. It's possible you could come with us, but we'll be moving as fast as we can. We will move as long as there's light enough to see. You'll be on your feet all day and Friss will probably carry through on his threat to teach you while we move. The New Gods help you if he does.

"We are going after the people who did this, but we are going after them to gather information, not for vengeance. We're going to find them, not fight them. Once we know who they are, where they are, and what's going on, we're going to skirt around them and make it to the next town before they do. From there it depends on what we find out. Maybe we fight, maybe we run, but that's a decision other people will make. I need to know if you can handle that."

"These bastards burnt down my life, Tara. I need to understand what happened and how. I can't do that on my own. Please."

She watched me with the slender index finger of her right hand resting gently on the tip of her nose. She shook her head, dropping her hand to her lap. "It's probably your only chance to survive."

I let out a breath I didn't know I'd been holding. "Thank you. It's probably the dumbest thing I've ever done in my life, but thank you."

She laughed and stood to help Serena with the dishes. I followed along, smiling as a thought hit me. "So..." I said. "What are sleeping arrangements going to be?"

Tara almost choked. "Cary!"

"What? Did you think one little kick would stop me?"

Serena's barking laughter cut across Tara's confused look. "*I'm* the one who kicked you." The elf barked. "I've seen starving dogs look less predatory."

My jaw dropped. "It was not that bad!"

Serena had finally managed to catch her breath. "You were almost growling!"

"I was not!" I almost shouted.

The three of us laughed until we were gasping for air, leaning against whatever would hold us. I stood against the bed frame with the blanket-wrapped bundle beside me on the bed. I reached down and flipped the bundle open to look at my sword.

The worn leather scabbard had been cleaned, oiled, and wrapped in strips of heavy cloth where the ancient leather had rotted through. The rust and dirt had been scrubbed away from the hand guard to reveal a cracked, black enamel finish. Friss had torn away the rotting cloth and rusted wire of the handguard, replacing it with thick grey sharkskin.

I reached down and gently picked up the sword. The pommel covered my hand completely, protecting my fingers. I wrapped my other hand gently around the midpoint of the scabbard and pulled.

The sword slid free. The dark gray steel curved slightly and the keen edge gleamed. I had never actually held a sword before, but it felt perfect in my hand, heavy and solid. I slid the blade carefully back into the sheath.

Serena held out a hand with a questioning look. "May I?"

I nodded and handed the blade over, watching her pull the blade free. She inspected it for several minutes, testing the edge. She smiled at the leaking blood along the edge of her thumb and handed the blade and scabbard to Tara. "What do you think?"

"It's a fine blade. One of the best."

Tara held the heavy blade by the handle, testing its weight. "It would have to be to survive so well."

I crossed the room and took the heavy sword from her outstretched hand, wiping the blade on a nearby towel before sheathing it again. My eyes caught sight of the strange club-like weapon leaning against the wall behind Serena. It was long and crutch-like with beautiful intricate silver gears and wheels flowing along one side. "What is that anyway?" I asked, pointing at it. "Some sort of weird club?"

Serena smiled. Her voice took on the tone of a chant or prayer. "This is an Elven weapon. It is my weapon. I forged it with my hands and quenched the steel in my blood. It is the manifestation of my soul, the embodiment of my Honor. My rifle and I are one and while I live we will not fail each other."

She spoke with strength and devotion. "Is that what it's called?" I asked in a small voice. "A rifle?"

She barked another laugh and gracefully swung the weapon into her arms. "The type of weapon is called a rifle, yes, but her name is Whisper."

The weapon was nearly as long as Serena was tall. She cradled it in her arms and named some of the parts. Scrolling silver vines ran the length of the barrel, disappearing against the dark engraved chestnut stock. The silver wheels and gears on the side were all the same dusky hue and both the silver scrollwork along the barrel and the dusky silver gears on the side had been treated so as not to reflect light. It was beautiful.

With sunset approaching, the three of us scoured the smithy's house for anything we could find that I might need. I added what little I found to the travelling supplies I'd already gathered. In the loft I found an old bedroll, a quality skinning knife, and a leather sling I knew had belonged to the smith's son.

6.

The next morning was a blur. They woke me at least two hours before dawn. Friss squatted quietly in front of the hearth, stoking the waning embers back to life. Serena looked perfectly refreshed, but Tara and I both grumbled, growled, and Tara actually threatened, when the elf pulled the blankets away from us. My usual morning ritual was replaced with splashing my face from a bucket of cold water and forcibly dragging my fingers through my unruly hair. Serena led me to a chair and attacked my head mercilessly with a brush, braiding my hair tight enough to sting. Breakfast consisted of the same stew as last night. I wasn't hungry, but I sat at Serena's scowl. "We waste nothing," she said. "And we won't be stopping until it's too dark to walk."

I grunted and shoveled down the two bowls of stew she threatened to force feed me. While I ate, the others began a final sweep of the house and area to obliterate the traces of our presence. I cleaned our dishes and claimed wooden bowl, mug, and utensils from the smith's cupboard and stuffed them into my pack. I also grabbed a small copper cook pot, a long wooden spoon, the smithy's supply of coffee, and a bar of soap, packing everything carefully so it wouldn't make any noise as I moved. Jason returned from his canvas of the area as I tied the drawstring on the pack closed. There was a smile in his voice. "You can't hang your sword like that."

"What? Why not?"

He grabbed my belt and tugged hard. The heavy saber swung forward and almost punched me in the belly. "If you tie it like that, it'll swing too much and bind if you have to draw it quick." He tugged the leather ties free, resetting the sword on my hip and tying it in place. "Hang it like this."

He whispered in my ear as he worked. "If you can, see me in the morning before Friss sees you and I'll check it." He winked at me. "Trust me," he said. "You do not want him to catch you doing it wrong."

We gathered outside the smithy. The others waited for me while I walked around the building. I shivered in the morning mist and said a final goodbye to everything I was leaving behind. The sky was still nearly black as pitch, but I used what little light there was to double and triple check my bag, standing to heave it onto my shoulders. Friss' massive hand caught the bag halfway up. He smiled and easily slung the bag over his own shoulder, pointing at his own pack. "Your training begins now," he said. "Your first lesson: Balance and strength are the same."

Friss' pack weighed almost as much as I did. I couldn't even heave it onto my shoulders without help. Friss helped me heft in into place and smiled, pointing after the others. I took a slow step and stumbled, falling to a knee. The weight inside the bag rolled and shifted back and forth, pulling me in every direction. I struggled back to my feet, the weight shifting and sliding with every moment. After two more tries, I managed to take a few steps, but each was a halted stumble that almost took me to the ground. I tried to adjust, scowling at Friss, but he just smiled and motioned me to walk. Jason gave me a sympathetic shrug of his shoulders and walked in front of me. I tried to stumble after him, but I had to stop every few steps to let the weight settle before I could keep going.

The other Landsmen were already disappearing in the darkness in front of me. I scowled and tried to speed up, but Friss dropped his hand to my shoulder and shoved. The weight in the bag shifted sharply, sending me sprawling to the ground. I hit hard, rolling onto my side. My lip curled in anger, but I bit off my tirade and dragged myself to my feet without help. Friss gave me a challenging smile and moved away.

I breathed deep and swallowed the second string of curses threatening to bubble free. Jason walked in front of me, easing his way forward with a steady, casual glide. He looked like he was striding at ease through a field, rather than hiking wooded trails in the near dark. He paused a moment to resettle his pack and glanced back at me from the corner of his eye. He slid his leg forward with exaggerated care. I smiled my thanks and watched the others fade into the distance.

Serena had the same ease to her walk, her hips rolled beneath her, her shoulders steady. I swallowed hard and raised my head, trying to hold my back straight, rolling my hips beneath me. The first few attempts were disastrous, but each time I tried I got it more under control. By the time the sky started to lighten into an angry gray, I was keeping pace.

An hour later it started raining. An hour after that we took a short break while Serena scouted the road ahead. Friss handed me a heavy stick and taught me the proper way to hold a sword, followed by six movements. Three blocks, two cuts, and a thrust. We practiced the movements until it was time to begin walking again. Friss actually laughed when I tried to put the stick down. "True understanding only comes from practice," he said. "You'll practice those movements on the march as well. You stop when I say you stop."

I practiced. And practiced. When my right arm could no longer lift the stick he made me practice with my left arm. When my left arm went out I went back to the right arm and I continued like that for the entire day. Near midday I was so exhausted in body and mind that everything beyond that faded to vague impressions of sound and movement.

When I wasn't moving fast enough, Friss would attack me with his own stick and force me to react. If I wasn't walking properly he'd give me a shove to send me tumbling until I got my feet under control again. By the time the sun was setting and it had stopped raining, I had already been walking in darkness for hours. When we finally stopped, Friss had to hold me in place because my feet wouldn't stop moving. When they did finally stop I fell where I stood, exhausted and already unconscious.

I fought briefly back to consciousness later, lying in the long grass at the side of the camp. My dress was open and Thomas' warm strong hands gently massaged soothing ointment into my back and shoulders while Serena's strong fingers worked it into my legs and arms.

In the morning I woke with the others, laying still and breathing slowly. My hand still gripped the curved stick I'd practiced with the day before. Someone moved nearby and I felt Friss' massive presence. Pain fueled anger rippled through me and I rolled to my side, lashing out as fast as I could, fueling my swing with frustration.

My training stick whistled through the air and slammed hard into the practice stick Friss swung casually into position. The sound of the clash echoed through the pre-dawn. It sounded like the hills were laughing at me.

Friss smiled down at me. "Good, you're up." He turned to walk back to where the others were eating.

Jason laughed from somewhere nearby. "You must learn faster than other people," he said.

He stood shirtless and barefoot in the grass near the foot of the small hill on which I rested. "What do you mean?"

"Most people don't try to hit him until the third day of training."

I grunted and sat up, watching Jason practice. His twin blades, one short and one long, danced through the air. He slipped over the wet grass without effort, his legs moving in harmony with every motion of his body. He turned again and I saw deep ladder-shaped scars on his left side; six instead of Friss' seven. He was a moving picture of grace and serenity.

"You're a master swordsman too, aren't you?" I asked.

He checked his movements and looked at me. "Almost. I have all the training and I've taught students, but Friss hasn't released me yet, so I can't call myself a master."

"Why not? You're movements are beautiful."

He nodded to a space behind me. "Ask him yourself."

I turned, already knowing what I would see. Friss sat behind me on the grass, calmly eating his breakfast. He was within an arm's length of me and I hadn't even known he was there. I scowled. The bastard had wanted me to know when he came to wake me. He had known what I would do. The big man chewed calmly in my direction, pushing a pair of bowls my way. One was heaped high with cooked oats and the other held a steaming soup.

The smell hit my nose and I yanked the bowls to me, turning back to watch Jason practice and stuffing myself silly before slowing my pace. I studied Jason's motions, learning as much as I could from watching. "Why won't you release him?" I asked over my shoulder. "He's amazing."

Friss nodded, pride filling his voice. "He's one of the best I've ever trained, but he still has one more test to face."

"Which is?" I prompted.

"Jason has never been in heavy combat. He's only seen a few skirmishes and some duels. He's never had friends at risk, never known what it's like to see the very land give birth to a sea of enemies bathed in raw hatred and screaming for his blood. Until he does, he won't know what it means to face a swordsman's true enemy."

I wrinkled my nose at him. "I thought the people trying to kill you were a swordsman's true enemy."

"They're just a nuisance."

I expected him to say something else, but he just sat, eating his breakfast. Finally, I cleared my throat. "So, what is a swordsman's true enemy?"

"Fear."

I looked back at Jason. He had moved away to sit near the others, lacing up his boots. I twisted to face Friss. "He's your son."

Friss looked at me oddly for a moment and only nodded briefly when Tara yelled for our dishes. I grunted and struggled to stand. Friss snorted and grabbed my bowls, walking them back to the fire. My entire body screamed at me, every joint and muscle hurt.

I moved slowly, struggling to make my body respond. The pre-dawn air was cool and fresh, but I could barely move. I heard movement in the grass behind me and looked up. Friss knelt in the grass and grabbed my arms. He pulled his arms out behind me and to the side. I shouted in pain, but his grip was iron hard and he kept pulling until my arms and shoulders strengthened and lengthened. I whimpered through clenched teeth and forced myself to keep breathing through the pain. He put me through a series of stretches and exercises that made my body feel like it was on fire.

We started walking again in the cold gray twilight and yesterday's rain returned in the form of a cold, persistent drizzle. The shifting weight of Friss' pack ground my muscles into shape, and I spent much of the day drawing my sword from my side and putting it away again until Friss gave me back my stick and told me to practice.

The next week of travel was entirely too much like the first day. We began hiking each day at least an hour before sunrise and Friss' pack got heavier with each passing day. I marched with the others, consciously shifting my walk into the casual glide required by the shifting weight. Back and neck straight, head high but tilted as I lifted my stick and went through the motions I was taught the day before. When it got light enough to see Friss would show me some more movements to practice along with the others I had learned.

The only difference between each day and the one before was one of pride. Each night, when we finally stopped, I was able to do a little bit more before collapsing. Each harshly muttered phrase or purposeful footstep was an accomplishment. They were little things and largely meaningless, but they were still a victory and I clung to them.

Late on the ninth night I woke to the feel of a soft touch, the hands of a man on my legs. I rolled on to my back, exhausted but excited. *Thomas.* I thought, my body arching as my eyes fluttered open.

I tried to scream, but a hard heavy slap knocked me sideways, stealing my breath. The face hovering above mine slobbered in lust, barely recognizable as human. A great scar ran diagonally across his face, leaving one eye a lifeless, milky white blot against his dark skin. Black chain armor hung loose from him as he pushed my legs open. I screamed again, forcing the sound out as he slapped me, struggling against him with every muscle. His pants were already open. His weight crushed against me. His clenched fist caught me under the jaw, snapping my head upward. I went limp and he yanked my face to his, forcing his lips against my skin. In the corner of my eye I caught a glimpse of my yellow hair covered in mud and froze. The beast continued to slobber, but I focused all of my attention on the hair. Something was wrong. Something didn't fit. I fought past the welling disgust and hatred and concentrated every thought on that single strand of mud-covered, straw yellow hair. Finally, it was there. I knew what was wrong. My hair was black.

The vision snapped like a bowstring and I gasped awake. My stomach twisted within me and I rolled out of my blankets. My hand closed around my sword hilt. I twisted around, snarling at every shadow and half staggering toward the light of the fire.

A figure rose in front of me, tall and lithe. Her pale eyes glimmered even in the darkness. "Tara." I croaked, still half blinded by the vision. "They were here. The main group camped over there." I pointed toward a small copse of trees I couldn't see about half a mile away. "The soldiers brought some women, bound and gagged..." I stumbled and fell into huge arms that appeared out of the dark, my eyes still fixed on Tara. "One of the men was riding my horse."

Moments later, Serena and Jason were running to where I said the camp had been. Friss worked nearby, searching the ground for any tracks the rain hadn't destroyed. Thomas eased more soothing balm onto my skin and murmured softly. Tara sat across from me at the fire and listened. "I saw them Tara. My horse was off to the side with someone sitting her. He was holding a long dark spear and was standing watch."

"Can you remember anything else from the dream?"

I started to shake my head and stopped, remembering something. "Th... there was something the woman was afraid of more than she was of being raped. Being raped was almost a relief. I could feel her fear running through her, but I don't know what it was from." I paused thinking. "That's it. That's all I can remember."

"Okay." She looked up, checking the stars. "It won't be light for another few hours. You should try and get some more sleep."

"No," I said. "I need to be part of this."

Tara sighed. "No Cary, there's nothing you can do. Not even the Landsmen will be able to do much at this time of night. Get some sleep. You'll need all the rest you can get."

I tried to protest even as my eyes drooped shut. I leaned back, sliding into Thomas' arms. The warmth of his body flooded into me. His smell filled my nostrils. The soft murmuring sound of his voice tickled my ears like a spring breeze and my eyes snapped open. I could feel his voice hit me, pulling at my mind. The world melted slowly in my vision and

Tara smiled softly. I tried to scowl and mumbled curses as Thomas' spell pulled me toward sleep.

7.

I woke late the next morning and stretched like a cream fed cat. The sun's warmth eased through me and the ache in my muscles was almost refreshing today. I sat up and blinked sleepily at my surroundings until the vision flashed through my mind. I lunged to my feet, fully awake. Thomas sat on his pack next to the fire, reading from a small leather book. A small coffee pot warmed in front of him. The others were nowhere in sight.

My eyes narrowed. I shouldn't have fallen asleep the night before. I had been on edge, ready to fight. I bent and retrieved my practice sword. I no longer held it in my hand while I slept, but I still kept it close. I walked toward the fire, weapon in hand. Thomas' salt and pepper hair was swept back, away from his face. His lips pursed slightly in contemplation at his book, but he looked up as I got close. His soft eyes glanced apologetically toward my practice sword. He put the book aside and smiled penitently. "Would you like some coffee?"

My paranoia fell away and was instantly replaced with deviltry. This was the first time Thomas and I had been alone. I smiled and let my practice sword drop. Thomas reached for the coffee put, but I pushed him back and swung myself into his lap, my skirt rising up my legs as I straddled his lap. His head snapped up and his eyes widened with unfiltered shock. I stopped his lips with mine and wrapped my arms around his neck, melting my body into his. I could feel his hands on my arms, trying gently to push me away. I shook my head and broke the kiss just long enough to whisper softly in his ear, letting my need for him flow into my voice. "You want this as much as I do. I know you do."

His body stiffened in shock and I wrapped myself into him, pulling him close. His protests died on his lips. His body shuddered softly and folded around mine, his arms reaching to encircle me. I wanted him close, I needed him close, but I stood up and turned away, grabbing the coffee pot and filling the empty mug nearby. Thomas sat speechless, his jaw hanging open. I sipped my coffee. It was warm and delicious, easing down my throat to burn pleasantly in my stomach. Thomas finally blinked, shaking himself back to the present. "What...?"

"That's for last night," I said. "Disappointment for disappointment."

Thomas cleared his throat, visibly trying to collect himself. "I really am sorry for last night," he said "but we did have our reasons. And I was able to work in some healing for you while you slept by way of an apology."

"You waited until I was asleep to run your hands over my body?" I said, raising an eyebrow. "Again?"

Thomas choked on his coffee. "It wasn't like that." He coughed. "The sleep was a healing sleep. It should have given you several days' worth of pure rest."

I sat on a log near the fire and nursed my coffee, thinking about the kiss over and over. I could feel Thomas' eyes on me. My heart was pounding. "I'm sorry for teasing Thomas." I took a breath. "But... That kiss wasn't a lie. For either of us."

"I know."

The silence stretched, but he didn't speak. "Is that all you're going to say?" I demanded. "What I said wasn't a lie either, Thomas. You want me as much as I want you. I felt it last night. I felt your feelings for me. You can't just turn away."

He gaped. "You... You couldn't. That's not possible. That's..."

I stiffened at the rejection and turned away. Suddenly, he was beside me, taking my hands in his. "I'm sorry," he said. "That's not what I meant. I...Yes, I have feelings for you, strong ones, but that's not what matters right now."

"It matters to me. You poured your feelings through you spell whether you meant to or not. I know how you felt with me in your arms and I know how long you've wanted me to be there." He swallowed hard. "I felt more than that too. I felt your strength, your compassion, your power. I'll wait if I have to, but I don't want to wait too long."

The words hung in the air for a moment. Thomas stammered, "I... I didn't... I..."

I turned away before he could respond. I wasn't sure I wanted to hear what he had to say. "Where is everyone else?"

His jaws snapped shut with an audible clack. "I..." He shook his head. "The others are out scouting. Serena and Jason went to follow the trail directly. Friss and Tara went over the hill to higher ground. They'll be gone most of the day."

"And you thought you'd keep a young and vulnerable village girl safe?"

His face reddened and he slid back to his former seat. "Actually," he said. "That may not be as far from the truth as you think."

It was my turn to drop my jaw, but Thomas just laughed. "Not that. There is something else I need to talk to you about." Thomas drew his brow downward. "Tell me again about your vision."

"I told you everything I could remember last night."

"Yes, but how did you know it was a vision?"

"I didn't at first. I told you that. I thought it was real until I realized I had the wrong color hair."

"No. I mean after you woke up. How did you know it wasn't just a bad dream?"

I thought for a second. "I don't know, really. Does it matter?"

"I'm not certain."

"I'm sure it's nothing to worry about. My father, I mean the Priest who raised me, was a Regent of Brill: New God of

Hearth and Song. His whole life was stories. He raised me on them. I'm sure it was something I heard when I was a kid."

"A Regent of Brill? That probably means you know how to read and write, don't you?"

"I can read, write, and sing in three different languages." I smiled. "Two of which nobody uses anymore."

"May I ask...?"

He let the question hang in the air. I studied the grass near my feet for a few minutes. "There was a pox in my village when I was about seven years old. Every healer in the area was called to help, but there was almost nothing they could do. Both of my parents died in the first few weeks and I was sent to a central orphanage. I was almost as terrified. I kept trying to run away. One day when I was trying to sneak out I found an old man lying on the ground. He couldn't breathe. I ran screaming through the orphanage until someone finally listened to me. That was how I met my father, Regent Kostya. He had been having a heart seizure. They said I saved his life.

"When he was finally well enough to leave the treatment of the other healers, he sent for me. He gave me a small paper wrapped bundle with a new green travelling dress inside and asked if I'd like to stay with him when he left the orphanage. To this day, that color green is still my favorite. I changed behind the screen in his room and he let me look at myself in a mirror. It was the first time I can ever actually remember seeing my reflection. From then on we were inseparable. Regents of Brill are always on the move, learning stories and songs wherever they can. He taught me everything I know. At first, I learned because part of me thought if I didn't he'd either die or send me back to the orphanage. Later, I learned because I loved him and grew to share his love of stories."

"Is he still out wandering around somewhere?"

"No. He died when I was twelve. He always believed that every story needed to end so that another could begin. He told me that although his story was over, he had given me everything I needed to begin mine. I stopped at the first town I came to and went to work at the inn. I needed to heal and figure out what to do with my life. Taverns and inns just seemed to be a small piece of the home my father had given me."

I wiped tears from my eyes. "I'm sorry. I wasn't trying to get sentimental."

Thomas pulled me into a hug. "I did ask."

His hand brushed against the pouch on my belt and he looked down. "Why do you still carry those bones?" he asked. "The ones from the grave?"

I shrugged. "Everyone needs a hand now and then."

Thomas groaned and my face split into a grin. A second later we were both laughing.

When our laughter finally faded I felt elated, freed. I sat up and untied my pouch from my belt. "I don't think I could really leave them anywhere. They feel so right in my hands. And they weren't wrong about the earlier directions. Why?"

Thomas sighed and stood up. "Because, there's something strange about you, Cary. Something special. I thought it was an old man's infatuated imagination until last night."

"Infatuated?"

He shot me a look and I smiled, shaking my head. "It was just a vision. I don't have any special training or anything."

"I know," he said "but there's no doubt in my mind that you should get some. There's more to you than you think. A lot more. Last night I put you to sleep, but I really shouldn't have been able to. Not with the feeble spell I used. I felt the strength of your resolve, the depth of your power. If you hadn't already been half asleep in my arms you could have scattered that spell like leaves on the wind."

"No, Thomas," I shook my head. "I don't have any special powers. I'm just a tavern wench with enough imagination to believe the stories I was told as a child. If the bones bother you, take them. We can bury them together." I tossed the pouch to the ground at his feet, spilling its contents.

He stepped over the spilled pile and walked toward me. "It's not the bones." He stepped close to me, his face calm. "You don't have to be afraid of this, Cary. I know how people like me are viewed by most people. It's like I'm not even human. I'm a Priest so people are more accepting, but even then they consider me an instrument of divine rule and not a man. But that's not how it is. I'm still a person. We are all still people. We just learn to use parts of our soul that most don't, that's all.

"There's something truly special about you, Cary. The others have noticed it too. It's not a bad thing. It's an expression of power and strength and you're lucky to have it."

I moved into him, our bodies almost touching. I looked into his eyes. His scent filled my nostrils. "Are you sure it's not a bad thing?"

"I'm almost three times your age. I have a son who's older than you. My wife died in childbirth giving him to me. I haven't really been interested in a woman since... until I saw you. When you kissed me I was helpless. I'm not sure of your powers. With regards to you I'm not sure of anything. You could be the greatest threat the kingdom has ever known, but I won't be the one to notice." He pulled me to him, his head bending to meet my upturned lips.

I leaned into him and my vision brushed the corner of his arm, slipping past him to rest on the spilled pile of bones on the ground. I stopped moving and turned to stare at the strange, sword-shaped cross pointing eastward. Thomas' soft lips landed gently on my forehead instead of my lips.

I pushed him away and looked into his face. My voice was grim. "Jason's in trouble." I said.

From the east the sound of distant thunder echoed my words and Thomas' face hardened. As one we turned and ran toward the sound.

8.

We pounded across the sloping ground, running for the copse of trees I'd seen in my vision. The sounds of combat grew as we got closer. The clash of steel on steel, broken regularly by the strange crack of cloudless thunder, and the occasional scream of horses and men flooded every sense. My legs slowed. Even after the magically enhanced night's rest I was still tired after the last few days. Thomas ran on, quickly getting ahead of me.

I reached the top of a small rise and paused, panting. From here I could see the fight. Jason and Serena stood back to back, moving slowly sideways toward the copse of trees. They were surrounded by men on horseback. Serena raised her rifle to her shoulder, thunder crashed through the air and one of the riders fell. Jason's blades wove a silver tracing in the air in front of him, knocking away arrows meant for his body. A rider got too close and Jason lunged forward, striking out with blinding speed. The rider screamed and swerved away, holding the freshly severed stump of his arm.

I ran down the far side of the hill and lost sight of the battle, clumsily pulling my sword free. Two riders galloped over the hill toward me. Thomas clung to the back of one of the horses, grappling with the rider. His right arm was wrapped around the man's neck and he held tight to the handle of a long knife buried in the rider's side.

The rider's face twisted in blind fury, struggling to throw Thomas from his back, but his jerking movements were driving the horse insane. The other rider swung a large axe single-handed, trying to cleave Thomas from his companion's back. I curved my steps, running to catch the axe wielder and bringing my blade to the ready. I felt the cold weight in my hand and leapt at the last minute, screaming in panic and slamming into the rider with a resounding clash.

The impact knocked me away and I landed hard, rolling several times. I scrambled to my feet almost before I had stopped moving. The rider lay on the ground a few paces away with my sword jammed in his chest. I ran to the body and grabbed my sword handle, wrenching it free. Both horses and the other rider were gone and Thomas went with them. Thunder sounded again and I ran, racing toward the sound.

I reached the top of the final hill and looked down the slope at the battle. Serena stood with an arrow in her thigh. Jason stood behind her. He was bleeding from a deep gash on the side of his chest, from his shoulder to his waist. Five riders still circled, taking turns charging against the pair. I held my bloodied sword aloft and screamed with all the power I could manage.

The air stirred around me, filling with my panic, rage, and fear. Power ripped through my voice. I charged forward, swinging my arms and pretending to signal people behind me. Thunder crashed in front of me and a rider's head vanished. An arcing band of silver clipped another rider whose horse had startled and stepped within Jason's sword reach. The remaining three turned and ran; their horses already wild.

I raced down the hill, sliding to a stop near Jason as he fell to the ground. Serena grunted and slipped to one leg beside him. I leapt to Jason's side, pressing my hands into his wound and squeezing it shut. He looked up at me with fear in his eyes until recognition dawned and he gave me a confused look. "Cary?"

Serena pulled off her heavy coat and pressed it into the gaping wound. I yelled for Thomas and tore off my belt, cinching it tight just above the arrow in Serena's leg. She grunted in pain and flinched back. Jason's wound spurted blood and I slammed my hand into his wound, squeezing it shut.

I held Jason's wound closed while Serena cinched the belt tight around her leg. Thomas stumbled over the nearest hill and leaned into a slow jog toward us. He collapsed onto his knees beside me. His face was covered in blood, running thick from a long gash on his temple. He shook off my look of concern and leaned in low, wiping blood out of his eyes and focusing on Jason's shallow breathing.

I bit my tongue and watched. Jason was pale white and barely breathing. The bleeding was slower than it had been, but I was afraid that it was because he'd already lost so much of it. Thomas used his knife to strip Jason's clothes away from the wound. His eyes and skin began to shine as he pulled power from somewhere deep within himself. "Strip him."

The surcoat was too heavy to cut free, but Serena and I managed to unbuckle it and peel it free from his body, trading hands with Thomas to keep the wound closed. Thomas leaned away from the body, retreating inside himself while Serena and I ripped Jason's shirt open.

Thomas leaned forward and placed his hands on Jason's bare skin on either side of the wound. His lips trembled open and began forming soft words I couldn't hear. The wind shifted direction and blew the echo of his words to me. They were garbled and unclear, but the power in them sent shivers through me. The wind grew stronger and the sky darkened. The ground below us began to tremble, shaking with the rhythm of Thomas' words. Part of me wanted to run, but there was nowhere to go. It felt like the entire world was trembling with magic.

I gaped at Thomas and saw he was no longer speaking. His mouth and eyes were closed, but his voice echoed on the wind and groaned out of the ground. Somehow he'd joined with them, molding them into part of his being and bending them to his will.

The landscape turned pale. Color faded out of the world, leaving only Thomas' hands in the stark brilliance of color. I could feel the power building around me like a string drawing taut. The earth bent, flowing upward through Jason's body and meeting the sky as Thomas pulled it down.

Thomas' voice roared out of the world and the opposing forces bent to his will, pouring through Jason's body until the bend in the world eased. The ground grew still and the wind died. Thomas' voice returned to a whispered softness and he slumped sideways, his eyes unfocused. I looked down. Jason's skin had returned to a more healthy pink. His breath was deep and steady. The gash in his side still bled, but it looked smaller and much less severe.

I leapt to Thomas' side, but he pushed me away, heaving himself up and reaching forward to bandage Jason's wound. I started to help, but Serena's hand caught my arm as she crawled closer. "Don't waste time," she said. "I'll help Thomas. You go to the trees and cut poles for a stretcher. We have to get Jason back to camp."

I ran to the trees, stopping along the way to wrench an axe from the cold grip of one of the fallen horsemen. A few swift swings brought down a pair of long sturdy saplings. I hacked the poles free of branches and ran back, reaching Jason just as Tara and Friss got there. The two moved without hesitation. They took the poles and stretched Tara's cloak across them, folding it in place and setting off at a run, carrying Jason on the stretcher between them with Thomas running alongside.

Serena sighed and watched them go, shrugging when I looked at her. "I could have used a stretcher ride too, you know." She shook her head. "Oh well..." She raised her hand. "Help me up."

I hauled her to her feet as gently as I could manage and hooked one of her arms around my shoulders. She settled her weight against me and we started walking. "You're pretty good at this."

"I've had a lot of practice," I said. "Usually it's just getting drunks to bed or to the stables, but every now and then it's an injury from a fight."

Serena gave me a pained smile. "I could definitely use a drink," she said. Suddenly, she flinched, sucking in a sharp breath as her wound started bleeding again. "Onward, wench!"

I laughed. "Careful," I said. "I can always drop you."

Serena laughed with me, though her face twisted a little more with pain than humor. "Bitch."

We continued in silence for a while and the taut muscles in Serena's body trembled with every step, but I could see nothing on her face that looked like pain. I looked around, grasping for something to take her mind off the pain. Finally, I nodded toward her rifle. "Whisper?"

"Yeah," she said softly. "My Whisper."

"I'd hate to see you yell."

She grunted. "You've got a hell of a yell yourself."

"It was the only thing I could think of."

"It worked. I'm not sure what those men thought, seeing you screaming your head off and charging like that. Hell, I'm not even sure what I thought." She shook her head. "That's not true," she said. "I thought you'd gone insane. There was so much rage and panic in your voice *I* almost wanted to run. But it worked. Thank you. Things would have gone very differently if you and Thomas hadn't shown up." She winced again. "Where is Thomas anyway?"

I hefted her higher and took more of her weight. "He'll get here eventually."

"Stupid son of a lesser deity," she grumbled. "Can't even hurry when someone important is injured." She waved her free hand toward her leg. "Not that this minor inconvenience really counts as an injury."

Friss jogged back with the stretcher and he and I held it low so Serena could settle herself into it without bending the wounded leg. He checked the wound and we started off, matching our steps at first to try and keep the ride smooth. Serena's eyes stayed closed through ride, snapping open the moment we set her down. She stiffened and glared toward Thomas as he turned toward her.

Jason was asleep near his gear, his wound clean and bandaged. Tara touched me on the arm to get my attention and led me toward the side of the camp where Friss was rekindling the morning's fire.

I stepped to one side and squatted on the ground, collecting my pouch and the scattered bones while Friss refilled the coffee pot and set it near the flames. Tara was the first to break the silence. "Thomas said you knew they were in trouble before the first rifle shot."

"Only by a few seconds," I said. "It was pure luck. I accidentally spilled my pouch and that's what the bones showed me."

Tara exchanged a look with Friss. "Can I see those bones of yours?"

I shrugged. "If you must," I said and handed the pouch over. "But Thomas already gave me the 'you're strange for carrying bones around' speech. I told him he was being an idiot."

"It's nothing like that." Tara smiled. "I just want to see if they'll work for me."

"They're not rigged dice, Tara. It's not a question of if they work. It's more like, are you listening?"

Tara swapped looks with Friss for a moment and shrugged, taking a deep breath. A moment later she upended the pouch and watched the bones scatter meaninglessly. Tara looked down at the scattered pile for several seconds before looking at me. "Well?"

"Well what?" I laughed. "I didn't ask them anything."

Tara smiled and swept the bones back into the bag. "I guess I just don't have the sight."

I rolled my eyes. "What sight? It's not magic, Tara. Magic is big stuff, scary stuff. Like what Thomas can do or what made you the way you are. This is different. It's just... It's like an old friend."

Friss grinned at the coffee pot without saying anything. "Fair enough," Tara said. "Tell us about this morning."

9.

We shared a few cups of coffee and I told them everything I could remember except some of the closer moments I'd shared with Thomas. When I finished, they stood and Tara tossed my pouch back to me. "We should go take a look at things before it gets dark."

I stood next to Tara and watched Friss walk over to talk with Thomas. "You two already heard the story from Thomas. Why did you need it from me?"

"We got his story on the run, but we wanted yours too. Besides," she added. "I wanted to see if you'd brag."

I laughed and blushed, stretching my muscles and grabbing my sword. "I was tempted."

Friss slipped into a shirt of mail and Tara slid her long curved blade into her belt before we jogged back to the battle site. The first corpse we came to was the man I had killed. Friss studied the fatal wound for a moment before turning to look at me. "He was on horseback?" I nodded and he smiled. "Well done."

I beamed and stood a little straighter until he pointed toward a patch of torn ground. "But that's probably where you landed."

We moved over the hill with Tara and Friss pausing to look over the bodies of the raiders. They studied the armor and weapons and followed the tracks of the fleeing horses at a run, moving out of sight around a hill. I stayed at the battle site and went back over the bodies, stretching them out and folding their hands across their chests. I didn't have time to bury them, but I said a few simple words over each one, wishing them rest. I didn't want any vengeful shades coming for us in the night.

I went through each of the bodies as I lay them out, emptying pouches and pockets and checking for hidden things tucked into gloves or boots. I wanted to collect anything that might be useful and life in taverns had taught me the normal places people hide things. I filled a pair of pouches with coins, rings, and small pieces of jewelry, and added a fine quality long knife to my belt.

I pulled the mail coat from a man who'd been decapitated by rifle shot and dropped it beside the pouches and a small hand axe in a furred shoulder satchel I'd collected earlier. Friss' low voice growled behind me. "What exactly do you think you're doing?"

"The bodies needed tending to or they risked becoming shades."

"And the rest?"

I straightened and turned to meet his gaze. "The jewels and coins may give us a clue where these people came from Even if they don't; I'm not leaving them on the decaying corpse of a murdering bastard. If I'm going to survive I'll need everything I can get. Thomas needs a bag to carry his surgical supplies and the mail coat is for your son." I stopped for a moment and barely stopped myself from sneering at the corpses. "Soldiers talk about the honor of a fallen enemy, but it doesn't apply to murdering scum."

Friss broke eye contact first. "Thank you for tending to their spirits first," he said. "I'm sorry. I'm angry and it's personal. Every soldier knows they may end up like this someday, with the buzzards beginning to circle and a stranger's hands in their pocket. Today I had to face the fact that Jason may one day be among them."

"I thought that kind of fear was a swordsman's true enemy."

Friss' head snapped up and his eyes blazed, but I put a hand on his massive shoulder before he could respond. "Jason will be fine. He was amazing today. He stood back to back with an elven warrior against at least twelve men on horseback, and won. You should be proud of him."

"Now, can I ask you a question?" I asked when he looked up again. "What the hell are you really doing here?"

His face didn't change but I felt his body stiffen. I shook my head. "Landsmen are supposed to be impressive, but even a tavern wench can see when something is up. This group is *too* impressive. Two master swordsmen, one of the King's Messengers, an elven warrior, and an ordained holy acolyte do not get sent chasing bandits, no matter how many villages they've destroyed. At first I thought you were all on escort duty for Tara, but that's not it, is it?"

"No." Tara's voice answered from behind me. "But how did you know?"

"Thomas." I said flatly. "He was testing me this morning, wondering if I'd get nervous and let something slip. Even his admissions of guilt were a test. And just now at camp you were trying to get some sort of response from me. You've been trying to see if I'd let something slip. I think you've even been testing me with the insane sword training. I think you're trying to see if I'm more than what I've said and you're doing it because you're worried about a threat. Not some distant half-imagined threat, but something real and something pressing."

Tara's smile was calculating but not unfriendly. "Let's head back to camp. The sun's going to set soon and I don't want to leave Thomas and the wounded alone after dark. The horsemen haven't attacked us yet, but they probably will."

We moved back toward camp. Friss slid up beside me with a smile. "The training wasn't a test. If it was you wouldn't have survived."

Thomas was back to reading by the fire and Jason and Serena slept comfortably nearby. The smell of warm coffee filled the air and soft tingles ran through me as I met Thomas' eyes. I moved toward the fire but Friss' heavy hand fell on my shoulder and he steered me off to the side. He showed me how to clean an enemy's blood from my blade in such a way to do honor to both my sword and my enemy.

"It is important to do it right," he said. "Blood is very bad for steel and if you do honor to your enemies blood and spirit, it prevents his hatred and fear from cursing your blade."

We drilled relentlessly for an hour afterward with our stout practice sticks replacing our blades. He moved almost faster than I could see even after he slowed down. When we finally finished I could no longer feel, or even lift, my arms. "You learn quickly," Friss said. "From now on you drill twice a day. Either with me or Jason or by yourself."

I started to groan, but Friss' look cut me short. His eyes were weighted and calm. "It's either practice or die," he said. "If anything good came of this day, it should be that idea cemented solidly into your head."

I stopped moving and felt the full impact of the day settle in. I had killed a man today. I had killed him with my sword because he was trying to kill me. I slumped to the ground, sitting where I had stood. Friss stood nearby and watched, giving me the chance to think without interruption. I had fought in a battle of life and death and won. I was proud of myself for winning, but just my being alive meant someone else was dead. Friss was right. I'd keep practicing.

10.

"The thing you have to understand first, Cary, is that there are only five of us." Tara's voice was quiet and calm. We stared at each other over the fire the following night. We had made what distance we could with Serena and Jason injured but not enough to be in the clear. Friss had slipped into the gathering darkness and disappeared on watch immediately after dinner. Thomas had finished the dishes and was checking on the injured. "We have three Landsmen, one King's Messenger and an Elven rifleman as acting protector. If we include you it brings us to six, with the addition of a homeless tavern wench."

I winced a little at the accuracy of her description, but I was definitely the odd duck in the group. "Somewhere ahead of us," Tara continued, "is an army of unknown strength and size. They are responsible for the destruction of at least six villages or small towns like yours that we know of. In each case about half of the townspeople are brutally murdered in some fashion, different every time, and the rest of the townspeople simply disappear. We assume they've been taken as slaves, but there's a problem with that idea. Can you guess what it is?"

I nodded. "The more people they take, the more people they would need to guard them. So they either started out in very high numbers or they've been gaining people as they go."

"There's more to it than that," Tara said. "They've taken several hundred people as prisoners and slaves. They've been kidnapped and forced on the march. You know what shape you're in. Can you honestly tell me that most of the people in your town would be any better off? My guess is they'd be in far worse shape than a strong young woman who is used to being on her feet all day.

"Most of the attacks have been at night. Many of these people are probably barefoot and poorly dressed. So, where are they? Forced to move at the speed they're going, many of them should have died from exhaustion a long time ago. We've found no bodies. If the army had brought enough food to feed all of the slaves that may explain some of it, but food for several hundred takes trains of wagons and supplies. This army doesn't have them. They have wagons and horses stolen from the same places the people were taken, but not enough.

"There's also a certain lack to the trail, no fallen shoes, no dropped items, not even scraps of torn cloth from the places where we know they've raped the kidnapped. We have found nothing except the ongoing trail of a well-disciplined army and the scattered footsteps of a large group of people being forced to march. The only thing they've left behind," she said, meeting my eyes, "is you."

I swallowed. "That's why you keep testing me."

"Yes. I've memorized every aspect of your being that I can sense. Thomas has had a constant eye toward any powers you might use, and Jason and Friss have kept you under constant surveillance the entire time. Oddly enough, the only person who has completely trusted you from the beginning is Serena and she doesn't trust anyone or, at least, no one human."

"I'm honestly a little sorry to disappoint you," I said. "I'm no spy trying to sneak along with you to learn the power of the realm. I'm exactly what I say I am. Which effectively ruins any chance we have of knowing anything, doesn't it?"

"It certainly does." Tara smiled. "But it also gives us some hope. If a tavern wench can beat them, with or without the help of ghosts, then maybe we can too. That's why we're here. We're chasing an invading army that we know nothing about. We don't even know where it came from. This is a pretty sparsely populated section of the kingdom because it's so near the mountains. We are at least two hundred and fifty miles from the sea, and at least five hundred miles from any inland border. Worse, they know we're here now and they know we're dangerous."

"What happens now?" I asked.

"One of three things." She said, raising a finger. "They ignore us completely and move on, which they can't actually afford to do." She added another finger. "They run from us because they're uncertain of our strength and numbers, which again they can't do because of their slaves." She dropped her hand back to her lap. "Or most likely, they attack us in force. Probably tonight."

My mouth dropped. "Uh-" I stammered, searching for words. "If that's the most likely case, isn't it really dumb us to be sitting and chatting in front of an exposed campfire?"

Tara sucked in air between clenched teeth. "Well...sort of," she said. "Like I said before, there are only five of us- Six, sorry. Since there are only six of us, that means we have to use all the resources we can find. It also means the worst jobs get passed to the people who are least useful in the situation. You and I aren't master swordsmen, or Priests, or even elven riflemen. So we get to be the bait."

My mouth worked like a beached fish and I whipped my head to the side, staring toward the places where Thomas, Jason, and Serena should have been, but there was only empty space. I stood up and grabbed my sword, turned left, stopped, turned back to the right, stopped, let go of my sword and sat down again.

I stared back at the fire, searching for the right response, or really any response that might help. Each pop of the burning wood, every noise from the hills and forest around us, each and every sound fed my panic. My head began to swim and I knew I was breathing too fast.

My fingers clenched around warm, threadbare leather and I looked down to find I was holding my pouch in my hand. I had pulled it form my belt without thinking, rolling the leather between my fingers as Tara watched my every move, trying to judge if they were genuine. To her, this was more than just our lives on the line. The entire kingdom was at stake and this was another test of my loyalty. I could fight and maybe die with the Landsmen, run and hide in the hills, or help the enemy. I hated her for it.

I looked back down at the pouch and drew in a ragged breath. It had helped me out of the impossible before. I pulled open the leather ties and upended the bag, scattering the ancient bones over the dewy grass. The skeletal pieces flickered in the firelight, splaying out like spokes of a great wheel with the longer, thicker, bones all gathered on one side, making it off balance.

I looked up, meeting Tara's eyes. "We're surrounded," I said. My voice was surprisingly calm. "Men on horseback are coming from behind me to the south. They've been holding in place to wait for the men on foot to arrive from the north, but they'll be here soon."

Tara's eyes blazed. "How soon?"

I looked back briefly at the bones and drew my sword. "Now."

Thunder struck nearby and Whisper took a charging rider from his saddle. I spun to face a pair of riders galloping toward us. I knew from the bones that there should be at least four more that I couldn't see. The first rider galloped into the firelight and the twisted rage on the man's face hit me like a bucket of cold water. I glanced down at the alien sword in my hand, suddenly very uncertain as to why I was here. I couldn't do this. This was too much. I stepped backward, away from the charging horses and bumped into Tara. I looked back at her, meeting her eyes for a split-second. Her face was grim and set, ready for battle. She turned away, stepping forward to give herself room to maneuver. I swallowed hard and turned back to face the horses climbing the hill. *If I die tonight,* I thought, *at least I won't be alone.* Whisper's thunderous roar sounded again and the rifle shot tore a man from his horse's back. His horse whinnied in panic and turned to flee, slamming into the other horse beside him. Both horses reared, screaming as the remaining rider fought for control of his mount. I ran toward his rearing horse, shoving my sword upward as the front hooves came down. My blade slid across the man's arm guards and bent deep into his belly. I turned, wrenching my blade free and running back toward the fire. Two men had closed with Tara, pushing her toward the flames.

I skidded to a halt. The first rider Serena had shot was trapped beneath the body of his horse, struggling to free himself. I pinned him to the ground with a sword thrust through his chest and yanked my knife from my belt, praying for time. The fire gave me an idea and I cut the horse's tail a few inches from the base with quick sawing jerks. The last of the hair came free with a quickness I hadn't been ready for and I stumbled, falling to a knee on the bloody ground. The knife fell from my hand and the air above my head whistled as another horse hammered by, the rider's sword missing me by mere inches.

I yanked my sword free and ran to the fire, tossing the severed horse tail into the flames and watching the oily hair catch instantly. The air around me filled with the acrid smell of burning horsehair and I lunged toward the nearest rider, screaming in terror and slashing my sword through the air. My blade bit deep into the charging horse and the beast reared, screaming in panic. I dove out of the way of the striking hooves, rolling to my feet as the terrified beast tried to turn too swiftly and fell, the rider's neck snapping as the panicked horse rolled over him.

The horse struggled to its feet and I took off most of its tail with a swipe of my sword. I dropped the extra hair in the fire and stepped to Tara's side. My side of the fire was clear for the moment thanks to the Whisper and Serena's aim. Almost a dozen men were clustered in combat in front of us with a single dark figure moving among them. The sound of clashing steel echoed above the cries of the wounded. Even with Tara panting at my side, my stomach aching, and the acrid smell filling my nose, I still stood in awe. Friss moved like a ghost. His body almost shimmered from place to place and paired silver gray swords wove gleaming arcs through the night as men around him died.

I sensed a presence behind me and spun, catching a glimmer of firelight along an exposed blade as the sword stabbed through the night. I dove to the side and pushed Tara out of the way. The blade buried deep in my shoulder and I screamed as the man yanked it free. I fell to my knees and looked up into a long familiar face, half hidden by the raised round shield. "Master Owen?!?"

His face was a mask of rage below his raised sword. The night no longer even seemed real. Tara's long light blade slid under his guard, plunging deep into his chest while he stared at me in raw hatred. The bloodlust in his eyes flared as he died and faded until there was nothing left.

Tara screamed my name and hauled me to my feet, wrenching my arm and filling my world with clarifying pain. I slapped my sword into my free hand and snapped it to the side, warding away another strike. Someone struck me bodily from behind and knocked me to the ground. My sword fell from my hand. I landed face down, my attacker's weight on top of me. His fingers dug deep into the wound in my shoulder, sending waves of agony through me while his other hand forced my head into the dirt.

I coughed and choked, flailing madly as I tried to breathe crushed grass and mud. I slapped my hand to my waist and tore the small skinning knife from my belt. I swung backward with desperate strength and felt the knife stick into bone. The man on top of me howled in pain and his weight shifted, ripping the knife from my hand. I bucked my hips and rolled, throwing him off and twisting free.

My right arm hung useless at my side. I scrambled to a squat and glared at my attacker in shock. The caravan's lead merchant grinned wildly at me from beneath an iron helm. He gave me the same leering grin he had given me before trying to lift my skirt in the inn. "You're a feisty little whore," he said.

I screamed as he came toward me. Shock and confusion tore through me. I stumbled backward, searching for a weapon. Color vanished from the world, leaving behind an impression of light and shadow. The air tore from my lungs and a brilliant flash of lightning split the night from sky to earth. It cleaved through the center of my attacker, leaving a charred corpse and an image burnt into my eyes. *Thank you, Thomas.*

The scent of charred flesh and burning horse hair filled my nostrils. Nothing moved on the hilltop around me except Tara. She bled from several cuts along her arms and torso but her face glowed. I crawled to my feet, moving to pick up my sword. The surviving horses had vanished into the night and none of the fallen enemy had survived. Blood ran freely down my arm and my shoulder throbbed.

I leveled a dizzy smile at Tara. "How's that for bait?"

Whisper roared a final time and everything fell silent. Only the sound of heavy breathing broke the quiet of the night. Tara returned my morbid smile. "Not bad at all."

I staggered toward the fire, looking for a bandage for my shoulder. Flickering firelight glinted off the pile of bones on the ground. The spoked wheel of bones had been broken during the fight. Now two of the smaller bones stood together in the center and the others were scattered. I would have been tempted to laugh if I hadn't hurt so badly. I found a spare cloth and pressed it deeply into my wound until Tara's light, quick, fingers tied it in place. The last thing I saw was stars when she jerked the knot tight.

11.

Fingers of fire Probed into my shoulder and I woke screaming. It felt like someone was shoving a red hot needle through my flesh. I flailed once and struck something solid before passing back into oblivion.

I could hear singing somewhere in the distance. Great deep singing that came from all around me. Dawn was rising in the sky and the great earth rumbled with a song more timeless than the wind. The earth heaved and cracked breaking, and flowing like liquid.

I tried to scream. I tried to get my feet beneath me and run in sheer rabbit-like panic. I couldn't move. I couldn't breathe. I was pinned by some force I couldn't see. The singing rose and fell in fevered pitch. My body splayed open and the ground ran liquid to pour itself through me, reaching upward for the whirling sky that came to meet it. I fought against it, pushing back against the tide as hard as I could. The singing faltered and retreated for a split second before hammering back through me.

The renewed onrush carried more than just force. It carried presence. Thomas' being reached out to me, carried by his song. He was there to heal my wounds and help me through the pain. I relaxed and the pain and uncertainty fled before his magic.

When the singing faded I drifted upward toward consciousness. I lay in my blanket on my bedroll. I blinked drowsily upward at a red eastern sky. The front of my dress was open and my shoulders bare to allow access to the wound. Thomas knelt next to me, his fingers gently kneading at my shoulder. His face was gaunt and a light bruise darkened his left eye. "Were you an orphan?" I asked, smiling.

He looked confused. "No. Why?"

"Because some orphans forget that a kiss makes things better."

I sat up and let the blanket fall to my lap, grabbing his shirt and pulling him into my kiss. I held him against me and let the feeling of warmth fill me to my toes. He finally pulled away, refusing to meet my gaze. "I was so afraid I would hurt you with that stroke of lighting," he said. "But I couldn't just sit there and do nothing."

"You did fine," I said. "I'm glad you were there."

"I'm just glad it worked. I've never been very good at aggressive magics and something like that... I barely controlled it."

I pulled him forward to kiss him again but a dry, cracking voice sounded behind me, "Thomas, if you're done trying to seduce one of your patients, perhaps you could check on the rest of us."

I blushed hard, yanking the blanket back up. I hadn't even considered that we might not have been alone. Thomas pulled away, his face flushed. I examined my shoulder as he moved away. The wound had been carefully stitched back together and was now well on its way to being healed. It looked like it had been healing for several days. I looked around carefully, closing my dress.

The bodies of two horses were visible a few hundred yards away. The bodies of our attackers began just past them. I studied the field slowly. I must not have been asleep for long. None of the others would have left the enemy dead untended for more than a day. I stood slowly, testing my body. Everything seemed to hurt, but everything also seemed to work. I grunted softly with the effort and looked toward the others.

Friss had few wounds and was only lightly bandaged but Tara had several long cuts Serena was stitching closed. When I looked at Jason, I was even more impressed with Thomas' abilities. He was shirtless and propped against a rock as

Thomas removed his stitches. His great wound was worn to a thick red scar and he looked like he'd had weeks of bed rest.

He gave me a friendly and pain-filled nod. I smiled back at him and bent to tie my boots into place and gather my things. My sword had already been cleaned and oiled. I nodded my thanks to Friss and buckled the sword belt around my hips, walking toward the scene of last night's carnage. There was something I needed to see.

I moved among the dead, searching their faces and stopping near the hill top where the fire had been. Master Owen's body lay where it had fallen. His blank and sightless eyes stared into the sky. I knelt and closed them, looking into his face for a long time. I had known and worked for him for years. I couldn't bring myself to believe he had betrayed the entire town and joined the enemy, but I couldn't find an alternate explanation. Nearby lay the charred remains of the lecherous merchant. My skinning knife was a melted nub of metal in his side.

"What is it, Cary?" Friss' voice was soft behind me.

"I know these two." I said, gesturing.

"I don't actually know this man's name." I said, pointing toward the charred corpse. "But he was staying at the inn the night my town was attacked. The man over there was Master Owen. He owned the inn. I worked for him for five years. I don't understand how he's here. He was too much of a coward for anything like this."

Friss frowned. "Do you recognize any of the others?"

"Not so far, just these two out of the ones Tara and I dealt with."

"I'll see to searching and stretching these so Thomas can see to them when he's better rested," he said. "Check the other two groups and see if you recognize anyone else."

I nodded and picked my long knife from the ground where I'd dropped it the night before. Friss had left almost a dozen bodies strung in a long train toward the north, covered in crows. I scowled at the birds and pulled the sling from my belt, picking a few small stones from the ground. Maybe I could scare them away. My first few attempts were horrible. The stones seemed to fly in every direction except the one I wanted them to go. I kept moving closer, the crows squawking mockingly at me.

The bodies were in pieces. Each bore at least half a dozen wounds. Many of the wounds were minor like Friss had struck at anything he could reach: fingers, arms, legs, anything he could get to until he scored the killing blow. I swallowed hard and kicked the crows away with my feet when I was close enough. I moved slowly, examining the men's faces and throwing rocks into the empty air with my sling.

When I'd finished looking over Friss' mob I searched the skies and let the clouds of squawking crows lead me to the bodies Whisper had left on the field.

I moved slowly, trying to be alert for any sign of survivors. I could hear the others talking in the distance but couldn't make out what they were saying over the incessant chatter of crows. One of the black birds seemed to lurk near the bodies. It wasn't eating and it wasn't squawking. It moved slowly, like it was watching everything around it. I swallowed and a chill ran through me as I remembered stories of the angry dead inhabiting nearby animals. The only way to bring peace to such a spirit was by the death of the animal.

I kept watching the area and drifting closer. Each time I got within a few dozen paces the bird would hop a few feet further away and lose itself in the tangle of bodies. I looked down at the sling in my hand and sighed, settling a rock into place. There was no way to warn the others without warning away the bird. I brought the sling up whirling and turned, letting fly as the bird leapt into air. My stone would've been high, but as the bird rose, stone and target collided with a sharp *Thwack!*

The bird screamed! High pitched and terrible like a broken child. I dropped another stone in the pouch. The birds head twisted to the side and screamed again, its mouth open impossibly wide. My second stone caught it hard in the side, snapping bone.

Friss appeared in my vision, running hard. I pointed at the crow and drew my sword. A dark snake sped through the grass away from the dead bird. "There!" I shouted.

Friss bolted to corner the hideous snake and my blade neatly split the snake in two. I lifted my sword and the two halves blurred back together, pouring themselves into a single dark pool of congealed blood. A near black tendril flashed out toward me, narrowly missing my legs as I jumped away. Friss leapt over the small puddle, crashing into me and taking us both to the ground. We rolled to a stop several feet away. "Thomas!" he yelled. "Get here now!"

Friss and I scrambled to our feet and scanned the ground. The snake-like tendril of blood raced along the ground at us. I dove to the side as Thomas stepped in front of me. His power shone like a mantle, bending the air around him with a blaze of white fire. "Enough!" he roared, stomping his soft-booted foot down on the creature and pouring his power into the ground. The tendril of blood blazed into white fire and twisted to ash.

I leapt to my feet, immediately checking myself to see if any of that *thing* had gotten on me. Tara helped look me over and Thomas checked Friss. "What was that thing?" I gasped.

"No time to explain," Friss barked. "We are leaving. Get your things."

I was still confused, but I ran with the others to our gear. In less than five minutes, we were packed and moving out at a jog, carrying our packs and dusting our trail. We headed due west, at right angles from the army's path, slowing to a fast walk after a few miles. No one wasted breath speaking and we didn't stop moving until well after dark. Almost no one spoke that night either. The few times I tried to ask questions I was met with little more than tired stares.

I woke in the pre-dawn without help. My body seemed to finally be adjusting to the grueling schedule. I stretched in silence and went through my sword techniques several times. Jason and I sparred until everyone was ready to leave. We moved out fast again. Friss set the same fast pace he had yesterday. I drew my sword on the move and fell into the training movements I'd been practicing for days, ingraining them in my muscles. I was starting to get a real bad feeling about the things that were coming and I wanted to be as ready as possible.

Later in the day I got close to Tara. "What was that thing yesterday?"

"I should ask you," she grunted. "I didn't see it. Thomas and Friss think it was the work of a Blood Priest. They use the essence of life to cast spells."

"That was really just congealed blood?"

"Yes. Probably enchanted from one of the corpses we left behind. Then it just waited to be ingested by a crow and became an instant spy. The Priest could see and hear everything the bird could." She gave me a dark smile. "Apparently, he could feel everything too."

I fell back several feet to consider everything. Practicing with my sword seemed to help me focus. A few hours later I had an idea I didn't like very much and headed over to Thomas. "Thomas, can Blood Priests control people?"

"Huh?" he grunted.

"Can these Blood Priests control people? It may explain why Master Owen was there."

"Oh," he said. He was silent for so long I thought he wouldn't answer. Finally, he nodded. "There are stories that say a strong Blood priest can perform a type of ritual they call conversion. All the blood in a person's body becomes imbued with a single specific emotion. Rage or lust usually. The priest doesn't really control them after that, but with all the blood in your body pulsing with a single idea..." He trailed off.

"Is that what's happening to the prisoners they've taken from the towns?"

"Probably. It answers every question we've had so far. If the Blood Priest is converting people on the march then there would always be plenty of guards to handle the new prisoners. The converted also eat less than normal people and don't suffer from exhaustion." He paused to consider a moment before continuing. "The converted are essentially insane and only barely controllable, but it might also give us an edge. The inner person is still there, fighting to regain control. It makes them a little slower than normal, not as smart, and extremely predictable."

"But to stop them we have to kill the person trapped inside too, don't we?" Thomas didn't respond.

"What do we do now?" I asked.

Thomas pointed forward with his chin. "We stay with Friss and finish our mission."

I followed Thomas' gaze to Friss. The large man strode forward at his ground-eating pace. His alert eyes swung constantly back and forth, watching every lengthening shadow. His body moved in the same state of relaxed tension he carried when fighting. I stayed walking next to Thomas for a while before dropping back again to practice. I wanted all the skill I could get.

12.

We turned north and pushed for another two days. Most of the signs of our passing were lost in the rocky foothills and Friss made certain to erase the rest. Each day, Serena would range far in front of us, running tirelessly on her short, elfin legs. She'd scout the enemy position from any vantage point she could find and both days she reported that we were gaining. We were closing the distance fast because we were cutting across the foothills and ridges while the army went around. According to Serena, the army had increased speed after they attacked us, but they hadn't turned to come after us directly. It looked as though they were in a hurry to get somewhere.

Friss focused mainly on our trail and our enemy, so Jason took over my sword training. He was relentless. He turned two days of forced march into pure torment. He crammed every lesson he could into my head and forced me to practice until my fingers began to bleed. When I could no longer grip the sword in either hand, he used leather straps to tie my fingers around the hilt. I didn't even try to protest. Something had scared Friss and that frightened me enough to put myself through the effort.

Thomas healed me whenever he could spare the effort at the end of the day. He'd use either his miraculous salve or whisper a gentle spell. Neither did much to provide relief, but they sealed the wounds and gave me back some strength though my muscles and joints burned worse afterward.

On the third night, I could only sit and stare at the food Tara had given me. It was a large bowl of hearty stew and half a loaf of bread. It was a feast compared to what I had been eating. She set it down with a meaningful look. "Eat well. Serena says we should catch them tomorrow."

I didn't really need the encouragement, just seeing that much food made me want to weep. Instead, I just stared at it. The smell of the food drove my stomach insane. It was almost half hour before I had enough strength to bring a loaded spoon to my mouth. Even still, I had to use both hands and bend my head to meet it. Even as the others gathered to plan, Thomas settled himself next to me. He smiled and placed his half full bowl of stew next to mine. "I thought you could use this more than me."

I was too tired to thank him with more than a grunt, but he seemed to understand anyway. He slid in behind me and started rubbing my shoulders. My arms shook. The tension in my shoulders flowed into the rest of my body in the form of a soothing ache.

He slid around to face me and took my hands. We sat together, my arms in his. The firelight flickered around us and he began to whisper. His words slipped away on the air, heard and lost as his magic flowed into the world and the color faded from his hands. Even the firelight faded from orange to flickering grey.

Thomas eyes had closed for the spell and the tension slid out of him. For a moment, I envied him. Then I felt something else. I felt something deeper.

Thomas opened his eyes and everything faded. "Thomas." I breathed, lost for words. "I... Thank you. I don't think I realized before but, when you use magic, you're not just casting a spell are you? You share yourself with us on some deep level."

He nodded, caressing my hands. "Magic is everywhere. It is boundless and eternal, but it takes a willing mind and a free soul to put it to use. When I act with magic, whenever I try to heal or harm, I'm drawing power from the world around me and channeling it through me to form and restrain it. When you do that, you can't hide anything. For a moment, part of you actually becomes what you want the spell to be. To heal;

you become peace, unity, and calm. To harm; you become an empty vessel of rage and aggression. All the while, the power courses through you, enlivening your being. There is very little more intimate for anyone using magic."

"But, is that safe?"

"No." Thomas laughed. "It's like climbing a mountain or smelting ore. Usually, it's safe enough if you know what you're doing and take the proper precautions, but any number of things can go wrong. Even if you do it right, there's a chance that you won't be able to contain it. It could explode in some unexpected way, or worse. The power could tear through you, changing you."

"What does that mean?"

"Well..." Thomas shrugged. "It has to do with how using magic works. Everyone has a certain type of things that they prefer. Most of them are formed by our lives experiences, but some of them we are born with. Simple things like: your favorite color, or what kind of music you like. It's usually pretty small, but they do help shape our lives. Some people like it loud, so they live in the city. Some people prefer to live near water, so they move to the coast and so on. The people who have stronger connections can sometimes get carried away."

"Are you saying some people just prefer to do magic over everything else?"

"Those people do happen yes, but it's more than that. That pull, those preferences, those are the start of the connection we call magic. It can shape our lives in many ways and if we know how, we can shape it."

"We're just people. We can't change big things like that."

"Is it really so difficult to believe? People who love to sing write new songs and find new music. People who love to explore will go out and find new places and new things. It's the same thing. People with stronger magic just share that connection with deeper parts of our world.

"For me, it started with the Earth. My gifts began as a teenager when I worked in the mines. I tended gardens and helped plant crops. I worked in the local mines. When my training in magic began, my wife and I lived in a stone cottage. We even had clay dishes. If I was at sea, I could tell you how far it was to shore, or how far down to the bottom. After working in the mines and learning about the stone around me, I was able to sense veins of ore through the rock. I made a fortune as a prospector while I completed my training."

I laughed. "That sounds pretty good."

"Yeah, but sometimes the force of the pull is too much. It begins to dominate our lives. We get obsessed. Sometimes a person isn't strong enough to resist. They get lost.

"I once met someone who had lost to the pull of the earth. He slept in a mud lined hole in the roots of a tree. He wore nothing beyond a thick coat of mud and when I met him, he was barely able to speak. The power twisted him until he stopped being entirely human. He became a Gnome: a being of great power and wisdom, but he lived only as a sentient extension of the earth itself. Meeting him forced me to find some balance in my life. It still serves as a constant reminder of what could happen if I forget to see the rest of the world."

Thomas' face glowed with intensity. "Using magic isn't really about what you can do. It's about how much you can stand. Use too much too often and you can lose yourself. Try to do something too powerful or outside your range of skill and it can rip you apart. The human body can only take so much."

"And then you become something else?"

"Little things begin to change first, but over time the entire body can change."

I smiled to try and lighten the mood. "You look fine to me."

"I was lucky. After my wife died, I had nothing to bring balance to my life. I grew obsessed with my power. It was a way to escape the pain of her loss. I went too far. My senses began to shift and my body with them." He pressed my hand against his chest. His skin was warm and solid. "My body now eternally radiates the warmth of the earth and my skin is as smooth and strong as worn stone. Had I not found balance, even more would've changed."

"If an earth Priest becomes a Gnome when they get lost, what would a lost Blood Priest become?"

"It's not pretty," he said. "It's a creature called a Wyrd. They say the Priest's body softens and runs liquid with the blood inside it. They can inhabit anything alive, controlling it as completely as you control any of your limbs."

"But if the Blood Priests are getting active..." My voice trailed off and I quickly reached for something to change the subject. "How does it all work anyway?" I asked. "I mean how do you do magic?"

Thomas smiled, relaxing as the mood changed. "It's really pretty simple. You're the bridge between what the world is now and what you want it to be. You have to let power flow through you while you shape it and let your intentions become reality."

"That's *simple*??"

Thomas laughed. "I said 'simple'. I did not say 'easy.' "

"Okay, how do you get the power to flow through you?"

"It already is flowing through you. It's just going the wrong way. It's coming from you and moving back toward its source. You've got to change the direction."

"How do you do that?"

"You pull back." He stopped to consider for a moment. "Did you ever play the game tug rope?"

"Sure."

"Good, now say you didn't care if you won, but you wanted to have fun with the other team. What would you do?"

"Let go half way through," I said. "We used to do it all the time."

"Exactly. And if you wanted it to be really spectacular, you'd pull with all your strength first, right? To make sure they're pulling back with everything they've got before you let go?"

"Yeah, I guess."

"It's the same with magic. First thing you do is pull the power into you. Then, when you're ready, you let go. Only instead of letting it go back to where it came from you let it explode through you into the world. All you have to do is aim it where you want it to go and shape it with what you want it to do."

"That's it?"

"That's it. It gets more complicated when you actually try to shape a spell and it's definitely tougher than it sounds, but that's about all there is to it. One of the most fundamental rules of magic is that everything has two sides. Everything that affects someone else, affects you and so forth. All you have to do is reach out, push past your own limits and find the source of your pull, discover what it *really* is and then pull it back into you. Once you learn to feel it you'll realize it's always been there, flowing through you.

"Later you'll learn that everyone has secondary connections you can learn to use. I learned how to channel the essence of Air as a way to gain balance against my Earth gift. Now I use them in concert to produce new effects. Some exceedingly rare people have strange gifts, like Magicians. They can sense the very essence of magic and work with it directly. Magicians are the people who can turn one thing into another like Lead to Gold, or silk into steel. Magicians created the Messengers."

"You're making it sound like anyone can do it. Everyone always says you have to be born special to use magic."

"Everyone *is* born special. Magic is part of the world and so are we. Anyone can develop new strengths or learn new skills. It's the same with magic, anyone who practices will get better, but being special isn't really something you have to worry about."

I shot him a look and he took my hand. "I told you, Cary. There's already something special about you. All you have to do is reach and you'll find it. Your power resonates inside you. I just don't know what power it is. I've never felt anything like it."

"Maybe I'm a Blood Priest." I said, laughing to break the tension. "Maybe I want your blood."

His eyes met mine. "As long as it can remain in my body, it's yours. As well as the heart that pumps it."

"Oh Gods," I groaned. "Is that the best you can do?" I asked. "Are you going to tell me that tonight may be our only chance to be together?"

He blushed. "I didn't mean-"

"It's late and I hurt," I said. "We should both sleep."

He nodded, but before he rose I leaned in and kissed him softly. "I won't have panic push us," I said. "Either of us."

13.

The next morning came gracefully slow. It was nearly midmorning before Jason's boot finally nudged me awake. The extra sleep showed in everyone's face. Even the unstoppable Friss showed signs of relief. I rose quickly and went through my morning regimen, taking care to limber without strain. Tara handed me a leisurely breakfast and sat beside me to enjoy hers.

"Why the late start?" I asked.

Tara shot me a look and pointed at her mouth while she chewed. "Serena says they've slowed," she said when she had swallowed. "We don't want to come upon them during the day. They know we're following them and they'll have outriders. With luck the dark will give us enough of an advantage."

"Advantage for what? If they've enslaved six villages there has got to be hundreds of them by now."

"That's why we're waiting for dark. All we want is a look, just enough to get a more solid idea on numbers and equipment. Then we sneak out and run for the next town."

I moved calmly through the morning, stretching and training until shortly after noon. Tara motioned at me to shoulder my pack. "You'll stay with me in the middle of the group," she said. "Keep your eyes and ears open. We don't expect to catch them till dusk, but we can't be too careful. Remember, all we want is a good look, not a fight. Be prepared anyway, we may have to deal with some of their scouts to get what we need."

We split apart, putting a couple hundred yards between each of us as we moved. We watched our chosen side, trusting the eyes and ears of the other to watch theirs. It was something that Friss and Jason had stressed over the last several days. We travelled fast, eating away at the miles that separated us from our quarry.

We slowed our pace at sunset and began feeling our way over the land rather than flying across it. My senses were strained to the limit so Tara's low whistle sounded as loud as a church bell. I cringed at the sound and crawled my way back to the center of the group where I could see Jason squatting on the ground, drawing in the dirt.

Using a combination of whispered words, hand gestures, and diagrams, he filled us in. There was a large encampment about three miles away. We had no reason to doubt it was the people we were following, but no way to be sure either. I pulled my pouch from my belt and poured its contents on the ground. The smaller bones flowed like liquid, dripping into the dewy grass with a dull splattering sound. "It's them," I whispered.

Serena and Jason slipped through the dark toward the camp. The rest of us spread out, settling to the ground to wait until full dark. I caught Friss as he was moving away. "What do you want me to do?"

His answer was barely louder than breath on the wind, "Stay with Tara. You'll replace Thomas as her guard and he'll move up with the rest of us. If we get separated, head north to the city of Sila. It should be another week on foot. If you hit any of the small villages between here and there on the way, get them moving toward the city. They won't stand a chance without the help of Lord Diea's militia. Remember, Tara's the messenger. If only one of us gets to survive, it has to be her. She can rally the kingdom and we can't."

I nodded and watched him move away, settling myself down to wait. A few minutes later, Tara slid over to my side. "Cary, I know what Friss told you, but you're an innocent in this, not a soldier. No one is asking you to die to protect me. Don't put your life at risk."

I looked at her for a moment and moved away. I was thinking of my town and all the other towns that had been raided. I wasn't a soldier, but I couldn't bring myself to think I was an innocent.

We waited for more than two hours for Serena to return. She slipped out of the shadows like a ghost, pausing at each of our positions only long enough to give us a few details of the camp and the position we needed to be in. After she left, Tara and I exchanged as few words as possible, sliding across the wet grass toward a small rise on the west side of the camp. I could almost feel the others move away, growing distant in the darkness as Serena gave them their jobs and positions.

Tara and I picked our way forward at a snail's pace, our dark cloaks blending easily with the shadows around us. My heart was racing and my breathing shallow. I expected to be caught at every second. When we finally topped the rise, crawling on our stomachs through the last several paces of tall grass, my breath caught and I longed for the apprehension of being caught.

The camp was massive. Almost three thousand people camped below us in the shape of a large seven pointed star. Fires burned at the tip of each point and torches circled the perimeter. A man sat near every torch and three or four circled the fires on every point. Every guard or soldier chanted rhythmically into the night. Their soft prayers rang in my ears like a great wind in the background, rumbling through the camp below and filling the valley with power. A great blazing bonfire burned at the center of the camp. Nine men sat cross-legged around it, murmuring their own chants and staring into the flames.

The banners spread through the camp all bore the same insignia, a double set of pale green crescent moons. Dozens of wagons circled the inner perimeter, cutting the camp into two sections, inner and outer. The soldiers moved restlessly through the outer points of their star formation while the inner camp was alive with power. Unsaddled horses were corralled on one side of the camp. Near them almost a thousand people huddled inside a high-walled corral. They'd been stripped bare and their skin hung from their bodies like they were starving.

Standing apart from everything, barely out of the reach of the central fire, was a handsome, lithe bodied man dressed in soft reds and blacks. He stood with an air of absolute authority, facing the flames with his eyes closed and his attention focused within. Twice he reached out and gestured toward the flames and twice I felt my heart flutter, responding to the wake of his power. He raised his head toward the crowd of slaves and pointed with a well-manicured hand. A pair of elaborately armored soldiers appeared out of the shadows at his side and strode into the crowd.

I expected screams. I wanted to see the slaves fight, but the armored soldiers moved through them like they weren't even there. People leapt out of their way, too scared to do anything but pray or whimper. My hands clenched. The people were practically dead already. There was nothing left in them.

The soldiers paused barely long enough to carelessly jerk a woman to her feet before turning to drag her screaming back toward the fire. The woman fought and screamed, but it was purely reflex, devoid of all real hope. I sucked in a breath between clenched teeth and held it, forcing down the urge to run to the woman's aid. I knew her. She'd worked in my village bakery. Her name was Nancy.

The twin guards dumped her naked body to the ground beside the fire. She cried out, tears streaming down her face. The lithe-bodied man smiled gently and bent low, grabbing a fistful of her hair and dragging her up to her knees. He spoke a whispered word of power and Nancy's throat burst. Her blood sprayed outward, boiling from her throat. The man reached down, letting the blood cascade over his fingers, soaking his hands. He smiled again, painting strange symbols on Nancy's body in her own blood.

The last of her life trickled from her throat, dripping onto the Blood Priest's fingers while I watched. He licked his lips, hungry with power, and bent to drink from the open wound. Cold shivers ran along my spine and color bled from the world, running like paint into the Blood Priest's mouth. My heart raced. I could feel the power growing around them, filling the valley.

The Priest pulled away, licking the last of Nancy's blood from his lips and singing out words of power. He stood tall, screaming into the night and bending the world around him. He raised Nancy's body into the air with one hand, pulling her limp form into a lover's embrace and kissing her deeply. The twisting power raced through him and poured into the body in his arms.

Nancy's body began to respond, her arms coming slowly alive to wrap around him. Color flooded back into her skin. Her hands moved in lust filled strokes over the Priest's body. The wound in her throat closed, healing to nothing more than a light scar in seconds.

Their kiss broke and Nancy giggled, twisting her feet beneath her to stand on her own. My stomach twisted at the sound. I wanted to vomit, but I couldn't look away. She stretched languidly, her face livid with ecstasy. She was flush and full, entirely possessed by lust and pain. I could feel the power in the spell as the world twisted and warped around them. My head reeled. The force of the spell was so close, so real, I could almost reach out and touch the warp of reality. I shuddered and rolled over to lie on my back, blocking the sight from my mind and sucking in a long slow breath of night air.

I opened my eyes, expecting to look up at the cloudy night sky, but my vision was blocked by the face of a startled young man on horseback. With my dark cloak around me, I'd been invisible to him until I'd turned. I'd been so focused on the ritual I hadn't heard him approach.

He wore the blackened steel armor of the army below and carried the double crescent device on his shield. My eyes widened even further in recognition. He was the son of my town's lord and he was riding the very horse he had traded for my virginity the year before. My vision from a couple of days before blazed into my mind. He had been there, sitting astride my horse and waiting for his turn with the captured women. I sprang to my feet as he yelled, "To Arms!" They were his last words.

My sword appeared in my hand and I lunged, slashing upward across his throat. The weight of his armor carried his headless body crashing to the ground and the encampment behind me exploded in fury. The Blood Priest's eyes locked on the hilltop, his face rippling in rage. Even in the dark, I knew he could see me. I roared out an insane cackle and swung into the saddle, yanking my sling from my belt and letting it dangle in the firelight. "Remember me?!" I screamed, kicking Varya into a gallop.

Varya leapt forward and I flung the leather sling into the darkness, clutching the reins and flattening myself to her back. She screamed a whinny and we were gone, flying for our lives. I let out another laugh, panic and adrenaline driving it to a still higher pitch. My body still tingled with the amount of power flooding the valley behind me. I could only hope the army would concentrate on chasing me long enough for Tara and the others to get out.

Varya and I fled blindly for hours, switching direction several times and turning to double back over our own trail. I guided her purely on instinct, ripping the reins first in one direction and then another, moving more by feel than anything. We'd slow our pace when we heard sounds of pursuit and race away as soon as their attention turned in a new direction. At first, I had wanted to gain distance and time, but with every second we weren't caught I struggled more to lose our trail in the night until they stopped following.

An hour or two before dawn I slowed to a stop, dismounting to let Varya rest. She seemed as glad to see me as I was to see her and I threw my arms around her neck, pulling her close as she nuzzled my side. She was thinner and filthy and the moment I pulled off the saddle and blanket she tore at the fresh green grass, eating like she'd had nothing in days. I rubbed her down with handfuls of long grass and scraped mud and dirt away with my hands. She nickered softly and kept eating, snorting as I patted her down.

Halfway through cleaning the mud from her hide I noticed the cut. The sleeve of my dress was torn open halfway up to reveal a long shallow scratch. It was nothing, painless and scabbed over, but it meant that sometime during the night I'd been bleeding, possibly enough to leave some behind. I didn't know what a Blood Priest could do if they had a few drops of my blood, but I knew I didn't want to find out.

Varya gave me a worried look, but I shook my head and finished the work as much as I could. I ate little from the supplies I had with me and lay back in my riding cloak, propped against the saddle. The clouds were beginning to break and I watched the stars, wary of every noise and feeling something I couldn't see.

I expected my dreams to be full of fire and blood. Instead, I saw images of swampland and large trees. They scared me more than fire and blood would have.

I woke a little past dawn. Varya was nearby, trimming some grass for her breakfast. I wished I could find grass appealing as I watched her. She was still in good shape even though it was obvious the past days had clearly been rough on her. She needed food and rest, but I wasn't sure she'd get either.

I stretched and went through my morning sword practice before taking a look at everything Varya was carrying. She still wore the same quality saddle she'd had when I left her. The rig was complete with saddle bags and trail gear. I found several days' worth of rations, a wooden bowl and spoon, a coil of rope, some more water, and a large piece of flint. There was also soap, a hair brush and a small hand mirror. The Lord's son must have been vain but I smiled and looked at my reflection for the first time in weeks.

The face in the mirror was filthy and had obviously lost a lot of weight in a short time. My nose slanted heavily to one side where I had failed to set it straight. Muscle showed on my arms and shoulders where none had been before and my face was sunken and hollow with exhaustion.

I ate slowly to save food. I had no idea how long this little amount would have to last. I gathered my gear and cleared the ground of traces the way the Landsmen had shown me. I wasn't sure if pursuit was still behind me, but it couldn't hurt to be careful. When I was sure I had the area clean, I saddled Varya but didn't mount. A few days without a rider would help her regain her strength and if the patrols caught us I'd need every ounce of her strength. I led us north, unconsciously slipping into the ground swallowing pace Friss had set since we left the village. If I was really lucky, I was far enough east of the camp to avoid patrols.

I drew my sword as we walked. I was proud of myself for remembering to clean it properly before sleeping last night. Varya gave me a few nervous looks while the razor steel flashed through the air in front of me, but I forced myself to ignore her and continue. I drove myself as hard as Friss or Jason would have, pushing every movement for speed and accuracy. I was in serious trouble and I needed to practice everything I knew as much as possible. I couldn't afford any mistakes.

My sleep that night was filled with strange dreams I couldn't remember. Varya and I slept in a shallow ravine on the edge of a washed out stretch of forest. I stashed my gear beneath my saddle and used Varya's saddle blanket to help me stay warm, but nothing seemed to work. In the back of my mind, I was convinced something was wrong. I woke several times through the night, hands grasping for something I couldn't name.

I moved through the day with my senses peaked. After we left the small stretch of trees we camped in, the land shifted to open grassy fields and small rolling hills. The terrain made travel faster and I kept as low on the hills as we could to avoid being seen.

Twice during the day, I snapped out of a walking dream and each time I found myself staring into the distance without being able to remember what I'd been looking at. I swallowed hard and tried to force myself to shake off the sensation, returning to sword practice.

The sun sank low in the sky in front of me and I shaded my eyes against the blinding light. I stopped in mid-step, staring into the sun while the realization dawned. The light in my eyes meant I was headed west, not north. Somehow, I had turned along the way. I had followed the wrong path around a hill or twisted my footsteps during one of the strange lapses. I swore and kicked at the dirt, trying to guess how long I'd been going the wrong way.

I grunted in disgust and turned north, freezing in place before finishing my first step. The world rippled in my vision. The ground in front of me fell away, opening into a vast black chasm. The abyss stretched out in front of me for endless miles, reaching around to my right and growing to swallow the world in every direction, but the east. The blackness pulled at me, drew me toward it.

My foot lifted, stretching toward the black. Tears streamed down my face. I could feel my body shake as I sobbed, desperate to fight my way free. Warm light poured along the still solid ground to my left. Brilliant hues of purple and red bled from the sunset, scaring me more than the yawning abyss. I fought against both sensations, trying to force myself to move. The brilliant hues faded to gray, leaving the sky bathed in blood red as the radiant image of the sun shrank into the infinite distance. Only a silhouette of light remained. It bent around the image of a tall man, beckoning toward me. "*Come...*" The Blood Priest called. "*Follow.*"

I screamed and threw myself backward, slamming into Varya. She whinnied and reared, knocking me sprawling onto the grass. The blackness of the abyss shattered like cheap glass to reveal the grass underneath. I leapt to my feet, grabbing Varya's saddle horn and throwing myself onto her back. I closed my eyes and sunk my heels into her flanks. She raced forward, picking her own directions while I held on for dear life.

Panic screamed through my mind, demanding I stop, insisting that at any moment I would fall into the abyss that was always only the next step away. Varya raced wild over the hills. Every time she started to slow I'd drive my heels into her ribs to keep her going. I nearly lost consciousness twice, clinging to the saddle. I screamed until the spell broke, snapping like a dry twig.

I tumbled from Varya's racing back and slammed hard against the ground. The breath rushed form my lungs and my body screamed in pain. I curled into a ball, whimpering in pain, until the world spun to a halt around me. When I opened my eyes, the waiting abyss was gone. The sky had gone back to normal. My stomach still twisted, but I pushed it from my mind and crawled to my feet. Every instinct I had was screaming to put as much distance as possible between me and what had just happened.

We camped on the edge of a large swamp I'd never seen before. It wasn't the best place to camp, but the small rise was at least dry and seemed free of snakes. I tethered Varya to a small bush on one side of the rise and spread my blanket on the ground, pulling my cloak tight around me and wishing for a fire. I knew better. My rise, though slight, was exposed. A campfire here would be visible for miles in any direction. I cursed and grumbled until I fell asleep.

I tripped over an exposed root several hours later and slammed hard to the ground. The impact knocked the wind from my body. Thick trees surrounded me, dancing in the strong wind. My body ached. Fresh bruises forming on top of the old ones. The dank smell of the swamp tickled my nose and I crawled to my feet. My hand slapped the side of my dress, my fingers scrambling for the sword that wasn't there.

I was on an island of solid ground in the midst of the swamp. Great dark trees rose from the muddy depths to tower menacingly over me. Long, razor-edged blades of grass bent in the slight breeze and Cat-Tail weeds danced to and fro. My legs were wet to the thigh, covered in shallow burning cuts and my boots were thick with mud, inside and out.

The night was alive. Eyes watched me from every direction and my skin tingled. Gooseflesh covered me from head to toe. The sounds of the swamp beat against my ears. Every crying insect or screeching bird sent shivers along my spine. I wrenched a broken section of root out of the tangled mass at my feet to use as a club and stepped forward. The only light filtering through the ancient tree limbs was scarcely visible starlight and a soft glow coming through the clouds obscuring the moon.

Something in the night changed and I was no longer alone. I couldn't see anyone, but I could feel them. It was a presence, like something on the edge of my senses, shifting and moving. I still couldn't see anything, but I turned toward the feeling, trying to focus. I strained with my senses, pushing with my awareness. The twisting in my stomach shifted, bellowing outward and my senses poured outward.

My anger and fear faded, vanished on the wind. I looked down at the rippling black water near my feet and the presence I felt split, multiplying around me. I felt giddy and drunk on the night air. My head began to spin with new sensations. A sliver of moonlight cracked from behind the clouds. The broken length of root fell from my limp fingers. I stood straight, staring into the swamp as the colors ran from the world, leaving only shades of silver and gray.

My senses kept expanding. I was more terrified than I'd ever been, but something inside me needed this to happen. I had to see how far this could go. I pushed myself further and further, letting my awareness flare outward. My senses and mind snapped outward, enveloping the swamp and locking onto the hidden presence around me.

The night ripped open. My soul screamed through me and panic tore at my mind. Power poured out of the darkness and raced toward me. The world bent and the entirety of creation poured itself through my mind.

It was power. It was feeling. It was unity. The wind rose. Cat tails danced back and forth. I could feel what it was to be a part of the weeds, bending before the wind. I heard a swallow's song and could feel wind beneath wings I didn't have. The moon broke free of the clouds and bathed the swamp in light. My mind flashed outward, ripping open to become one with the world. I ran screaming.

I crashed through the swamp, stumbling over rocks and slamming into trees. The feelings coursing through me were too much, too strong. I screamed again and the sound echoed off the trees around me. My thoughts started to blur and disappear, bleeding out of my mind and merging with the world around me. My feet ran of their own accord, numb at the end of my legs.

I couldn't feel warm or cold, wet or dry, living or dead. My whole being was ripped open and scattered on torn currents of wind. Everything I thought I knew about myself was fading away. I couldn't even remember my own name. Somewhere deep within the chaotic tumble was the remembered sensation of a young, shy little girl, desperately running through an orphanage, screaming for help.

I tried to focus on the memory, tried to cling to the shred of identity it represented. We knew the girl in the memory. She was the same girl running through the swamp and she was still screaming. But this time she wasn't trying to save anyone else, she was trying to save herself. Panic gripped her completely. She had the bones of a dead man strapped to her side and her thoughts kept repeating. *Go Away Go Away Go Away GoAwayGoAwayGoAway!* If only we could remember who she was.

The world skittered through our awareness and left us nothing to hide behind. We could feel everything. We felt the impressions of every tree and blade of grass. We knew every fish and bird by name. Every insect screamed for our attention. We sorted their minds, feeling what they felt and knowing what they knew. But something about the girl was different, she had purpose, she was aware, she had memories of sadness and joy. Recent memories of great pain and loss mingled with a sudden sense of happiness and belonging.

The distance between us and the girl grew and it troubled us. Why couldn't we feel her the same way we felt everything else? Why wasn't she part of our awareness? We watched from afar when she lost her footing. She slammed sideways onto an exposed tree root. Our unity with the world ripped open and pain lanced through us. Our awareness twisted around us. We reached toward the blossoming pain and found a ripped dress, filthy with flowing blood. My awareness of the world shattered, my mind focusing on the sudden pain. I knew who I was.

"Stop this now!!!" I shouted.

My words thundered from my ragged throat and the pain ran through me. The swamp was quiet and the moon had once again hidden itself behind the clouds. I lay in the aftermath of panic and gulped air. My body burned from bruises and scratches and the gash in my side was deep and long. I slumped, exhaustion forcing the abyssal gulf of sleep upon me as the world quieted.

14.

I woke to the sound of Varya's whinny and the searing pain lancing through me. I opened my eyes and the harsh morning light slammed into my skull like a blacksmith's hammer. I clenched my fists and sat up with a groan. The world rippled and bent in my vision. The night before ran through my mind and I vomited on the ground.

My stomach twisted around itself long after it was empty and my head ached worse than I had thought possible. I curled into a ball and begged the world to be still. I felt disconnected from my body, like the only thing anchoring my mind in place was pain. I gagged again and tried to focus, pulling my awareness back into my body. The world fell slowly still and I shuddered through several deep breaths. Tears streamed down my face and I cursed every god I thought might be listening.

The gash in my side was ragged and torn, but it had at least stopped bleeding. I crawled along the soggy ground to a nearby tree and pulled myself to a standing position, blinking blearily at my surroundings in growing surprise. From where I stood I could see Varya, still tethered to a bush at the base of the hill. Somehow in the hell run of last night I had managed to make it back to the edge of the great swamp.

I staggered toward the rise, hunched from the pain in my side. My head throbbed horribly and my stomach ached from lack of food, but the world had stopped reeling. Near the base of the hill I stumbled to a knee. My head ached with blinding pain. I winced and shook my head, stopping when I caught sight of the slender sapling to my right. It was a white willow. I breathed a sigh and stumbled over. The bark of the tree had a special medicine in it to reduce pain. I moved slowly, carefully making it clear to the gods that I recanted some of my earlier curses.

I grabbed a slender branch and stripped it bare. The bark was tough and vile tasting, but I kept chewing, sucking down the juices. By the time I had reached my camp the pounding in my head had faded to a dull roar.

My gear was exactly as I'd left it. I buckled my sword into place the moment I reached the camp, immediately reassured by the weight on my hip. Something caught my eye and I turned to stare. A thin column of smoke drifted lazily into the sky. Dawn was already a few hours old, which meant it was a cook fire and not a camp fire.

I walked slowly down the hill and saddled Varya. I doubted the Blood Priest's outriders would take the time for breakfast if they were still on my trail. I had enough food for another day, maybe two and I was helplessly lost. I grabbed the reins and started walking toward the trail of smoke, looking myself over.

My hair hung behind me in a solid, snake-like mass that used to be my braid. My dress was torn in several places and caked in mud and grime. My feet were covered in mud inside my boots and every step squeezed more liquid outward through the leather. I decided not to use the mirror.

I walked slowly, chewing on some dried meat and thinking about what had happened. I could still feel it, a sensation of power and awareness resting inside my skull. I pushed the feeling away and focused on my sword practice keeping an eye on the column of smoke. It was good to have a destination, for better or worse. The pain in my head was fading and I was drying quickly in the morning sun. My sword whispered through the air for more than an hour.

My focus shattered at the sound of a fear-filled scream. I leapt to one side and landed in a fighting crouch. Varya startle-stepped to the side and both of us watched the sides of the low valley. I had automatically kept to sheltered areas where I wouldn't be seen and the low hills blocked my line of sight. The bleating scream sounded again and my senses tore outward. I bit back a scream of my own and dropped my sword, wrapping my arms around my head and struggling to keep myself under control.

The grass and wind sang in my mind. The rolling hills tried to tell me stories and somewhere to my right a frightened calf was being attacked by a snake. I swallowed another confused scream and the calf's fear filled me. I slammed my mind shut with an effort of will and the sensation cut off with staggering suddenness. I reeled and sucked in several deep breaths before climbing the hill to my right.

The calf was wedged, wild-eyed, against a wall of thorny bushes. He stamped frantically at the ground in front of him. I could see the hissing snake darting back and forth to dodge the heavy hoof. Small traces of blood trickled from the calf's nose and flanks from where he'd pressed against the thorns. He must have startled the sleeping snake while eating the bushes. I glanced past the frantic scene to the heavy bushes. My stomach growled and my mouth watered at the sight of the juicy black berries.

The cow's panicked bleating pulled my mind away from my stomach. I dropped Varya's reins and stepped on them, trusting her to stay tethered in the soft soil. The calf was too frightened to be calmed. I eased my sword from the scabbard and waved it slowly, pushing the snake backward. The snake snapped and coiled several times, but I kept pushing it toward the bushes on the far side of the thicket.

All my attention was on the snake. I'd almost forgotten the calf until he gave a panicked bleat and leapt out of the thicket, slamming into me as he ran bleating into the hills. I fell to the ground in front of the enraged snake. I flinched and my mind poured outward. Fear lashed out through me, slamming against the snake's feeble presence and crushing it like paper. The snake snapped straight as a rod, gurgling in terror. Blood leaked from its eyes and it collapsed dead to the ground.

I screamed. My new awareness raged outward to swallow the surrounding hills. Thick thorns tore at my skin and the pain brought me back to the present. I clamped down on my mind, stifling my panic and fear. My senses fell away from the hills, coiling back inside me. I needed to get a handle on what was happening to me. I needed to find Thomas.

I stared at the dead snake and tried to breathe. I had felt its presence shatter as my fear rolled over it, killing it as certainly as if I'd used my sword. My stomach twisted inside me. Revolt combined with fear. I felt Varya near me and turned to the sound of her eating, catching sight of the berries again.

I closed my eyes to everything but the hunger and tore into the bushes. I ripped berries free by the handful and ate until my stomach was full. Varya pushed into the bushes beside me, nickering and munching happily.

Finally, I turned back to the snake and drew the long knife from my belt. I couldn't understand what was happening to me. The snake's mind had cried out in panic as it died and the feeling of that cry still rang in my memory. I pushed it to the back of my thoughts and went to work, skinning the snake and adding the meat to my meager supplies. I couldn't let its death be for nothing. I slipped the fangs of the snake into my pouch, adding this memory to the other bones at my side.

I found the calf grazing on a patch of clover less than a mile away. It wasn't old enough to have gone very far on its own. The herd it came from had to be nearby. I eyed the trail of smoke in the distance. It hadn't moved. It might be a cattle train or a nearby farm. The fact that it was still going also meant that there were people still alive. Maybe they were the Blood Priest's people, but it was worth the chance. I slid off Varya's back and managed to get a rope around the calf's neck without much trouble.

With the calf tied in place, I let Varya go. She moved to the other end of the clover patch and I settled to the ground. I made a small fire of dry sticks to limit smoke and slow roasted the meat from the snake, eating as I went. Thomas would know what to do about what was happening to me if I could find him. I needed food, supplies, and directions. The calf might get me most of it. I ate some and packed the rest of the roasted meat into my rations.

Two hours later, I stood in my stirrups on top of a hill and watched several hundred cows mill aimlessly in the valley below. They all wore different brands and the sight put me on edge, but only slightly. Each family had their own brand and often several families would band together to move their cattle to pasture or to market. There was always someone looking for free cattle and the more help you had the less cows you'd lose along the way.

The little one with me bleated hungrily, pulling at the rope. I smiled down at the anxious calf and shushed it softly. The first outrider I'd flagged down had told me to wait and ridden away, refusing to come close enough to fetch the cow without backup. Only a few minutes later I heard the rapid approach of hoof beats and turned Varya.

A trio of horses approached at an easy lope. The young boy I'd first seen was in the lead and two men followed. One of the men was older, near his fifties and worn as hard as the leather on his saddle. The other man was younger, but old enough to have his own stake in the herd. Both men carried stout prod clubs in calloused hands with careworn crossbows slung over their saddle horns.

I sat calmly in the saddle and waited for them with my hands folded in front of me. I was sure I looked like exactly the type of trouble they wanted to avoid. I was filthy, starving, and armed. The calf bleated up at me again and tugged on the rope. I watched the approaching riders and sat still, hoping the calf would buy me the hospitality I needed before they booted me to the road.

They drew their horses to a stop a few dozen feet away. Well within crossbow range, but far enough away that my sword would be useless. I kept my hands in sight and waited for them to speak. The older man gestured and the boy in front loped down the hill back toward his part of the herd. The young man folded his hands on top of his readied crossbow and waited. He didn't try to hide the move and the message was clear. If I was dangerous I'd be in trouble.

I nodded toward the older man and shifted Varya slightly sideways with my knees. I wanted the rear rider to see the sword at my side and the shift put my long knife conveniently out of his line of vision. The older man nodded at me and moved closer. "Ma'am."

I smirked. He probably had a granddaughter my age. "I found a stray a ways back," I said. "I was hoping if I brought it in we could trade kindness for kindness."

He grunted and said nothing, looking me over. I dropped the smile and shifted in my saddle to rest my hand on my thigh in easy reach of either of my weapons, making sure they saw the movement. "If there's a problem, I can just take the calf and go. I'm sure someone else would be willing to trade me what I need."

Something stirred within me. Tension and warmth tingled near the base of my spine. I swallowed hard, holding my awareness in check by an act of will. Colors started to fade in the distance and slowly drained toward me. The old man relaxed. "Nah," he grunted. "I guess you're alone. We can't do much for kindness, but you throw me that rope and we can do you a hot meal and a bed for the night." He eyed me up and down. "Maybe a place for you to wash up?"

My hands shook as I untied the lead rope and tossed it toward him. The power still stirred inside me, my awareness threatening to overrun everything. I could feel the slightest shift in wind or grass. I swallowed and nodded. "Thank you," I said. "I'll take that wash first if I can."

He grunted and turned away. "Marcus can show you where."

My eyes locked on the younger man, but he sat his horse calmly and smiled at me in a lopsided friendly way. His hands slid away from his crossbow to grab his reins. "Sorry about that," he said. "Things are bad these days and we don't expect a lady to be carrying a sword."

I took a deep breath and smiled to try and shake off the feeling stirring inside me. "I sort of inherited it."

"Lots of people inheriting things lately."

I nudged Varya into motion behind him. He was tan and hard bodied. His medium sized frame easily carried the heavier arms and shoulders of a farmer or ranch hand. "There's a small pool nearby we use for bathing," he said. "It's clean and we keep the cattle toward a bigger pond just west of here while we're waiting."

He stiffened and his face went blank. My hand inched toward my sword and the power lurched inside me, but I held it back. "What are you waiting for?" My voice was surprisingly mild.

I could feel him lie to me. "Just another family with some more cattle. We're going to drive them all to market together."

Something flashed in my awareness behind me and I whirled in my saddle, reaching for my sword. There was nothing there, but I could still feel something. A presence I couldn't see, cold, hungry, and watchful. I twisted back slowly, still shaking. Marcus' watched me with wide eyes. "Are you okay?"

"Fine," I lied. "Just thought I saw something."

Marcus shrugged and pointed toward a small slow creek. "Follow that down the hill and you'll reach the pool," he said. "You can take your time and bathe. I'll swing back around in about an hour to take you into camp." He turned his horse and paused, smiling as he looked back at me. "Don't worry, I'll whistle as I'm coming in."

Varya and I watched him ride away before following the stream around some low hills and into a shallow valley. I breathed a sigh of relief as the hills closed in around me. The strange powers that were stirring in the base of my spine had me on edge, but the sensation eased as I neared the valley bottom. There was still something out there, twisting in the wind behind me and burning like an ember in my mind. I knew for sure it hadn't come from Marcus or the older man, but that didn't leave me more comfortable.

The stream wound through the valley until it reached a small, deep pool near the base of a rocky ledge. The water swirled against the base of the rocks before flowing out and along the stream again. The surrounding hill sides sloped sharply away at the top and were too steep to climb on horseback. It felt secluded and safe.

I eased from the saddle and walked Varya to the edge of the stream to drink. The flare in my awareness was fading and I allowed myself a few moments to relax. My awareness still threatened to boil out of my skull at a moment's notice, but I was getting better at keeping a handle on it. I leaned against Varya's side and just let myself get lost in her closeness for a little while. So much had happened. So much was going to happen. I sighed and shook my head. I didn't think Marcus or his people meant me any harm, but there was definitely something he'd been hiding. I would have to watch out for whatever it was.

I dug through my saddle bags and found the lavender scented bar of soap the Lord's son had left behind. I left my sword, belt, and boots on a rock near the edge of the pool and jumped fully clothed into the water.

The shock of the cold ripped through me. I broke the surface and gasped for air, shivering as I swam toward the side. Varya shook her head out of the swirl of muck draining off me into the pool and moved upstream to drink. I undressed in the water and scrubbed my clothes as clean as I could get them, laying them on the rocks to dry. I washed my body and attacked the muddled mass of my hair with the thick-bristled brush I'd found in my saddle bags.

The bath felt so good I almost forgot I could be in danger. I relaxed in the water and wondered at Marcus' people. A summer cattle drive was fairly common, but why were they here? Marcus had let it slip they were waiting for something. What was it?

I splashed to the edge of the pool and gripped the edge of the rock where my sword lay. The Blood Priest's army had thousands of soldiers. The converted may eat less than normal people, but they still needed to eat.

My clothes were only half dry, but I threw them on as I climbed out of the water, buckling my sword into place. The valley air was warm and still. The stirring in my spine was gone, but now I reached for it. I tried to push my senses outward and let my mind expand like it had before. Nothing happened. I kicked a stone into the pool and swore. What good was magic if I couldn't do anything with it?

I yanked the pouch of bones from my belt and moved forward into the grass, squatting on a piece of dry ground and dumping the pouch. Most of the bones clustered together to one side, leaving a few scattered around the edges. The camp was to the west, but there were riders coming toward me from several different directions.

I scowled and swept the bones back into the pouch, shoving my feet into my boots and running to Varya's side. I swung into the saddle just as I heard soft whistling coming from upstream. Marcus was coming back for me. I wheeled Varya downstream and kicked her in the flanks. We raced away along the valley, hoping to find a hill I could climb.

Hooves splashed along the soggy ground behind me and I urged Varya faster. We followed the bend in the stream along the bottom of the valley until it opened on a gentle slope to my left. I twisted the reins and sent Varya galloping up the hill as a pair of riders came into view behind me. Marcus yelled. I turned Varya to the east and saw a dozen riders, scattered wide and coming fast. Power stirred deep inside my spine and I yanked the reins, racing along the top of the hills to the west, searching for an opening.

Horses raced along behind me and my heart pounded in my ears, echoing the sound. A brilliant, predatory presence blazed into my awareness. The intensity almost knocked me from my seat. I twisted the reins and sent Varya leaping to the top of the hill. She reared and skidded to a stop at the sudden loss of ground in front of us.

A large camp spread out in the valley below the cliff edge. There were a dozen wagons and several strings of horses corralled behind them. Sentries stood guard on every accessible route and the smell of cooking meat mixed with the sweat and smell of hundreds of people. In the center of the camp, nearly a hundred people, most of them children, were shuffling toward the cook fires in long lines, dressed in rags and carrying an array of cast off bowls past a great black lantern hung on a post. *Slaves!* The thought screamed across my mind.

I spun in the saddle and yanked my sword free as a hand grabbed my reins. Marcus' face was flushed and desperate. "You don't have to run." He gasped as the dozen men behind him closed fast.

Something swept low in the air behind me. Its presence flared in my awareness, alien and angry. It screamed and the stirring power in my spine poured outward through me. The power flared out and slammed into Marcus, engulfing him like it had the snake. I could feel his mind struggle against it. I could feel him scream nightmarishly inside his own head. I yanked my awareness back, desperately trying to pull away as the man beside Marcus moved. I heard the whistle of hard wood and a club slammed into the back of my head.

15.

My head ached like it was on fire and my stomach threatened to turn itself inside out. I opened my eyes to soft firelight and instantly regretted it. Someone pressed a cold cloth to my forehead. "Lie still," a woman whispered. "You'll be okay."

I pushed at her hand and tried to sit up, but she held me in place. "Lie. Still."

I stayed down. I didn't have the strength to resist anyway. A couple minutes later I managed to open my eyes. The woman was careworn and middle-aged, silhouetted against the fire light. "Water?" she asked.

I shook my head and the world tilted with the movement. "I'd rather die."

"What did you say?"

"You'll never make me a slave."

She slapped me hard. The world spun and my stomach emptied. She dragged me back to sitting and slapped me again. Things went dark for several seconds, but I shook it off and crawled back toward the firelight. Her face swam back into view. Keen eyes glinted without emotion from a hard face. "Take it slow and you'll live."

I moved slowly, sitting up a little more with each breath. Six fires burned in the camp, despite the number of people I could see huddled together for warmth or comfort. Cattle moved along the far edge of the camp. The woman held the cup forward again and this time I took it. "You'll live," she said again.

She handed me a bowl of steaming broth without waiting for me to respond. "Drink this. It's got some herbs to help you recover and something to keep you awake. Do not go back to sleep, understand?" she asked. "If you go back to sleep, you die."

I grunted and watched her leave to crouch next to someone else lying nearby. The smell from the bowl tickled my nose and I took a cautious sip. It was beef broth, spiced with herbs. I sipped from the bowl and looked around, studying my surroundings and absently caressing the worn wooden bowl I was holding.

The bowl was warm and familiar, too familiar. I peered at it in the light of the fire. It was my bowl, stolen from my saddle bags. I whipped around, slamming my eyes shut as the world tilted around me. When the nausea faded I tried again. My saddle bags, pouch, and sword belt were on the ground behind me. I pulled them close and checked the contents of the bags. Everything was where it belonged except for the bowl and spoon in my hand.

I picked up my sword and drew it from the scabbard. The blade gleamed in the firelight and the hard-faced woman turned to stare at me with menacing eyes. I glared back and belted the sword into place around my hips. When she turned back to her patient I pulled the worn leather pouch from my side and upended it. The snake's teeth stood poised and still and the rest of the bones scattered in front of them. "Refugees." I breathed. Pain and guilt flooded through me. "You're all refugees."

"Most of us, anyway," a strong voice said from my right. "Nearly a dozen villages and towns have been wiped out by an army moving northward. Most of these people are the survivors."

I shifted position toward the voice and the world tipped dangerously. When it righted again, I saw a tall man with broad shoulders walking to me. Firelight danced in his eyes and, for a moment, I thought of Thomas, but as the man moved closer the sameness faded. He had a lantern shaped pin holding his cloak in place and I hadn't heard or sensed his approach at all. For a moment, I wasn't even sure he was real. "Have there really been a dozen attacks?" I asked. "I didn't know it was so many."

The woman's hard voice stopped his answer. "He hasn't changed, Travis."

The man drifted forward like a living shadow and knelt beside the man on the ground. The woman glared in my direction and hissed something I didn't catch. The man called Travis cut her off with a gesture and turned back toward the man on the ground. The woman spat into the fire and stalked away. Travis cast a look at me over his shoulder. "Eat your soup."

I sipped soup and watched him tend the injured man. His hands moved slowly over the man's body, prodding and kneading. Color faded from the firelight around us, running into Travis' hands like one of Thomas' healing spells. I put down my bowl and crawled slowly toward them. "I want to help," I said. "They destroyed my village too."

Travis shot me a look. "What's your name?"

"Cary."

"You can start by telling me what you did to him."

"Huh?" I frowned, struggling to focus on the man on the ground.

It was Marcus. His eyes were open and unblinking, staring at nothing. His chest rose and fell in steady movements but his skin was pale and cold. I shrank away in horror and dizziness swept over me. Strong hands gripped my arms, catching me before I fell. "Breathe, Cary," he said. "Just breathe."

I bumbled through some words, attempting an apology and explanation at the same time, but rendering both into gibberish. Travis smiled and shushed me like a frightened child. "Take it slow," he said. "He's getting better on his own, but it would be easier to heal if I knew what it was."

I shook my head and jerked out of his hands. "I didn't-" I stammered. "I... I don't..."

"Woah," he said. "Take it easy. We've all been through a lot."

I fought back tears. The memory of Marcus' last thoughts screamed in my mind. I retched on the ground and blacked out.

16.

The sound of Marcus' screams tore me from sleep the next morning. I woke, gasping for air. My head rang with the sound of Marcus screaming, but the morning air was silent and empty. I looked across the cold fire pit from the night before. Marcus lay on his side, sweating and panting, but his eyes were finally closed. I buried the memory of his screams and looked away. Dozens of people moved through the camp and dozens more slumped in the vacant-stared lethargy of recent horror.

I shifted my sword around my hips and walked toward a patch of open ground nearby. The ache in my muscles eased slowly as I practiced and after almost an hour my mind was clear enough that I could finally focus. Travis' deep voice sounded immediately behind me, almost in my ear. "Nice form."

I spun toward the voice with my sword raised and stopped. Travis stood more than twenty feet away, leaning casually against a wagon. I narrowed my eyes. I could have sworn he was right behind me. His smile rang with confidence and he eyed my battle stance with a critical eye. "Pivot your rear foot a little more when you spin," he said. "It will put you in a far better position to lunge."

I shifted my foot and felt my entire center of balance change. "Isn't that more of a child's trick?"

"Proper balance is for everyone."

"No, I meant-"

He cut me off. "I know what you meant." He picked up a tray from the wagon bed beside him. "Lunch?"

He took the tray in one hand and threw me a towel with the other. I dried my face and followed him toward a patch of shade, watching him walk. He strode swiftly across the ground, testing every step before putting his weight on it, like a man who didn't always expect the ground to be beneath him, but wasn't really bothered by the thought. When we got to the shady spot he squatted easily on his heels and handed me a plate of food. I didn't even wait for my stomach to growl. I tore into the heaping slices of meat and gravy and washed it down with fresh milk from a clay pitcher.

We ate in silence for a while until something tickled the back of my mind. "I thought I wasn't supposed to sleep last night."

"You were in pretty horrible shape," he agreed. "I did what I could and left you to heal. I'm just glad it worked." He chewed for a moment before adding. "Marcus is doing better."

I didn't say anything and Travis gave a snort. "Don't be embarrassed about last night Head wounds tend to make people emotional, but I'd still like to know what you did to him."

"I don't know, okay?" I said. "These things only started a few days ago. An earth Priest told me I had the potential to do magic, but he didn't tell me what the hell that meant and I don't know anything else." I scowled at my plate. "I wish I could help. I really do, but I'm just a homeless tavern wench."

Travis chewed on his lip for a moment. "If you're telling the truth, then you're in more trouble than we are. When did this start?"

I sighed. "A couple days ago."

I set my plate on the grass and tried to explain what had happened to me in the swamp, but it was a lot tougher than I'd thought it would be. I didn't even have the words to express most of what had happened. At first, I had to fight through it, trying to force myself to be able to explain, but a moment later the damn broke and I told him everything from the attack on my village to the mind-ripping experience in the swamp and the attack on Marcus.

Travis listened and ate while I talked, but when I finished he let out a slow breath and shook his head. "I'm sorry, Cary. That's all way beyond me. I mean, I've got a few talents, thing's I've picked up: a little healing, throwing my voice, things like that. But what you're talking about is out of my league." He put his plate down on the grass. "I can try to give you a little help while we're waiting to leave. There are some basics that are pretty standard for most spell casters. It might be enough to help keep your powers from overwhelming you again."

"I'll take all the help I can get." I said. "Where are you heading?"

"At the moment we're not heading anywhere," he said. "No one knows anything about the people who attacked the villages. Everyone here either hid until it was over or was outside of town when it happened. Without knowing who did it, or where they might be going, I can't lead these people to safety."

"I can help you with that."

"Yeah?"

"Yeah." I went back over the details of the army. Adding in the parts I'd left out about the flags, the Blood Priest's, and the enslaving of villagers. Travis produced a map and showed me where the camp was. From there, we tried to track me back toward the camp to guess where the army was going next. I was much farther west than I'd thought. If I had continued going north I would have missed the city of Sila by several days.

Travis asked me further details about the camp and his eyes widened a little at the description of the Blood Priest's camp. "What is it?" I asked.

"The standard: two crescent moons, one above and one below. I've seen it before."

My pulse quickened. "You have?" I asked. "Where?"

Travis made certain we were alone before answering. "It's the personal emblem of the Queen."

"Which Queen?"

"Keep your voice down," he snapped. "Our Queen."

I laughed, but lowered my voice anyway. "Travis, we don't have a queen. She died in childbirth years ago. The whole kingdom mourned for a month."

"Yes," he said. "That's the official story, but the truth is the queen was exiled because she refused to accept the King's other son as the royal heir because he was birthed by the King's favorite cook. The King had the Queen and her son exiled in secret with little more than a personal guard. Then he officially pronounced her dead so she couldn't return with a claim on the throne."

"Are you saying this is about revenge?"

"Sure could be," he said. "The King is getting older and some people say he's not well. The Queen was not yet twenty when she was exiled and it's only been about ten years. Enough time to find some allies and let the insult fester."

"But how would she find a Blood Priest?"

"It was always kept quiet, but the Queen was a Priestess of Mystery. She could've found almost anything she wanted."

"So, the Queen's alive and she's a Priestess," I said, "and she just may be the driving force behind the invading army that has destroyed the lives of everyone here." I shook my head. "I had always heard she was a beautiful and kind lady."

"She was certainly beautiful. Green eyes, golden skin, and the kind of curves men dream about. Far more beautiful than the King's favorite cook, that's the truth." He smiled. "She's a cranky, round old woman, but she does roast a fantastic turkey."

I raised an eyebrow. "How do you know so much about the Queen's curves and the cook's turkey?"

He laughed. "I've eaten in that kitchen a few times."

"You've eaten with the King?"

"No. Just in his kitchen."

I shared his smile for a second. "So, what do we do now?"

He rolled up the map. "I'm going to go make sure that a little more than two hundred people are being fed and then I'm going to check on Marcus. I suggest you check on your horse. I had her corralled with the others."

I watched him walk away before moving off in the direction he had pointed. The horses were all gathered on one side of the camp where the valley hills helped form three sides of a natural corral. I wound slowly through the wagons, studying the camp and its people. Something felt wrong to me, but I couldn't place it until I watched a pair of children panic and run as I turned a corner.

No one in the camp would make eye contact. And many of them seemed to be trying to avoid looing in my direction all together. I tried several times to catch someone's eye, just to see if I could, but I was steadfastly ignored by almost everyone I came across. No doubt word of what happened with Marcus had spread fast through the camp. I was a stranger and these people were already frightened enough. I pursed my lips and kept walking, trying not to take it personally.

The small group of horses had largely been allowed to wander freely in their pasture. Only a couple had been tethered in place on the back of a small wagon. I headed there first. Varya was new. It was most likely that they hadn't just turned her out into the herd right away.

As I got nearer the wagon, a small boy bolted from his hiding place and ran screaming in front of me. "Mama, Mama!" he cried. "Witch!"

I raised a startled eyebrow and stared after the scampering child. He raced between scattered piles of supplies and hid behind the skirts of a red-faced woman. I tried to laugh and failed, settling for a half-sick smile instead. "It's okay," I said to the boy's mother. "I'd probably think I was a witch too." I pointed past her toward the wagon where I saw Varya tethered. "I just want to check on my horse, then I'll go."

A man on the far side of the wagon straightened and grunted in the woman's direction. She turned away, taking the boy with her. The man watched her go for a moment before turning back to me. He was a bald-headed fat man in a farrier's apron. "Sorry about that, miss. People around here been used pretty badly. You shouldn't judge 'em too harsh."

"I don't. Too much has happened to everyone lately." I pointed toward Varya on the far side of the wagon. "How is she?"

The farrier's face soured. "She's been used too hard and not taken care of," he said. "She needs food and rest."

"I'm glad she's in good hands. I had to kill the last man who mistreated her."

The farrier studied me a moment, considering my threat. He snorted a laugh "Okay," he said. "You leave her with me and I'll make sure she heals. And no more doubts about how you handle her."

"Thank you."

After visiting Varya and watching the farrier work for a while I walked back through the camp. This time I noticed all the stares and whispered words. Twice, I saw older people make an ancient sign of protection to ward away evil, but I ignored it. I could too easily understand what these people were going through. I'd almost run screaming the first time I'd met Tara.

Travis' voice drifted across the air as I got closer to the hospital area where I'd left my gear. I turned around a final wagon and almost collided with Marcus.

"Marcus!" I shouted with glee. "Thank the New Gods, you're alright!"

His golden face twisted into an evil scowl and he spun on his heel, marching away. My stomach fell and I watched him walk away. Travis also watched him leave, turning to face me when Marcus stepped out of view. "That welcome I offered you is probably going to get a lot colder."

"They're already calling me a witch," I said.

"Marcus isn't going to help you change that, either. He's utterly terrified. He says he can still feel you inside him, like part of you is still there, dragging him back down."

"I wish I knew if that was true." I sighed and looked around. "Look, if my staying here is going to cause trouble I can move on in the morning. You've done more than enough already."

"Don't gather your things yet. The farrier said your horse will need at least three or four days of rest. I can hold them that long."

I nodded and together we walked across camp to a readied cook wagon, bypassing the line already forming. We sat near Travis' tent and watched the sun set while we ate. Near dark, Travis dug into the supplies in his tent and handed me a long thin shirt. "One of the women in camp suggested I loan you a shirt and give you a needle and thread. There have been some concerns about some of the rips in your dress."

I flushed red and Travis laughed. "You can use my tent for tonight," he said. "Needle and thread are by the lamp."

The tent was small and low with enough room for a thick bedroll and a small folding table that held a lit lamp, a needle, and thread. A high quality pack lay in place of a pillow on the bedroll and everything looked well used. I struggled out of my dress and gratefully slipping into Travis' shirt.

From outside, Travis gave a warning whistle slowly stuck an arm though the tent flap, holding my saddle bags. I laughed and took them, watching his arm withdraw before making liberal use of the brush and mirror.

The dress was a mess. The patterned weave was stained beyond recognition and several holes of varying sizes were scattered everywhere. I sighed and wished I was more of a seamstress. It took a couple of hours, but I finally managed to stitch and patch all the holes before climbing into bed.

17.

I sprang awake several hours later, sensing the cold, hostile presence that had watched me arrive. It was clearer this time, harsh and searching and circling the tent. Animalistic hunger radiated through the night and I rolled out of bed, pulling my sword from its sheath. Outside the tent I could hear a voice speaking too softly for me to understand. I crept to the tent flap. The presence was very near. It couldn't be more than a few feet away.

I threw the flap door open and lunged into the night, spinning toward the source of the presence. I cleared the corner of the tent and stopped short. Travis stood shirtless a few feet away. He held an arm out to his side and a large hawk rested on his outstretched forearm. I stared, confused. The hunting presence wasn't coming from Travis. It was coming from the bird.

Travis turned to face me. The bird hopped once before resettling on his outstretched arm. "You can put down the sword, Cary. This is a friend of mine."

My sword point sagged to the dirt and I peered at the strange bird, watching it watch me. I could feel the hungry presence of the bird wondering if I was predator or prey. "You can control birds?" I asked.

The bird snapped its beak in apparent anger. "No." Travis chuckled. "No one controls birds. I just talk to them." He raised his bird arm. "This is Lula. She's a friend."

The bird made a sound. "She wants to know why you came charging out of the tent to kill her."

"I sensed a presence that was harsh and searching. I thought it was something bad." I flushed. "Tell her I'm sorry."

"What do you mean, you sensed a presence?"

"You know how it is. You just know someone's there."

"No...," he said. "I don't know. I've felt the presence of another person before, but only when they were right next to me. I've certainly never felt the presence of a hungry bird twenty feet away while I slept." He cocked his head at me the same time the bird did. "Have you always been able to do that?"

I shrugged again. "Sure," I said. "Sometimes I can feel a person approach, or tell who was hiding somewhere because of how the presence felt and sometimes I get vague impressions of people or places, but that's extremely rare."

"Have you always been able to sense birds? Can you sense the cattle?"

I shivered in the cold night air. "I've never been able to sense a bird before. That's why Lula scared me. I thought she was a person."

The bird chirped and snapped her beak. Travis whispered something and straightened his arm as the bird flew off into the night. "She was hungry." He said by way of explanation. "Cary, I think we may have found part of your power. Let me think and we can talk more in the morning."

I nodded, painfully aware of the cool night air blowing through my thin shirt. Travis gave me a long lingering look. His gleamed and a small smile played across his lips. "You know..." He leered. "It is a little chilly tonight."

I rolled my eyes and turned toward the tent flap. "Build a fire." I stepped inside the tent.

The following morning, I lounged in the soft warmth of Travis' blankets and listed to the camp come alive around me, stretching slowly and working the kinks from my muscles. I wanted to take every as much time as I could to relax and enjoy the moment before it ended like something inside me told me it was going to.

The scent of breakfast being prepared finally pulled me from the blankets and back into my dress and riding boots. Travis was waiting when I stepped out of the tent. Shirtless and sweating, he held a carved wooden practice sword that was sweat stained from hours of use. He saluted me with the sword and backed away a few paces before kicking a second practice sword across the ground toward my feet. He winked a sparkling-blue eye without saying a word and fell into a ready stance.

We sparred for almost an hour. Travis moved through at least a dozen different styles of sword play, each time moving faster than he had before, testing me. I stuck to what I knew and improvised only when I had to. We moved each other around our small field, the speed and noise of our clattering wooden swords drawing a crowd of onlookers. Sweat poured down my face. My arms were numb with effort and impact, but I refused to stop. I could beat him.

In the middle of a pass of swords I stabbed low and Travis' counter paused in mid-air a beat too long before it came crashing down. I was so stunned I didn't even pull back on the force of my strike. My wooden sword splintered against his bare chest, knocking him windless to the ground. Travis gasped in pain, clutching at his chest as I lowered my sword. I felt cheated. He'd held back his block on purpose. He'd let me win.

The crowd of onlookers erupted into cheers and laughter. Coins swapped hands and bets were paid off. People and children stared at me in awe and joy. One older farmer even winked at me before turning to leave with friends. The same people who had been afraid of my yesterday were now laughing and celebrating, looking at me with admiration.

I scowled at Travis' crumpled body on the ground and staggered over to slump on a barrel and catch my breath. He was gingerly testing the rib where I'd hit him. The mark was already turning purple. I should have felt bad, but instead I wanted to hit him again. He'd cheated and I was pissed.

A wide-eyed young boy ran over and reverently handed me my sword belt before racing away again. My arms shook so badly from exhaustion that it took me several tries before I was even able to get the belt buckled in place. The crowd filtered out through the camp as Travis crawled to his feet, hobbling toward a large bucket of water. He drank deep for a moment, but before he could empty the dipper I lunged across the ground and slapped the water out of his hand. "I didn't need your help," I said. "I could've beaten you."

Travis shrugged, splashing water on his face with his hand. "Probably," he agreed, "but I needed to be sure, and it needed to be good."

"Why?"

"Because everyone would expect me to lose to one of the King's Landsmen."

I blinked at him, not really understanding. "I'm not a Landsman."

"Really?" he asked in fake surprise. "Then I guess it's too bad the entire camp has heard the same rumor by now."

His words sunk in as I was bending to retrieve the ladle I'd knocked on the ground. "You bastard." I gaped at him. "You cheated the entire camp."

Travis pulled the ladle from my limp fingers. "Yup."

"People are going to find out."

"It will work long enough to get you the rest you need," he said. "You've trained with the Landsmen. You've traveled with them and fought beside them. That's good enough for me and more than good enough for any of these people."

"No. I won't do it. I won't say I'm something I'm not."

"So don't." Travis sneered. "Just keep your mouth shut and let people assume what they're going to. Surely you have practice at that."

I glared but was too tired to argue. We drank and washed our faces in the cold water. My stomach loudly complained about missing breakfast and Travis' answered. He led the way to a cook wagon and handed me a plate heaping with meat and gravy and a pitcher of milk.

"They feed us well here," I said.

"For now anyway. We've got about two hundred people and over six hundred cows. Several families had banded together before the towns were destroyed to drive cattle to the Midsummer market at Sila."

"Sila! But that's-"

"That's where the Blood Priest was heading, yes."

I dropped my loaded fork to the plate. "We have to warn them somehow! If the festival was there then it's going to have hundreds of extra people, maybe thousands. The city gates will be open. The army can just walk in and take the city without a fight!"

"If none of your friends got through then that's exactly what will happen. The entire city will be converted or destroyed."

"We can't let that happen!"

"We're not *letting* anything happen, Cary. Anything that's going to happen at Sila will happen long before we even get close. If the Landsmen got there in time the city will be under siege. If not it will fall. Sila is one of the richest provinces in the Kingdom but they have one of the smallest city militias because they're so far inland. It's at least five days to the city on horseback. Any attack by the army you saw is liable to have started by the time we get there."

"There must be something we can do."

"Not much," he said. "I've already sent what word I could. With luck it'll get there in time. But until we know for sure what's going on, I can't ask these people to head toward what might be a walled city fortified by the very people who've destroyed their lives."

I mumbled into my food and began to eat, snapping my head up suddenly as an idea hit me. "You could use a bird!"

"No one uses a bird. They occasionally agree to do me favors." He sighed and visibly calmed himself. "And I already did. I sent Lula with a message for the Lamplighters in the city. They're the only ones I know for sure I can trust."

"Who are the Lamplighters?"

Travis looked hurt. "The Lamplighters are an ancient guild of explorers and wanderers," he said. "We try to bring light to the dark areas, whether they are of history, on the map, or in the heart."

"Never heard of them."

He laughed and threw a bread roll at my head. I dodged and ate it as soon as it landed. "Until we get word back from them I think your time would be best spent learning the extreme basics of handling magical abilities," he said. "I've picked up a few things over the years. It's not much, but it may help."

"What do you need me to do?"

"First, tell me everything that happened in the swamp again, then everything that happened with the snake."

I told him everything I could remember, stopping sometimes to describe things in different ways and fighting for the right words. When I finished he asked, "Is it still getting stronger?"

I swallowed and nodded. "I can feel more than ever," I said, "and now it's like I can almost touch the things I feel."

"Can you feel everyone?"

"No. I can't feel you and I couldn't feel Swordmaster Friss either, but that was before the swamp. It's like you're hidden, like you're not even there."

Travis nodded. "That makes some sense. Hiding your inner essence is a trick some people learn when they're used to dealing with Mages. It helps keep us normal people safe. What if I do this?" He closed his eyes and concentrated.

It was like someone had lifted a curtain. Travis' presence flared into existence in front of me. My jaw dropped and I stared at him. "How did you do that?"

Travis blinked and let out a breath. His presence faded from my senses, slipping away on the wind. "It's not important."

"Teach me."

"Maybe later. What's important right now is the trick works on you. That means part of what you're sensing is the inner essence of things, the form behind the form. If you can learn to do it on purpose you could do some amazing things."

"Are you saying I can sense a person's soul?"

"I have no idea. I told you before, this is all way beyond me. The best we can hope for is to get you to a point where you can use your powers on purpose and control them when you need to. Beyond that you'll need someone who knows a lot more than I do."

We spent the rest of that day and all of the following practicing. Travis taught me how to control my breathing and start to access power in smaller and more controllable amounts. I practiced as much as possible, meditating for hours at a time. I built my will around my powers to protect my mind and practiced the most basic aspects of how to feel my power and gradually let it come into my awareness.

It felt incredible. I wanted more, but Travis refused to even try without knowing what we were dealing with. It upset me, but I focused instead on what I could do and focused on learning to control my powers. I also learned how to shift my presence until I became one with my surroundings rather than standing apart from them. It wasn't exactly what Travis had called 'hiding his inner essence' but it worked for me.

By the fifth day I could feel the power without fear. I practiced slowly, playing a kind of hide and seek Travis had come up with using the cattle. I forced myself to relax and breathe deeply. I was blindfolded and watched constantly by herds of children making sure I didn't cheat. My awareness slowly stretched out past me and blossomed into the surrounding camp, looking for the calf Travis had hidden.

My awareness swept over the children and other onlookers, feeling each one before moving on. My mind locked on the cattle. Sometimes the herd felt like a single creature. The sheer size of it threatened to overwhelm me. I forced my mind away. It was dangerous to stay near the herd too long. If I stayed I almost started feeling like one of them.

I extended my senses outward to fill the air again. Lula shrieked in the air above me and my grip on my powers slipped. My awareness roared outward, flaring through the valley and filling the area. I grit my teeth and grunted with the effort of pulling myself back, forcing my powers back down inside me. I slumped and reached for the blindfold. Travis had a glass of water ready. "Are you alright?"

I dropped the cloth and drank deep. "I lost control for a moment. I felt everything. The farrier is sleeping with the midwife. The calf is tethered behind your tent. Two of the Dawson children have snuck away to go swimming again and Lula is on her way back to camp." I gave Travis a grim look. "She doesn't have good news."

"How bad is it?"

"Let's find out."

I knelt on the ground and tugged my belt pouch free. The crowd of onlookers moved closer but I pushed them out of my mind. I placed my water cup on the ground in front of me and emptied the pouch onto the ground. The snake fangs fell directly into the center of my cup. The other bones all fell to the ground outside. Many of them clattered violently against the rim before bouncing away. I looked up at Travis, aware the others could hear. "The city is besieged. The defenders are still fighting but it doesn't look promising."

Whispers rippled through the crowd around me. The few adults present exchanged worried looks and put on happy faces for the younger children while the older children slipped away, running through the camp to spread the news. Travis helped me to my feet and raised an eyebrow. "You didn't tell me you had an oracle," he said.

"You didn't ask."

Travis turned and grabbed a pair of gawking youngsters who hoped they could learn magic by watching and sent them after the calf. He looked back as I collected the bones from the ground. "You should probably go check on your horse," he said. "I'll go hear the news straight from the Hawk's mouth."

Varya milled in the open pasture with the other horses when I got there. I whistled and beamed as she loped toward me. I stroked her neck and checked her over head to tail before slipping her a smuggled carrot and sending her back to the other horses. The farrier came across the hillock toward me and I turned with a smile. "She looks great," I said. "Thank you."

"She's from good stock." His face was uncertain. "I was actually coming to find you. I just heard a rumor..."

"I don't have all the details," I said with a nod "but Sila is under siege."

"Is it the same people who destroyed our villages?"

I let out a breath. "Probably," I said. "It looks like they were gathering-." I stopped. I hadn't told any of the refugees about the Blood Priest and the conversions, only Travis. I shook my head. "It looks like they were raiding the villages for supplies and slaves to lay siege to the city."

"Any ideas on where we go from here, Landsman?"

"Travis is getting details now. I'm sure we'll have a plan soon."

"I hope so." He said, turning. Before he could take a step he stopped. "Miss..." he sighed. "I don't judge no one by their birth or what they do." I raised an eyebrow as he continued.

"I've always judged people by how they take care of their horses. How they treat those under their care. But...There's something I think you should know. That Marcus character, the one you hurt, he's been saying things. He talks about you constantly, and not in a good way. Calls you a Witch and warns people to watch their children."

"I know. I've heard some of the things he's been saying. I wish I could tell him it was all an accident, but he won't listen."

"No." The farrier nodded. "No, he won't. Last night he got to drinking, bartered for some liquor with the cooper. Anyway, I happened to come up on a small group of people with him in the center, raving like a madman about how you hurt him, how he thought you'd tore him up inside, and how he was gonna get even. Gonna find a way to hurt you as soon as he knew how." The farrier leaned close to make his point. "I've seen drunk men rave before. Normally it's nothing to worry about. But Marcus-" He shook his head. "I don't think it was just talk. I think he means it, miss. You just be careful. He'll turn the whole camp against you if he can."

"Thanks for telling me."

"Just be careful."

Travis stood behind his tent, hidden from the rest of the camp as the fierce looking hawk circled low, landing on his outstretched arm. I watched close, trying to catch some meaning from the useless series of chirps and clicks the two exchanged, but I came away with nothing. Finally, Travis smiled, slipping the eager hawk a large stream trout. The bird screeched in glee and flapped away to feast on her reward. "She loves fish," Travis said with a grin, "but she hates getting her feathers wet."

I smiled briefly at the flying bird before turning back to him. "Is it as bad as I said?"

"Worse." He shook his head. "The city is under siege. The warning got through in time, but only barely. The army attacked at night, shortly after your landsmen friends arrived. Most of Lord Diea's personal guard and a lot of the city militia died holding back the initial attack so people could get inside the walls, but over half of their livestock and supplies got left in the fairgrounds outside. The city is now crowded with over twice the normal number of people fighting for supplies and the Blood Priest's army is sitting comfortably outside the wall with enough food and trade goods to live like kings until spring.

"And to make matters worse, the Blood Priest's army is growing. Nearly every traveler who makes it to Sila for the festival is added to the army. Those who won't serve willingly are converted. The ritual bonfires light the sky every night and according to my information, Sila will fall within the month."

"By the Gods... We've got to do something."

"I've already started spreading the word through the camp to get ready to move. There's a royal garrison three weeks west of here at Narissa. I know the ground well between here and there. If I cut straight through, push hard, and chance running a horse to death, I can make it in a week. If Sila can hold, we could have the royal army there four or five weeks after that. You'll need to stay here and help get the camp moving toward. They'll look to you to lead them. It's a downside of the Landsman rumor, but that's the price you pay. You can meet the garrison on their way to the city. The army will pay well for the beef and people will need it once they break the siege."

"I can't just play nursemaid, Travis. Let me come with you."

He shook his head, already moving to gather his things. "No one here can travel as fast as I can. You can keep the tent. I won't need it."

I wanted to argue, but I shut my mouth and helped him pack, flagging down passing children to run errands. By the time his rucksack was packed, the farrier was bringing up two stout horses and a small crowd had gathered. Travis made last minute changes to his gear while the farrier and I packed the horses. The camp cook brought a pair of bundles packed with dried meat and trail food while another horseman brought bags of rich feed for the horses.

Travis said a quick round of goodbyes to those present and turned to the horses, but the farrier held the reins. "At least wait till morning, man."

Travis snatched the reins from his grip. "No time. I can get at least six hours of riding in before it gets too dark to see and I lose more of the moon with every day. It's only half full now and rising later each night." He swung into the saddle, wincing from his bruised ribs, and addressed the people gathered. "Start preparing to move. Listen to your camp leaders, and if there's any question about your course of action," he pointed at me, "listen to the Landsman." He turned his horses west and kicked them into a gallop.

We watched him leave and wished him well. When he was gone from sight everyone turned to look at the person who was left in charge. With a start I realized they were all looking at me.

18.

The farrier saved me from having to speak. "Okay everyone," he said, "get a good meal and start packing. We move in the morning."

The crowd faded as everyone headed back to their families or adopted families to gather what few belongings they had. I stole a final look at Travis' fading back and turned to face the few camp leaders who had remained nearby.

The five middle-aged men formed a circle with me and introduced themselves. I already knew them all by sight, but didn't yet no their names. I shook every offered hand and moved the discussion toward the nearest wagon with a map. We talked briefly. The camp had been kept ready to move and we had more than enough food to feed ourselves and any stragglers we met along the way. The people might get really tired of beef, but that would pass. The ranchers divided the pre-move tasks equally among themselves, splitting the responsibility for horses, cattle, wagons, and people, with a practiced ease. I tried not to be surprised, reminding myself they had mastered this particular type of logistics years ago.

I stayed at the wagon after they'd left and studied the maps I had available. Sila was only four or five days away, while reaching the city of Narissa would take these people almost four weeks. With luck we'd meet the garrison on the move in three.

There was just no way I could lead these people north to help my friends in the city. The ranchers were good with their crossbows, but over half of the camp was women and children and most of the rest were untrained refugees with nothing but the clothes they were wearing. They'd be slaughtered in minutes. Whatever happened in Sila was going to have to happen without me.

The rest of the night passed in a frustrated blur. I tried to keep myself busy by lending a hand wherever it was needed. I hate feeling helpless. When everything was as ready as it could get I ate a light meal and burned away the rest of my nervous energy with an hour of sword practice.

I woke that night on the verge of screaming. My stomach wrenched inside me. Something was terribly wrong. I swung out of my blankets and ran from the tent with my sword drawn. The light of the half-moon covered the valley in a silver glow. I touched the power within me and stretched my senses as far as I dared.

The camp was still and dark. Every camp fire had been smothered hours ago. The cattle slept calmly and the only people awake were the few perimeter guards and a couple hard working women around the cook wagon, trying to bake enough trail bread before the morning. I walked along my side of the camp, hunting for any trace of what had woken me, but found nothing beyond the uneasy twist in the pit of my stomach. After nearly an hour of searching I went back to the tent and slept.

The screams started as soon as dawn lit the valley. I sat up without surprise and stepped out of the tent, calmly buckling my sword around my waist. People ran toward the source of the screams or huddled together with their belongings, waiting for someone to tell them what to do. I strode across the camp, giving a few reassuring words and encouraging people to get ready to leave.

A crowd of people huddled on the far edge of the camp. The circle opened for me without comment and I stepped up to view the scene. The pair of bodies lay cooling in a pool of their own blood. Both were young boys who had often stood night guard over the horses. I looked at them more closely. They had fallen one on top of the other. The one on top had managed to draw a knife before he had been gutted at close range. The other looked like he'd been clubbed from behind. I motioned to one of the men standing nearby. "Count the horses," I said. "See how many we've lost."

The heads of the ranch families arrived a few minutes later and I waved them to the side. "Get some blankets to cover these two and start digging graves," I said. "Then get your people up and moving. Take a head count of the people in camp and find out who we're missing."

An older woman standing nearby dug an oiled canvas tarp from the back of a wagon and helped me cover the boys. The camp leaders moved out and called their people to them to get a head count. The farrier stood nearby and I beckoned him to me. "Send someone to get my horse ready, along with an extra if you've got one to spare. If I'm right, I'll have to catch them before they get where they're going."

He left and I turned in time to see the camp scouts returning with a body tied to a saddle. The lead scout saw me and rode over. "Three men on horseback," he said. "Riding northeast without even trying to cover their trail." He gestured toward the body. "The Braddock boy was on lookout on that point of the camp. They shot him in the back with a crossbow and road on." He spat. "They didn't even stop to make sure he was dead."

We laid his body beside the others and one of the scouts passed the word to dig a third grave. I jogged back across the camp to the tent and packed my saddle bags, adding Travis' bedroll, lamp, and tent. The riders were heading northeast toward Sila.

Varya was saddled and waiting next to a stout chestnut gelding when I'd finished. The camp was a flurry of activity, everyone was prepping to move. I tied my few belongings into place around Varya's saddle as a group of riders approached behind two of the camp leaders. The older men eyed my horse.

"Three men are missing," one of them said. "Marcus and the two Mallory boys."

I stiffened. "They'll be headed to Sila to bring the army down on us. I've got to catch them before they get there."

One of the riders kneed his horse forward. "We'll ride with you."

"I can't allow that." I said, swinging into my saddle. "You all need to stay here and get these people moving. And you've got to get them moving today. The best thing you can do is ride with your families and the refugees. Keep a wide perimeter, the wider the better. Any armed men you see who aren't waving the King's banner should be killed on sight. It just might be the only way to keep these people safe."

The riders exchanged shocked looks, but I stared them down. "The army besieging Sila is taking slaves and forcing prisoners to fight for them. If they even get an idea that your train is here, they will surround you by the thousands and slaughter anyone who fights. You can't let that happen."

The camp leader who'd spoken earlier looked up. "Do you need anything from us?"

"Food for the trip and a crossbow."

The ranchers split through the camp to gather what I'd need while the camp leaders stayed behind. "Move west toward Narissa," I said. "Don't worry about speed. Just keep your people together. I'll make certain no one reveals your location."

I rode out of camp before the sun had finished cresting the sky and met the small group of scout ranchers. The rider in the lead handed me his crossbow while two others flanked my sides and tied a pair of heavy sacks onto the pack saddle on my second horse. The lead rider pointed toward a point on the hill on my right. "They killed the Braddock boy up there and took off down the hill at a run. You can see the trail pretty clear from the top. It's as good a place as any to pick them up."

On my way up the hill I hung the crossbow and quiver from my saddle horn the way I'd see several of the other camp riders had theirs. I didn't really know how to use a crossbow, but it looked like it couldn't be that hard.

The trail was impossible to miss from the top of the hill. Torn ground led directly away to the northeast. The trio had run from the camp at a gallop, kicking dirt and grass the entire way. Marcus' face floated through my mind, followed by the almost forgotten echo of his mind shrieking in terror. I rolled my neck to loosen my muscles. Rage was making me tense. This was exactly what he'd been waiting for. This was Marcus' promise to hurt me.

I travelled as fast as I safely could at first, sometimes losing sight of the trail completely in favor of a faster or more secluded route. Twice, when I left the path I lost it completely and had to rely on the bones in my pouch to point me back in the right direction. I couldn't help but smile when I did. Serena would have been mortified.

Near the middle of the day their trail led me to a small stream. The muddy hoof prints were clean and fresh. I couldn't be more than a couple of hours behind them. I slowed Varya and the gelding to a stop and slid from the saddle. I wanted to eat, stretch out the kinks from my ride, and let the horses rest. I couldn't see any other footprints in the mud beside mine which meant they'd passed without stopping. I didn't know if that meant they were driving themselves and their horses hard or if they planned to stop later, but I did know that both my horses and I would have to be rested and ready when we caught them.

I rode until it was too dark to see the trail clearly. My horses were tired, but not exhausted. Switching my saddle between the two had kept them from being run down. I rubbed them down and turned them loose. Varya would keep them close enough. I ate, stretched, and forced my tired limbs through some practice swordplay to try and loosen my clenched muscles. I was quivering with nervous energy and afraid I wouldn't rest, but I was asleep the moment I settled under the blankets.

Marcus' voice screamed through my mind and I sprang awake, rolling to a crouch with my sword drawn. The screams were new, filled with hate and fear. I could still remember the terrible sound his mind had made as it tore under my assault, but these new screams were worse. They meant I was still connected to him somehow. His mind was still attached to mine.

Varya snorted awake and eyed me carefully, waiting. I sheathed my sword and held out my hand, murmuring softly. She blinked sleepily and ambled over to shove her head under my outstretched hand. I rubbed her neck and took comfort in her presence for a short while. Dawn was still a few hours away, but the half-moon in the sky gave me enough light to walk by and I was still behind.

I trailed them through the day, inching my way closer with every passing step. Finally, late in the afternoon I caught site of a dark line of movement topping a hill in front of me. It could have been anything, even trees waving in the wind, but I drew rein and stood motionless in my saddle, watching. After another few minutes, three horses topped the ridge, silhouetting themselves against the sky. I had them.

When they dropped out of sight again on the far side of the ridge I eased the gelding forward. Part of me wanted to race after them, but I kept myself in check. I didn't know how closely they were watching their back trail. I didn't want to spook them into running and I didn't want to ride into an ambush either.

They settled in to camp a little before sundown. The three of them wandered away from the open areas and moved into a small section of woods where their campfire wouldn't be seen from a distance. I slid out of the saddle and led my horses into the nearby trees where I could find a secluded spot to wait.

My whole body trembled with nervous energy while the last few hours of daylight passed. I pulled the crossbow from my saddle and fired several practice shots at a fallen tree. My aim was horrible. I might be able to hit a horse at twenty paces. I wasn't sure I could hit more than that, but it was worth a try. I gathered the few bolts I could find in the last of the twilight and settled in to wait.

The horses milled through the narrow glade. I dozed until long after sunset, waking to find strange lights dancing in the northern sky. The clouds rolled through the sky, flickering with light. It was the reflected light from the Blood Priest's bonfires. My mind focused with razor clarity. I loosened the tethers of the horses in case I didn't come back and slipped toward the other camp.

19.

The glowing embers from their campfire lit my way the last half mile through the woods. It had taken me hours to get this far. I had been forced to back track several times and let my pouch of bones show me a better way. But now it was easy. The horses they'd stolen recognized my scent and barely stirred when I moved past them.

One of the Mallory boys was alone in the camp, asleep in his blankets. He woke too late as my sword found his throat. Cold rage clutched my belly tight and sped tingling along my limbs. I shifted my sword to my offhand, moving into the shadows around the camp and stretching my senses outward. Marcus and the second Mallory lay together under their shared blankets on a hilltop a short distance to my left. They were content, sleeping under the firelight that still danced across the clouds.

The instant my senses touched Marcus' mind, he snapped awake gasping and trembling in fear. I could feel his mind stir. The link between us rang vibrant with his terror. I crept soundlessly closer while his lover stroked his naked flesh and offered soft, soothing words. I raised the crossbow and paused. A sense of certainty washed through me and I squeezed the trigger. My crossbow bolt leapt through the night and lodged deep in Mallory's chest. His last words of emotional solace were lost in a fit of coughing blood.

Marcus screamed in terror. I dropped the crossbow and my sword rang as I pulled it free. My voice was a rage filled hiss, "Marcus."

Marcus flung the body of his lover aside, shedding the blankets and struggling to his feet as I closed. He stumbled and fell, his arm flailing upward and catching the thrust I had aimed for his heart. My blade bit deep into bone and Marcus screamed. Blood poured from the wound and he lurched away, jerking the sword from my grasp. I yanked the long knife from my belt and tried to go after him, but my feet slipped on the edge of the blood soaked blanket. I stumbled to a knee. Marcus tore the sword free from his arm and ran. I could hear him crashing through the woods. His panicked screams echoed through the night with the high pitched abandon of the insane.

I scrambled to my feet and grabbed my sword. I didn't know for sure how close we were to Sila, but if the army was anywhere nearby Marcus' screams might bring them. I didn't think he would live for long anyway. My strike had nearly severed his arm. He was running mad and had nothing to bandage the wound. My job was done.

I grabbed my fallen crossbow and ran toward the light of the fire, grabbing packs and saddles. I loaded the horses with everything I could find, leaving only the bodies of the Mallory boys alone in their blankets. The fight and the smell of blood in the air made the horses nervous, but they followed me out of the camp. I led them out of the woods, listening to Marcus' screams fade behind me.

Varya and the gelding were awake and waiting for me back at my camp. I lit Travis' old lantern to have enough light to see while I repacked the packs and horses. I saddled Varya and strung the horses in a line behind her, putting the pack saddle on the gelding at the end of the line. The gelding was used to following Varya and having him at the end would help keep the others in line.

We moved due east, walking and riding toward the rising sun until we finally came upon the royal road. It was a ribbon of hard-packed dirt, two wagons ride and stretching from horizon to horizon. It was one of the main trade routes of the kingdom and passed directly through Sila, joining with three others. I turned north toward the city, losing my tracks in the wake of thousands of other travelers for a pair of hours before turning off into a shallow, rock-bottomed stream.

I followed the stream until it wound around the base of a hill. Once I was sure the rise and the trees would block all sight from the road, I slid from Varya's back. My tired horse nickered and sighed, slogging toward the greenest patch of grazing she could find. I agreed completely. I could barely remain standing long enough to tend to the other horses before passing out in my blankets.

My stomach woke me. I crawled to my saddle bags and choked down some dried meat and trail biscuits. My arms trembled with exhaustion, but I forced myself to keep moving. I adjusted the tether length on two of the horses to allow them more room to graze before turning back to my supplies. I cleaned and oiled my sword, letting the night air fill me as my awareness slipped outward.

The next morning, the frigid water of the stream washed away the grime and sweat of the past few days. I let the horses off their tether, trusting Varya to keep them close and went through my morning routine. I let my hair dry in the breeze and took stock of the supplies. I had two sets of blankets, four saddles, four crossbows, four quivers of bolts, three bullwhips, about a hundred feet of rope, a tent, and five horses. I was also well supplied with food, utensils, tools and other odds and ends, including several sets of clothing and a bottle of strong, homemade liquor.

I cocked an eyebrow at the clothing. The younger of the two Mallory's had been thin and slightly built and my dress was definitely on its last legs. His pants were too long, but they fit around the waist and hips. I cut off the extra length with my long knife and washed them in the river along with a thick, dark tunic I found in one of the other bags. I wrung them out and dressed. There was still enough extra length to tuck the pants into my riding boots so it wouldn't drag or catch on my stirrups. I stowed the ragged remains of the dress in my pack and swung my cloak across my shoulders.

I practiced with my sword again to get used to the new way my clothes moved around me and to give me time to think. I wanted to help my friends and the city, but I wasn't sure what I could do. On the other hand, I was better outfitted than I had been in my entire life. There were plenty of areas in the kingdom that could be a lot safer. I sighed at myself in frustration, knowing the decision was already made. Sila was a day away at most and if there was any way I could help, I would.

But instead of moving out, I rested through the day. Hunting Marcus and the others had taken its toll, mentally more than physically. I needed the rest and so did the horses. I had pushed my two as hard as I dared and the three stolen by Marcus and the two Mallory's needed time to adjust to Varya and the gelding.

I went through every sword move I knew, working through the movements for hours and switching hands until both arms trembled. I took some time to eat and rest and switched to my crossbow. The rest of the afternoon I fired at a makeshift target of dead wood I'd braced against the base of the hill.

By the time the sun set, my arms quivered with every movement. I ate slowly, leaning against my saddle. My awareness drifted slowly outward to fill the surrounding area. I pulled it in with a breath and shifted my senses, scanning the area again and again to practice feeling my new powers until I could barely keep my mind focused.

I tried to extend myself outwards one last time and failed. My mind drifted away from the valley and locked onto an idea of Serena. The picture of her odd pointy ears bracing against her strange hat filled my mind and expanded as I concentrated. She stood upon a ledge. Black smoke rose behind her as she fired arrow after arrow into rows of the enemy, saving her rifle for later. Her hair drifted behind her in the wind and the screams of the dying drifted to my ears, lost in the rapid twang of the bow string. I pictured myself beside her, speaking softly in her ear, "I'm coming, Serena."

She spun to face me and the bow slipped from her startled hands. "Cary?"

My eyes snapped open and I came to my feet, breathlessly looking around. I was still in the shallow depression. There was no trace of fire or battle. The horses meandered in front of me. Varya cocked her head at me, trying to decide if I needed anything. I waved her off and settled back against my saddle, trying to shake off the strange dream.

20.

The next morning came easily. I rose early and rode due north to stay out of sight of the road. I'd been to Sila once as a child with my adopted father, but I could only remember a thick walled city surrounded by dense old trees. The maps Travis and I had looked at back at the cattle camp had only shown the main roads that cut through the forest. If I was lucky, I thought I might be able to find a logging trail or farm path through the trees.

The forest I rode through thickened through the day, growing dark and dense. Not only could I not find a trail or path through the trees, but my horses grew more skittish with every passing step. By late afternoon even Varya seemed reluctant to move forward.

The smell of the city tickled my nose and a roar of distant sound broke through the trees, punctuated occasionally by distant horn calls. The shadows seemed to move through the forest. I could almost feel something pressing on my mind and urging me back. I slid to the ground and panic rippled through me, pounding on my mind.

The ground pulled the warmth from my body, feeding the growing shadows around me. Something flashed in the corner of my eye and my sword arced silver in the afternoon sun, springing to my hand as my senses blossomed outward.

I froze. There was nothing there except forest. I looked around and could almost feel the trees grow. My breath came in short gasps and I pulled my senses back to me. The shadowed ground rippled with small amounts of power. I could feel it pushing outward from the city and driving me back. I drew in a deep breath and gathered myself around the feeling of my power, using it like a shield to block the force of the spell coming at me.

I staggered with the effort, almost falling to my knees. I clung to the nearest tree, panting for breath and dripping sweat as I pulled more power forward, extending and thickening the shield. The spell split around me like the wind and I gasped for breath. After several minutes, I stood up, moving forward. Varya snorted in fear behind me. I mustered my strength and pushed harder to slide the spell away from the horses as well.

The forest was thick and savage. Huge trees grew several feet thick and the underbrush wove traps of vines and thorns, but it they weren't the evil shadows they'd seemed before. I moved forward slowly, but the strain of holding the spell at bay grew with every step. Finally, I was forced to turn back and tether the horses in a small clearing.

I wrapped my power around me like a blanket and forced my way through the forest alone. The effort of keeping the spell at bay was a lot smaller without the horses and I was able to cut a path through the thickset trees. The distant sound of conflict grew louder as I moved. I focused on my ears and let the sound guide me to the city, hoping I could get a good look without being seen. The taller trees slowly faded as I reached the forest wall and I crawled forward beneath the woven mass of twisted trees and looked out on Sila.

Nearly a mile of torn ground land lay between the city and the forest. Boulders jutted up at odd angles with broken wagons impaled on the top. Great open crags crisscrossed the ground and ended in boggy mires or twisted sinkholes. It was a stretch of ground out of someone's nightmare, but the besieging army still owned the ground.

There were thousands of them, tens of thousands, surrounding the city on all sides. They straddled the great rips in the earth and tamed the bogs with wagon loads of dirt they brought from the tree line to the east. Horn calls cut through the air as I watched and siege weapons rumbled, hurling great boulders against the massive city walls, shattering the stone and sending razor sharp shards through the air.

The walls of the city were thick, but not high enough to be a deterrent for long. They stood massive and slate grey, rippling with vine work and topped with spear-like thorns. The decorative wrought iron structures of the three great gates stood well above the walls, braced by stone archways. Two of the gates faced the main roads entering the city from the south and the third gate straddled the road from the north. The Lord's keep rose in the center of the city, surrounding by its own tall, heavy wall.

A horn call sounded in a field to the west of my position. The assembled siege weapons rang against the wall, splitting rock and shattering the vines as the Blood Priest's infantry charged the walls, carrying ladders and ramps. The city walls shuddered under the assault. I thought they were starting to buckle, but instead they began to ripple, responding to the attack.

My eyes widened in shock. The vines on walls moved on their own, undulating with a predatory hunger while the very stones of the walls thickened and grew perceptibly higher. The row of stone thorns on top of the wall gleamed and the wrought iron gates wove tighter together, shifting like a spider's web.

Thomas' presence flared through the air in front of me, a fleeting impression of his face warped in concentration and rage. The ground split beneath the charge, heaving men to their knees and ripping open a great chasm. Men and women fell screaming into the abyss alongside horses and machines. The ground twisted and shut, swallowing their screams.

The enemy infantry attacked again without fear, but this time they reached the walls. The vines reacted. Tendrils reached past the ladders and ropes to grab at the people climbing the walls. The city defenders swarmed the top of the wall, screaming in rage and hacking at the swarming invaders. My breath caught in my throat. The defenders on the wall fought breathlessly and brave, but mixed through the ranks of the militia were barely armed men and women, screaming as much in terror as rage.

The waves of infantry hit the wall three times. Converted threw themselves over the wall with each assault. The fighting was brutal and bloody, but I forced myself to look away, taking stock of the enemy positions from my vantage behind them.

Each gate faced out from the city toward an encamped group of men. Each besieging army was arranged in a large seven-pointed star. Each point of the three stars burned with small sacred fires guarded by armed soldiers and stoked by a man in orange robes. I breathed and shifted my awareness toward the nearest army. Thomas' spell was blocked by the sacred fires. It split around the camp and left the people and cattle inside unharmed.

I pulled my senses back with an effort and studied the rest of the siege. There was an army camped in front of each gate and a wall of tents running along the sides of the city. They were heavily manned and supported by wagons. I crawled away from the field and sideways through the trees, inching toward the camp on the nearest side wall.

I smiled. The wagons supporting the side camp were cook wagons and more than half the men moving through the camps were injured. Hospital tents flanked the side camps to make them appear bulky and stronger from the front. A large herd of cattle milled in a protected corral to the south of the city alongside the road to the eastern gate and an equal herd of horses were corralled to the north.

I watched the enemy camp for hours. I lay in the heavy brush as the sun sank low over the surrounding hills. When their attack began to falter against the wall, the enemy vanguard pulled back and rotated the remnants of their tired infantry away to be replaced with fresh troops. I was exhausted and depressed and my mind began to drift.

My daydream was of Serena again. She was covered in soot and stood in a long line of people. Her greatcoat was almost solid black with ash. She held a battered bowl and waited until a scared looking woman gave her a ladle of broth and a chunk of bread. The people around her were gaunt and hollow eyed, waiting for their daily ration. Her grimy silver hair flowed as she knelt and offered a hungry child her bread. The little girl snatched it away hungrily and ran to share it with her siblings. The rationing was strict, one bowl of soup a day.

Serena walked to the side of the road and sat with her back pressed against a building, slowly drinking her soup. She was tired and hungry and somewhere behind her eyes there was a trace of despair. I spoke softly to her in the dream, wishing she could hear me. "I'm here, Serena. I'm just outside the city. Gods, I wish you could hear me. The formations on the east and west sides are just for show. They're mainly wounded men, hospital tents, and cook wagons. You're wasting man power on those walls. If you can hold out, help is on the way. The royal garrison at Narissa is coming. They're weeks away yet, but they're coming. You just have to hold on."

She raised her head with a tired smile, her glittering elven eyes fixing directly on me. "We'll try, Cary. The food won't last much longer. Much of what we had was poisoned, but I promise we'll try. Thank you."

I snapped awake. My heart pounded in my ears and the tips of my fingers were numb. The dream had been so real. I swallowed and looked back down into the valley. Bonfires burned in the center of each army. The same type of ritual bonfire that I'd seen before. Crowds of people shifted around them, chanting rhythmically. I wanted to shift closer, to see if they were the conversion fires I was afraid they were, but movement drew my eyes to the ground in front of me. A squad of men on horseback raced across the ground toward my position with readied weapons.

I leapt away from the tree and ran back into the dense brush. I threw myself into a deep thicket and curled into a ball, pulling my cloak around me and trying to blend my presence into the surrounding forest by force of will.

The scout party crashed into the forest exactly where I had been sitting only moments before. They threw open the shutters on massive lamps to flood the area with light. They cursed and growled, snarling at the shadows. I stilled my breathing and froze, praying to all the New Gods the scouts wouldn't see me as they dismounted to check for tracks. They moved north along the forest edge, reluctant to enter the spelled trees. I kept as still as I could, afraid to even breathe until long after the sounds of movement faded.

I lay perfectly still for another hour before I crawled from the thicket. The forest was black. The thickset trees blotted out all light from the moon or stars and I had to pick my way along. The bones in my pouch led me unerringly back through the forest toward the horses. I gathered the reins and led them deeper into the woods and out of range of Thomas' spell, finding a deep ravine where we could spend the night.

The drizzle woke me first, followed by a biting cold wind that ripped through the ravine. I shivered with the cold and grunted angrily while the horses nickered and stomped in complaint. We stumbled, half-blind, through the gray of morning for nearly an hour before finding a suitable spot of open ground. I tethered the horses and tucked my equipment beneath an overhang of branches to stay dry. I ate breakfast while sharing warmth with Varya and moved forward again, aiming for the tree line a few miles south of where I was yesterday.

Hundreds of cows milled through the thickening mud below my position. The fairground's corral was large, well-fenced, and within easy view of the city gate. The Blood Priest's camp was well to the side of the paddock. It left the line of sight clear to taunt the starving city.

The wind blew harder in the open areas near the city, driving freezing rain through the ranks of the Blood Priest's men. Thomas' presence rode the wind and the city walls were almost lost in the swirling fog, but looked far more crowded with defenders. I scanned the camp and positions below me as well as I could, judging the toll the rain was taking before moving away again.

I led the horses away from the city and far around the eastern side. We crept through the dense trees to avoid any patrols and moved back to the north. I left the horses tucked neatly below a cathedral canopy and wormed my way back to the city near the northern ramparts. Along the tree line to the north the enemy's horses stamped and blew against the cold while I eyed them. Ribs showed against the hides of many of them and their eyes spun wild in feral hunger.

The camp facing the north gate was larger than the two southern ones. It straddled the northern road and dominated the landscape. Their seven pointed star stretched wide, but the lines of the formation were arrow straight and well manned. The greater discipline from this army showed plainly in damage to the city walls. The great ornamented gate was blackened from fire and bent from repeated blows. Thick vines fell blackened from the wall to smolder along the ground, burning from some source of heat I couldn't see. Cracks ran the length of a man through the city wall and sections of the heavy gate doors were missing.

A horn call cut through the air and siege weapons roared. Massive boulders soared through the air to shatter against the walls and gates of the city and sea of men and women formed into blocks before the camp, readying for the attack.

My breath quickened, but I held myself in check. Defenders flooded the walls and horns sounded to the south. The wind roared, twisting the light drizzle into a driving rain and battering against the soldiers. A single rider moved calmly through the ranks, holding a lit torch. His features were hidden beneath a dark gray hood. He raised the torch and the assembled horde screamed, charging toward the wall.

Arrows fell like rain into the ranks of the attackers, but the charge didn't slow. They carried ladders and long wooden platforms to brace against the wall for use as ramps. Once they got close, the ladders and planks were thrown against the wall and people struggled to the top, weapons drawn.

Brutal fighting erupted along the top of the wall. Swords and axes clashed, ripping open armor and flesh. Screams echoed across the field and blood painted the outer walls. The attackers kept coming, raging against the driving wind and fighting like crazed beasts.

The rider with the torch watched the carnage from behind his forces, out of bow range from the city. As the fighting on the walls neared a fevered pitch, he stood in his stirrups and thrust the torch toward the gate. The world melted like wax before him and the gates shook with a thundering crash. He swung the torch once over his head and thrust it forward again, tearing power from the world and channeling it through the torch. The wall rang with the force of the blow. Pieces of wood and stone splintered and shattered. I could hear Thomas' voice on the wind, screaming in pain.

My feet tore across the open ground. My feet narrowed to a single point. The rider shoved his torch forward again and again the world ran like melting wax. I threw myself into the air, vaulting onto the rear of his horse. My sword blade split the rain and lodged in the side of his throat.

The horse reared, dumping us both to the ground. I rolled to my feet and tore my sword from the spurting wound in the man's neck. Two steps and I grabbed the saddle horn, swinging myself onto the horse's back and kicking hard. Enraged shrieks rang behind me as the horse leapt forward, flying toward the city wall.

The air was wild with screams. Hundreds of men and women boiled out of the driving rain toward me. They tore themselves free of the walls, racing back toward me. The walls defenders slaughtered them from behind, but they kept coming. I rode low and clung to the horse's neck, slapping his flanks with the edge of my blade, driving him faster with the madness of pain.

The wagon-bed ramp was a mass of battle-cries and flailing weapons. We hit it with the force of a thunderclap. People screamed and tumbled in all directions. Something tore deep in my side and weapons flashed through my vision. Attackers and defenders alike grabbed at my legs and arms, trying to tear me from the horse as my momentum carried us forward. For a moment we were on top of the wall. We were the center of conflict as the two armies crashed together. Something struck me low in the chest. The horse screamed and we tumbled to the stone ground.

My body went numb with the impact. I was trapped beneath the screaming horse. My sword was gone. A boy of about fifteen ran at me, raising an axe above his head. A shadow stepped between us and blocked the boy's path. I caught sight of long, strange side-burns below a steel helmet. Friss looked at me with a mixture of awe and sorrow. He grabbed the boy by the shoulder. "Tell the watch the assault is breaking and to send more men to the south wall. Then go to the temple and tell Master Thomas the city defenses are a tavern wench stronger. He'll know what it means. Go!"

The boy ran off and the large man launched himself back toward the wall, brandishing a pair of swords. I smiled dimly and felt myself slip into the darkness. He had been talking about me.

21.

Pain brought me, staggering, back to the waking world. Pairs of hands gripped me by the shoulders, holding me in place as a dozen people leveraged the dead horse off me. I screamed as they heaved the massive corpse clear. The moment the weight cleared my feet, the hands holding me pulled me clear. There was a crossbow bolt imbedded in my chest and blood poured from the gash in my side. I whimpered in pain, coughing blood. Black spots warred with flashes of light in my vision. Thomas' face loomed in front of me, his salt and pepper hair slick with sweat and rain. He touched my cheek and I slipped back into blackness.

Magic filled the air, dragging me back to awareness some time later. Strong hands probed at my wounds and Thomas' deep voice sang. The strength of Earth and Air flooded through me. It bent and shaped the world as Thomas twisted reality around his will.

My vision sharpened as my wounds healed. Thomas' hands rose to my temples, rubbing slow circles of magic into me. The tear in my side was gone, replaced by a deep and desperate itch. I breathed the magic into my lungs, reveling in its purity. Finally, the song came to an end, letting silence ring through the large room.

Thomas looked awful. His hair was unkempt and unwashed and his face was sunken. He smelled of sweat and exhaustion, but he still spared me a smile. I reached out a trembling hand and brushed the hair from his face. His shirt hung from his collar bones and the color of his skin was more yellow than his normal tan. I turned painfully and hugged him close. "Oh, beloved," I whispered. "What have they done to you?"

His thin arms were still warm and strong. He held me tight for long enough to drag several shuddering breaths between his clenched teeth. "Cary, I..." He pulled away and gave me another tired smile. "I can't stay long. I have to get back."

His face was still tight, but his eyes shone. I pulled him to me, kissing him deeply as a tingle ran through my body. We held each other again until he broke away. "I'll try to visit you later tonight. I promise." He pulled himself out of my protesting arms and staggered away.

I watched him leave and Serena step into view. She carried Whisper slung over her shoulder. Her greatcoat was black with soot and ash and her strange tri-cornered hat was singed on one side. She carried her bandaged left arm in a sling and her high boots were scuffed and caked in mud. She smiled at me and her elven eyes blazed. She pulled me into a one-armed hug and kissed my face. I held her tight, laughing and beaming. "You look terrible," I said as we pulled apart.

She barked a laugh, her face glowing beneath the grime. "We thought you were dead."

"It was close a few times."

"I'm sorry, Cary. The others wanted to go after you, but Friss and I forced them not to." Her voice trembled. "I wanted to help, but my mission was to protect Tara. I couldn't let her go."

I kissed her gently and pulled her into another hug. "It's better that you didn't. It was a nightmare of running and hiding. Coming after me would have just gotten the rest of you killed. I did what I did to save Tara's life, not risk it."

Serena nodded. "She told us what happened. I'm not sure where you got the courage to taunt an entire army, but it was an act worthy of any rifleman."

"You should see some of the tavern brawls I've had to break up with nothing more than a bar tray and an empty mug." I laughed. "Insulting an army is easy."

Serena smiled, but before she could respond I plucked at the sling on her shoulder. "What's with the bandages? Hasn't Thomas gotten to you yet?"

"Thomas hasn't been healing anyone," she said. "You're a special case."

I glanced in the direction Thomas had gone. "He looks like he's been fighting this war by himself."

"He has, in a way. Thomas has been the city's only magical defense since we discovered the Lord's personal Mage poisoning the food supplies." She shook her head. "The city wall is thick, but not high enough to withstand a long siege. Thomas is the real reason this city hasn't fallen. He's kept the wall intact and upright, practically single-handed."

I drew back. "Isn't there anyone to help?"

"A few temple priests and a few travelers with enough power to amuse children. No one with any real magical talent. We're all worried about him. He hasn't been able to sleep more than a few hours a night since we got here and the enemy knows our strength is fading. Every day they increase the pressure a little more."

"New Gods, Serena. I wish I could've helped."

"You already have," she said with a dry smile. "Thanks to you we have some meat for the cook pot tonight."

"What meat?"

"The horse you came in on didn't survive the fall."

"Horse meat?" I made a face. "You must really be desperate."

Her smile twisted a little. "It's about what we have left. The city has a few thousand more people than it should and almost nothing to feed them. Lord Diea has already sacrificed most of his stables and the remaining livestock is under continual guard, but the Lord's Mage turned traitor long before the army got here. He poisoned most of the city's reserve food stores and laid a plague on the animals. The bastard even killed off most of the city's pets before he escaped."

I scowled. "Someone should gut him."

Serena's laugh was full bellied. "You already did."

"Me?"

"The Magician you killed on your way in here; the one with the torch? That was the Lord's personal Mage." The laughter suddenly fell from her eyes and she smacked me hard in the shoulder. "What in the hell were you doing charging out of the woods like that anyway?" she demanded. "That was the single dumbest thing I've ever seen. If that Mage hadn't been so engaged in battling Thomas he could have killed you with a wave of his hand."

"I didn't even really think about it," I said. My voice was small. "It just happened."

"Make sure it doesn't happen again. I thought it was another ghost at first."

"Ghost?"

She looked sheepishly at the floor. "I've been seeing your shade recently. I thought it was your ghost coming back to help us. Elven stories are filled with such things, but I guess it was just me seeing things, or a message from the gods."

I shrugged. "Who knows? I actually had dreams of helping you while I was watching the siege from the forest. I let you know I was coming, and then later I told you reinforcements were coming and about the troop distribution on the side walls." Serena gave me a strange look and I suddenly realized what I'd said. "By the New Gods, Serena! Reinforcements *are* coming! The garrison at Narissa! They'll be here in a couple of weeks! I can't believe I forgot to tell you until now. And the troops on the sides of the city-"

"Are mainly hospital wagons and injured people."

"Yes! How did you know?"

"You told me, Cary. That is exactly what your ghost said."

"But I told you that," I said. "In my dream. I came and spoke with you while you were eating."

Her eyes widened. "Yes! I was sitting against a building near the cook fires at the center of the city. How did this happen?"

"I...I don't know. I thought it was just a dream, but I've developed some abilities lately. I guess this is one of them."

"Like, what kind of abilities?" she asked.

I half shrugged, shaking my head. "I don't really know. A friend told me it was a kind of magic, but he didn't know what kind and I can't actually do much. I can sense some things and, apparently, talk to you."

"Does it work with anyone else?"

"I didn't know it worked with you. I thought I was day dreaming. I don't know what I'm doing with this stuff. Mostly it just kind of happens."

"It's alright," she said. "I was hoping for word on those reinforcements. We could really use it."

I struggled to my feet. My legs shook, but they held. "Let's get a drink and you can tell me how bad it really is."

"That I can do. The city's taverns were well stocked for the upcoming festival."

I buckled my sword belt into place and looked at the empty scabbard. "Did they find my sword?"

Serena smiled a little wickedly and nodded, handing me my cloak. "Friss has it."

"Oh, great..."

It was still drizzling rain and the wind whistled between the buildings. Children ran through the streets chasing rats for food. Horse stalls and hitch posts were barren and nearly all the shops were locked and shuttered. We walked through the streets until we found a tavern with a door we didn't have to kick open. It was empty and abandoned, but the shutters were intact enough to keep out the wind.

I sank into a chair not far from the door. Serena searched behind the bar for anything the looters had left behind. "It seems pretty picked over," she said. "Not much left back here except empty glasses."

I grunted and jabbed a finger toward a section of wall on the side of the bar. I smiled. "Try looking for a hidden cupboard below the price list. Most tavern keepers like to have a place to stash the expensive bottles."

Serena disappeared behind the bar for a few minutes before I finally heard a clasp slide open. She grabbed a dusty bottle and a pair of glasses and came back to the table, filling our glasses with the fine brandy. "You'd make a good wench," I said.

"Whisper could collect my tips."

We raised our glasses to each other and drained them. I reached for the bottle. "Okay," I said. "I know it's worse than I thought. The army outside numbers in the tens of thousands and the city is packed with starving people. Tell me the rest."

"If we don't get food in the next week or two, we're all dead. We've got almost fifteen thousand people who've had little more than one bowl of horsemeat broth a day for over a week and the rest of the food is gone. Thomas is on his last legs and won't survive more than another few days if he doesn't get a chance to rest." She took a breath. "And the army outside is three times larger than we expected because we're not dealing with one Blood Priest. We're dealing with three.

"They've converted or destroyed dozens of villages in the past few months. They've hired mercenaries and every thug they can find and they've managed to buy off some high ranking people in the kingdom, like the Lord's Mage. So far our only respite has been a rivalry between the three the Blood Priests. Each one wants to take the city first. We have three Blood Priests, three armies, and three gates. And all three armies serve the same banner."

"The Queen."

Serena raised an eyebrow. "A friend told me what the banner meant," I said. "I assumed Thomas and Friss knew."

"They do, but we've been keeping it quiet. It might divide loyalties we can't afford to lose."

I finished my drink and set the glass down. "What do we do now?"

Serena stood and tucked the bottle inside her jacket. "We go see Friss and get your sword back. Then we put you on the wall."

22.

We found Friss standing near a campfire giving words of encouragement to the men shivering around it. I stopped Serena before she stepped into the circle of light and stood back, watching Friss. He'd never talked much while we marched and it was surprising to see him at work. His gruff, short-spoken nature lent every word extra weight. He stood tall and strong; somehow gleaming through the grime that covered him. He addressed people by name when he could, singling out moments of bravery on the field of battle or thanking everyone for their determination. If inspiration and courage could win, Friss would be our greatest weapon.

He turned away from the men and walked toward us away from the fire. He nodded and waved us away under a low-hanging eave. He bent low and pulled my sword from under a pile of blankets. He handed it to me hilt first. "You dropped this."

I checked the blade and slid it into my empty scabbard. "Thanks for picking it up for me."

"You've taken care of it."

"It's saved my life too many times not to," I said. "I also practiced every day I wasn't running for my life."

Friss opened his mouth, but I cut him off. "What are you planning?"

"We hold for now. They know we're getting desperate so they'll be ready for a raid, but if we don't try it we may as well surrender."

"Then we do different than expected."

Friss grinned predatorily. "I was hoping you'd have enough sense to scout the enemy positions before hurling yourself to what should have been your death." He paused, meaningfully.

"Again." He pointed toward a shadowed doorway. "Let's go inside. I'll need everything you can tell me."

We walked inside. Serena poured the brandy and I outlined my plan. "I've got five horses with equipment stashed in the woods east of here. These wagons here," I drew a diagram in the dirt floor, "are full of medical supplies and guarded only by the wounded. The green canvas wagon in the northern camp is a fletcher's wagon. It's full of arrows and supplies. We get five people still strong enough to go. We slip east over the wall and straight into the hospital tents. We raid as many supplies as we can and then leave, but not back to the city. We head into the forest where we get the horses. Then three of us head north to raid some wagons and get back to the city, while the other two head south. Two small groups, two chances at supplies."

Friss shook his head. "Five people aren't enough. A good raid would take at least a dozen people. Five people just can't carry enough to matter. And you haven't told me how you plan to get back into the city."

"At this point a bag of potatoes would be enough," I said. "The people I've seen in the last hour need any victory they can get. And as for getting back into the city? That's where Serena comes in. While we're gone, Serena builds two ramps that will reach the top of the wall. She puts one inside and when we signal her, she drops the other outside and we all just ride up and over."

Serena shrugged at Friss. "It could work," she said. "Any success would perk our people up for at least another couple of days."

The large man grunted. "The real prize will be the information we get. Five men worth of supplies is meaningless beyond a symbol, but five men worth of information may give us a real chance."

I studied him with narrowed eyes. "You were already planning on going."

"I've been out twice already." He smiled. "I just wanted to hear your plan."

"When did you want to go?"

"Tonight. During the conversions. Most of the armies gather to watch the rituals. Their people will be night blind and tired."

"Okay. Where do you want me?"

"I'll get the men. Meet us by the east end command post. Serena can show you where it is." He turned and walked away.

Serena led the way back outside. "It's a good plan, at least," she said. "You set it up well."

"I didn't come up with anything new, though." I studied Serena's arm. "It's too bad you're injured," I said. "I'd love to have you along."

"Sorry. If you want to embrace death tonight, you will have to do it without me. I've got other plans."

"Jason would be perfect and Tara if she's willing." I stopped. "Wait. Where are Jason and Tara? I haven't seen them."

"You won't, either. We sent Tara north to the capital to report. Jason went with her as an escort."

"Oh."

Serena led me through the city, detailing fortifications and troop placements as she went. The people seemed to be working in shifts. Most of the people we saw were foraging or getting ready to fight, but others just slumped against buildings or lay on the ground. They were filthy, and starving. Anyone who couldn't fight: children, the elderly, the sick and wounded, were all stashed within the main keep. Tradesmen searched the town in droves, ransacking buildings and shops for anything they could find. Engineers tore apart houses. Bowyers and Fletchers tore down poles and cut trees from the city parks. Volunteers who were strong but unskilled were set digging trenches or building barricades with whatever they could find. Before long there wouldn't be much of the city left to defend.

Our tour of the city defenders ended more than an hour later as Serena led us to an old general store on the eastern side of town. Four people stood around a table in the center of the main room. Friss introduced the three I didn't know. Rhiannon was a tall, strong looking woman with short black hair and a spear. Lord Diea was a surprisingly young, well-built man who carried himself confidently. He was master of the keep and the official owner of the surrounding lands. The final person was a spindly old man in his late sixties who looked like he had trouble getting out of bed. He wore a long black cloak and carried a short sword on his hip. A lantern shaped pin held his cloak shut. "You're a LampLighter," I said.

He nodded and smiled at me in a grandfatherly way. "Larson," he said as an introduction. "Most people don't recognize us that quickly." He winked. "And fewer still know anything about us."

"I was with Travis when he sent Lula."

The old man shifted position and his whole demeanor shifted with it. I was no longer an outsider. I was someone worth talking to and perhaps even worth trusting. He looked me over for a second before Friss spoke, "Cary, outline your plan for us."

I went over everything I could think of, answering questions and listening to suggestions, fully conscious that I was a tavern wench giving orders to Landsmen and Lords. We finalized the plan and moved out to a section of wall where Friss had widened the distance between the perimeter torches. We wanted our night vision to be as crisp as possible when we went over the wall.

Each of us grabbed a pair of empty sacks and settled our belongings into position. It had started to rain again. We checked each other over, removing or blacking out anything reflective. Serena's elven eyes gave us the final inspection as we climbed to the top of ramp she'd placed on our side of the wall. At her nod, we slipped over the top, one by one.

23.

I hit the ground with a hard thump and clamped my teeth together to avoid groaning. I managed to catch my breath and lunge sideways in time to avoid having anyone land on me, but it was a close thing. Larson and Friss landed on noiseless, catlike feet and the sounds of the rest of us were swallowed by the wet ground and the falling rain. Friss had warned Thomas of our raid and the spell of confusion he had laid on the ground split away from our feet, leaving us unaffected.

We met near the corner of the wall, crouching low and waiting. Larson vanished according to plan, the spry old man disappearing into the night. I stretched out my senses to blanket the area, trying to feel everything and everyone. I couldn't feel Friss or Larson. They were invisible to my extra senses, even though Friss stood close enough that I could hear him breathe. I let them go, trusting their abilities far more than mine, but focused on the presences of the others carefully. I was hoping I could identify them later. Rhiannon squatted easily on the ground beside me, calm and relaxed. Lord Diea's presence was more what I expected. He was tense and anxious, but forcing himself to stay calm and deal with the situation. I swallowed. I felt the exact same way. Larson crept out of the night and signaled us to move. We spread out and ran toward the wagons.

Larson led the way and Lord Diea followed him. I counted to ten and ran after Lord Diea. Serena had helped me bind my sword in place so it wouldn't clatter as I ran. I kept as low as I could, straining my senses against the dark and the rain. My new awareness flooded through the area around me. It was uncomfortable, but it worked. I could feel people moving throughout the range of my new senses. Some of them felt awake and alert, but most of the people I felt, seemed to be asleep or drunk. Which was what we'd been hoping for. I felt two people clash to my right and turned to watch Lord Diea lower a wondering guard to the ground, pulling his dagger from the guard's throat. I turned away and kept running.

The target wagon loomed out of the darkness in front of me. It was on the end of a string of wagons, picketed with a torch and a few sleepy guards. There was a ripple of black cloth as Larson snuffed the torch with his cloak and a second later I ran past another dying man, struggling silently against Rhiannon's throat crushing grip.

Larson and Friss accounted for the other two guardsmen and I stretched my awareness ahead and around me, casting it outward like a fisher's net. Every presence I could sense that I didn't recognize I tried to sooth and ease, trying to calm them all to a point beyond the reach of alarm, especially the animals. I didn't know if it would work, but it was worth trying.

I reached the wagon in time to replace Friss. Larson was inside, choosing supplies and passing them out. Friss tugged the drawstring on his second sack closed and slung it over his shoulder, running past the wagon and toward the forest. I swung my empty sacks over the side of the wagon and turned away to stand guard. Lord Diea jogged the last few steps to the wagon as I watched. He moved cautiously, his face half coated in blood. I moved forward to check his injuries in the faint light from the distant fires, but he waved me away. I turned and grabbed the full sacks from Larson, hoisting them onto my shoulders and running east after Friss.

I took the second half of the run far more cautiously than the first. Even though I was behind the main guard positions, it was far more dangerous. People wandered through their camps despite the rain and with a heavy sack in each hand I couldn't draw a weapon if I needed one. My awareness stretched outward, trying to sense and calm the area around me.

I risked a glance backward and cast my new senses toward the wagon to check on Rhiannon and Lord Diea, but I should've been paying attention to where I was going. A presence flared up to my left and I turned in time to see a man stumble out of the rain, a bottle in his hand. I locked eyes with him, reacting instinctively as he opened his mouth to yell. My awareness collapsed. It narrowed to a single thought and I thrust it into him like a knife point, carrying the single unspoken command, *Sleep.* The man staggered as though struck, stumbling backward and slumping to a heap on the ground.

My mind reeled with the sudden effort and I lurched forward, stumbling to a knee. A gust of wind blew the rain into my face and I forced myself to breathe. I dragged in a cold shuddering breath and rose. I hefted the sacks with suddenly leaden arms and leaned into a stumbling run to cover the rest of the distance to the forest wall.

The brush at the tree line was thick. I spent what little strength I had left in my arms to heave the heavy sacks clear of the brush so I could stay silent as I shifted through the heavy underbrush. I could feel Rhiannon and Lord Diea crossing the distance between the wagon and the forest and squatted against the shadowed base of a tree to wait and watch. Something hissed softly on my left and I snapped my head to the side. Friss caught my eye with a short wave and together we turned back to watch for the others.

Rhiannon arrived first. The moonlight shone softly on her rain covered skin. She eased her way into the forest between a pair of trees and dropped to a squat near me when. She rested easily on her heels, her face split by a toothy grin. "Are you enjoying yourself?" I asked in a whisper.

"Immensely."

Lord Diea arrived before I could respond, loping out of the darkness at the forest edge until Friss hailed him with a faint bird call. Larson followed him by just a few seconds. His sacks slung carelessly over his shoulders. He smiled as he stepped into the forest. "Shall we?"

Rhiannon shrugged at my confused look, still smiling. I turned and led the way, ,moving deeper into the forest. My senses ranged through the forest ahead of me. I had lied to Friss and the others when I said I remembered exactly where Varya and the horses were waiting. I was fairly certain I knew roughly where they were, but I was betting my reputation on my new found powers and my ability to sense Varya from a distance.

We moved almost two full miles before I could feel Varya with my senses. She and the other horses were still together. I breathed a sigh of relief and felt my shoulders slump, hoping the darkness would conceal it. Varya's presence acted like a beacon, guiding me through the forest toward her. Within another mile, the five of us slipped into the clearing where I'd left the horses. They had slipped their tethers but were all still present.

Varya nickered softly and came to meet me as I entered the clearing. I stroked her neck and pressed my forehead against hers, sharing her warmth and her strength. The other four settled alongside the horses, selecting their mounts. Lord Diea, Friss, and Larson each took one of the saddled horses while Rhiannon vaulted carelessly onto the bare back of the gelding. We checked and tightened saddle straps and gear. Rhiannon cut a length of rope to tie into a make-shift bridle.

We squatted together in the clearing when the preparations were finished. "From here we split up," Friss whispered. "We may not have much time before someone finds those bodies. Lord Diea, Rhiannon and I will head north. If Cary's right, we should be able to lead the horses a good half mile from here without risking being seen. Then we make our break toward the city wall. Larson, you go with Cary and raid whatever food supply she has lined up."

Everyone nodded and moved toward their mounts. We'd been over everything already. Friss caught me as I moved to Varya's side, whispering, "Are you sure you know what you're doing?"

"No," I answered honestly, "but it's got to be done. Remember, even a sack of potatoes is a victory."

He nodded and started to turn, but I caught at his sleeve. "You were right not to let them come after me." He squeezed my shoulder and moved away, leading his horse.

Lord Diea and Rhiannon followed Friss north while I led Varya and Larson south. We didn't speak to each other, but we weren't overly concerned with being quiet either. This far into the trees sound didn't carry very far before it died in the rain and brush. We had decided before leaving the city we would take our time moving south. Once we got where we were going, we'd sit and wait for at least an hour to give Friss and the others time to make their run into the city. If everything went perfectly we wouldn't hear a thing until it was our turn.

There was a bark of thunder from the northwest corner of the city as Serena fired a single shot from the mighty Whisper to signal Friss. A few moments later, chaos erupted from the northern encampment. Men yelled, horses screamed, and fire blossomed into the night. Larson raised his eyebrows, but I could only give him a baffled shrug in response. We held each other's gaze for a moment before turning back to the south. They were on their own, just as we were.

Half an hour later we reached the southern tip of the forest as it wound around the city. We stashed our horses deeper in the woods and crawled forward to scout the area. Flames still danced north of the city despite the rain and I could see the dim shapes of people and animals running. I shared another bewildered look with Larson and he shrugged softly. "We must let it be as it is, I fear," he said.

I turned my eyes south and Larson did the same. "Where is this food stash you know of?" he asked.

I gestured with a nod and pointed westward. "Right down there. About a mile away across open ground."

Larson turned slowly to face me. His eyes were with astonishment. "You mean the cattle?"

24.

"Yes, I mean the cattle."

He let a breath out slowly. "Some bag of potatoes."

Part of me was thrilled I could shock the old man, but I shook my head. "Friss is right. A bag of potatoes is a symbol that keeps those people going for a day or two, but there are thousands of people starving to death in that city. A herd of cattle feeds us for weeks and cripples the siege." I paused. "Are you with me?"

The old man grinned like a playful child. "You're insane," he said. "Still, it's worth trying. If we can even get a couple of those cows over the ramp it'll be a tremendous help."

"It would," I agreed. "But we're not aiming for a couple and we're not aiming for the ramp. We're going to take the whole herd and run it straight through the open city gate."

Larson's jaw dropped slack. "How do you propose to do that? The city gate is nearly two miles away from the paddock. You'll never get those cows there unseen, and when you are seen the army will mount and take them back, butchering you in the process."

"That is certainly possible," I said. "And you don't have to come if you don't want to. That's why I wanted you with me. If anything goes wrong, you're good enough to get away and survive. But I don't plan on being unseen. I want them to see me. We're going to stampede the cattle toward the city and watch the army jump out of our way."

"And how are you going to get the city to open the gate?"

"You stand watch and I'll take care of that." He shot me a look, but turned his attention back to the encampment without comment.

I slid back into the shadows and calmed my mind as completely as I could manage. Gently, I reached my senses outward, sliding my awareness toward the city. Serena stood near the wall. She was talking to someone, but I couldn't make out who it was. I pushed my senses toward her and she whirled to face me. "Cary?" she hissed. "Is that you?"

"It's me. I'm south of the city and there's been a change of plans. I need you to do something for me and I'm going to need you to trust me."

Serena listened carefully as I told her what I needed her to do and when. Her eyes were hard and cold when she answered. "I'll do it because I owe you, Cary. You were willing to spend your life to protect Tara when I was too far away to do my job. I'll risk the lives of everyone else here to give you the chance to do what you think you can. But you should know, if your plan doesn't work, you will have single-handedly given them the city and all our lives."

I nodded, uncertain if she could see the gesture. "It'll work," I said. "It has to."

I snapped awake again. My head ached like crazy and my stomach twisted, but I shook it off. I took a second to re-adjust to my surroundings and crawled forward. Larson was where I had left him. "The plan is set to go."

He nodded and pointed toward the camp. "*We* should also go."

I looked at the camp in front of us. Four men on horseback were pounding over the open ground toward us. They held torches high and spread out to scour the ground toward us. Larson looked at me. "I don't know what you did, but it got someone's attention."

We slid back into the woods and ran lightly toward our horses. I pulled the crossbow from my saddle and fitted a bolt to it. "We can't let them find us or follow us," I said. "We put them down here."

Larson grunted and tied his horse to a branch before climbing into a tree several yards closer to the oncoming riders.

I slid into a narrow thicket and crouched with Varya tied securely in a stand of trees behind me. The riders thundered into the forest in front of us, grunting and throwing light everywhere. Larson's horse whinnied in surprise and the horsemen came at us in a rush.

They split on the run. Two of the riders rushed toward Larson's horse and the other two charged straight for Varya. As soon as the riders were in range, Larson leapt from the tree, plunging his dagger into the rider's throat and knocking him from his rearing horse. I came to my feet and fired my crossbow. The bolt went wide, sinking into a tree several feet away from the man I'd shot at. I dropped the useless weapon with a sneer and pulled my sword.

One of the men kicked his horse forward and stabbed low with his spear. I stumbled backward, losing my footing in the thick brush. Another rider circled behind me. I turned and swung. The rider shifted his weight and caught my sword on his spear shaft. I twisted away, reversing my swing and plunging the point of my sword into the horse's throat. It reared and screamed, sending the rider to the ground.

My senses flared open and I dropped to the ground as the other horseman's axe whistled through the air. The swipe took loose strands of hair from the top of my braid and the charge carried the horseman past. I stepped forward and buried my sword into the fallen horseman to ensure he'd stay down. The axe man had started to charge again when he suddenly stiffened, the smooth wooden hilt of a knife protruding from one of his eyes. He tumbled from his saddle and his horse thundered by. I looked up. Larson was standing calmly a few feet away. The other two horsemen lay dead a short distance from his feet. I grabbed my crossbow from the ground. Larson bent and grabbed the two still-burning torches from the ground.

"What are you doing with those?" I asked.

He smiled and pulled his cloak hood low. "We ride out the back side of the forest and hold the torches high. Let them think we're part of the patrol."

I swung onto Varya's back and grabbed one of the offered torches. We wheeled and rode hard through the woods with the torches held high. We came out of the back of the forest onto the main road and rode like hell, our torches hissing in the rain. The wind drove the cold under my cloak. We turned north toward the city and rode hard. A rear posted sentry waved as we neared. "What news?" he called.

I hit him in the face with my torch as we thundered past. The impact ripped the torch from my hand. Larson threw his to the ground as well, leaving them to sputter out in the rain.

We slowed our run as we approached the fairgrounds and eased our way up behind the corral. A pair of guards huddled at the front of the paddock. I pulled my crossbow and reached for the quiver, but Larson stopped me with a gesture. "I've seen you shoot, lass."

He slid from his saddle and handed me the reins. "As soon as that gate is open, you had better do whatever you're planning to do to move those cattle. We won't have much time."

He vanished into the dark before I could respond. I pulled the bullwhip from my saddle and let the rain slicked leather dangle loosely. I stretched my senses forward to touch the herd. I could feel their mood, their energy, and their anxiety. I tried to work quickly, pushing at them, raising their level of anxiety and fear into a state of near panic. I brought my rage into their minds and let it stir.

The whole herd stood tense and their aggression grew with every splattering raindrop. It swirled between them, waiting for something to set it off. I opened my eyes and looked up. One of the huddled guards had already vanished. The other guard disappeared behind a swirl of black cloak.

I took the cattle higher, pushing at their minds. I took their rage and hate to the boiling point and gave it a sudden direction. Their mood flowed back into me, pouring into my mind, thundering through my being and threatening to engulf me. Larson threw open the gates at the front of the paddock and I raised the bullwhip. The soft leather whispered through the air. I snapped it down hard. The night split with the sharp crack and the cattle leapt forward. I screamed into the night and let the rage and terror flow through my voice and fill the herd. I kicked Varya's flanks and she lunged forward, chasing the storm of cattle.

We plunged forward. The stampede gained speed and power as it destroyed everything in its path. I rode behind the storm, urging it onward with every whip crack. I was linked with the herd, part of it, in control of it. They moved in response to my will. I poured my awareness into them and through them, sending panic to radiate through the herd and into the surrounding camp. I let the terror and rage flow through me, becoming part of me and feeding it back into the herd.

I felt my awareness shift. It slipped past the point where I'd always stopped before. Fear ran through me like lightning. The lines between me and the herd blurred. We were becoming one. The strength and unity of the stampede pulled me in, merging my mind with theirs. A dozen slow men had already been crushed beneath our hooves and more were coming. They were too slow or too stupid to move out of our way.

Something hit us like a wave of thunder. It struck at our minds and threatened to split us apart. A wall of rage grew within us and we turned to thunder toward the man responsible. He was foolish to try and stop us. He was alone with no herd to strengthen him. We thundered toward the group of men who rode tall in their saddles and shone in their armor. They rushed forward and their hated whips cracked.

They were nothing. They stood near each other but they each stood alone. They knew nothing of strength. The mind creature that opposed us appeared. He stood behind his men and his power built like a wall around them, but our rage turned us toward him.

The man's arm waved wildly and he threw something into our midst. I felt the spell hit me and instantly severed my link with the herd. The momentum of the charging cattle carried them thundering forward. The stampede slammed into the Blood Priest's personal guard, crushing the men and scattering the horses. The Blood Priest stood behind the chaos and yelled words of power. Varya thundered forward, still moving with the force of the herd. The Blood Priest shifted to the side and his face became visible in the fire light. He wasn't the Priest who had attacked my village, but he was still a murderer. I raised my whip and he thrust his arms forward. His power hit me like a net, weighing me down. The weight gained on me with every step forward Varya took. My arms sagged to my sides and my legs went numb.

The spell must've hit Varya too. She slowed as we neared the Priest, coming to a stop in front of him. The Blood Priest grinned and screamed for his people. I fought against the spell, tearing and screaming with my mind. The stampede raced on in front of me, but without guidance they were beginning to come apart. I gathered my strength and raged against the spell, forcing myself to move. My arms trembled. My heart pounded. The effort was incredible, but even as the Blood Priest gave me a gloating smile, my hand slid forward and landed on Varya's bare neck. As soon as I touched her, her presence linked with mine and I flooded her being with all the hatred and rage I held. In an instant, my fight became *our* fight.

Varya' whinnied in rage and reared, lashing out with her heavy hooves. The Blood Priest flinched in surprise and tried to leap back, but he was too late. One of Varya's massive iron shod hooves slammed hard into his temple, knocking him to the ground. The spell holding me shattered. I slapped my hands to the pommel as Varya hammered at the ground. The link between us was fading, but my rage still filled her mind. She ground the Blood Priest beneath her hooves, crushing the life from him.

I kicked Varya hard in the flanks and cracked the bullwhip. She leapt forward, racing after the stampede. I poured my awareness through her and sent it rippling into the night to join with the herd. I gave myself to the spell, becoming one with the herd. Instantly, the disorganized rout became a single living entity. We were the herd, thundering over anyone in our way.

The city loomed before us. The wall was massive and threatening, but from within us we knew what to do. We screamed. All of us, every cow, every ox, the horse, even her rider screamed with a single voice and purpose. The wall opened at our signal, revealing the strange buildings of the city as we thundered toward it. That place deep within told us peace, safety, and food lay within. More slow and stupid men were trampled beneath our charge but we barely noticed. We funneled through the open wall into a large open space. The open streets leading away were blocked by wagons. The stampede raged through the air, butting against buildings and trees while something calmed from within, slowing us until we eased. The master part of the herd within us told us we were safe. We heard the walls slam shut behind us and men ran forward with long logs.

I broke contact with the herd. My mind reeled as men ran past me with lumber to brace the gate shut again. Serena was standing on the ramparts looking down at me. She smiled in awe. I swiveled my head around, searching. Dozens of city defenders fought with the enemy that we'd pushed through the opening in front of our charge. Larson leaned hard over his horse's neck. A crossbow bolt stuck out of his leg and he bled from a gash in his arm, but he was still smiling. When I knew he was safe I collapsed, falling from my horse to the cobblestone below as a great cheer rose through the city. The world twisted and I slept.

25.

Even in the darkness of sleep the world kept twisting. Lights appeared and faded. Strange shapes moved in the darkness around me. Some joined together and others broke apart. Sounds appeared suddenly. Voices grew out of the darkness. Whispers that screamed through my head and shouts so faint they were lost on the wind. I felt the sun wheel through the heavens above me. Strange flashes of images rotated through my mind: cows, Blood Priests, weapons. I grappled with what I thought were core traits of myself, only to have them ripped from me. My memories were parceled out like rations only to be thrown back into me. Finally, everything slowed and settled, calming again into the plain blackness and dreams of sleep. I thanked the New Gods and let myself slip away.

I awoke in darkness. My head rang like a cathedral bell. I was laid out on a cot again in the domed temple. I sighed and immediately winced. The soft sound of my breath escaping had spiked the pain in my head. A few feet away a cup of broth sat on a table. I forced myself to reach for it. The liquid was no longer warm but it wasn't quite cold. I drained the cup in a single pull. The liquid filled an empty place in my stomach and pushed away my headache. I put the cup down and wiped my mouth.

I turned toward the soft sounds of someone breathing deeply behind me. The movement was slow, more from stiffness than caution. Thomas lay on a bunk a few feet from mine, snoring softly at a pillow. I leaned toward him to get a better view. His face was gaunt and pale, but I thought he looked to be sleeping peacefully rather than unconscious from exhaustion. I rose softly on bare and unsteady feet. My boots, belt, sword, and saddle bags were resting on the end of my bed.

I left them where they were and made my way to the privy on the side of the room.

There was a bucket of water near the wash basin and I bathed my hands and face, freeing my hair from its confinement to attack it with my brush. When I finished, I let my hair flow freely over my shoulders and made my way back to the cots. I debated for a moment about crawling into Thomas' bunk for the rest of the night but didn't want to take the chance of waking him.

Serena walked in carrying a small bundle as I tied my boots into place. She smiled as I stood and motioned me to follow, her arm still wrapped in a sling. We walked across the temple floor to a small alcove in the side of the room with a bench and table and she kissed me lightly on the forehead. "I'm sorry I doubted you, Cary. Forgive me."

"You're forgiven. I wouldn't have believed it either."

"We've been worried about you. When you collapsed, we all thought you were under a spell. Larson saw you fight the Blood Priest, but Thomas said it was something else, though he wouldn't say what. You've been asleep for almost a week."

"A week?" I gaped at her. "What's been happening?"

Serena sat on the bench and placed the bundle on the table. "You and Larson both collapsed after getting back with the cattle. You were suffering from whatever it was and we pulled four crossbow bolts out of Larson." She held up a hand, forestalling my reactions. "He'll be fine. They didn't hit anything vital, he just needs to rest.

"They butchered almost two dozen of your cows immediately after you brought them in and a few more were stolen. They would have kept at it but we were able to force the people back. They would have destroyed their only chance of survival in the celebration of having gotten one." Her voice was bitter.

"Now the cattle are under strict guard in the keep courtyard. There have still been several attempts to steal a cow and we're still rationing food to one meal a day, but now there's some meat to it and it might actually last. We hung the heads of three of the butchered in plain view, one head on the top of each gate. Just to make sure the sting of your raid sticks."

She shook her head to clear away her budding rage and held the bundle she'd been carrying out to me. "This is for you. It's a gift from Lord Diea. He had a seamstress see you while you slept."

The bundle contained clothes: a shirt, bodice and pants, all of high quality. I finished bathing in the wash bucket and changed while Serena continued. "Things have been quiet since the raid. You took down one of the Blood Priests and we think the other two are competing for control of his camp. It seems to be keeping them too occupied to think about us. Thomas has been asleep for almost two days now, his first in about a week."

"I didn't take the Blood priest down," I said. "Varya did." Serena shot me a confused look and I laughed. "Varya's my horse."

"Good horse."

I laughed and slid into my new shirt. "She is that. Reliable too. She's the horse they stole from me the night my village was attacked. I got her back the night I led them away from Tara."

Serena's smile broadened. "Then she is meant to be yours."

"What about the others?" I asked. "Friss, and Rhiannon? There was a lot of noise that night."

"They all made it back. Friss used some alcohol in his supplies to set the horse paddock on fire. Then they pulled down the fence. With all the horses running wild, the guards didn't seem to notice an extra three with riders. Which reminds me," she said with a grin. "Friss sent along a gift as well." She reached into her pocket and drew out a large, lumpy, potato. "He calls it your symbol of victory. Rhiannon managed to capture a sack of them on the way back."

I laughed. "I should stick this on a spear and make it into my personal standard."

Serena shook her head. "It's too late for that. You're standard has already been chosen for you, at least in this city." She pulled me forward. "Come and see."

Serena led me out the front door of the temple. Planted in the soft grass outside was a long wooden pole with a banner hung from the crossbeam to flap in the evening breeze. It was a long green cloth with a cow's head painted on it. Long black horns gleamed above soft brown eyes. I beamed at it for a moment before heading back inside. "What else has been happening?"

Serena raised a questioning eyebrow. I shot her a look, buckling my sword into place. "You don't honestly think I'd believe that you've spent a week doing nothing but resting while they're pre-occupied, do you?"

She shrugged. "Who knows how bad that fever damaged your fragile human mind?"

I kicked out at her shin, but she dodged easily. "Friss has led several raids against the camp you trampled with the herd. Both destruction raids as well as supply raids. They've been successful, but very costly. Half of the last raid didn't return, including Rhiannon. She went down while setting an herbalist's wagon on fire after they raided it. The next major move is planned for tonight. About an hour before dawn we're going to launch a full scale attack against the northern camp. We hope to break their front line of forces long enough to pull in some of the wagons. Several of the caravan drivers that came here for the festival have been practicing with quick hitching teams." She gave me a wry smile. "You've inspired them. It seems if you humans see stupidity, half of you think it's a good idea. Now everyone wants to spit in the enemy's eye and be a hero. Your crazy stunt may have saved us all, if we can keep it going."

"I didn't do anything worth praising," I said. "I put the lives of thousands of people at risk on a slim chance and got lucky. Just because it worked doesn't mean it wasn't a bad idea."

Serena beamed at me like I had just spoken my first words. "A human who can reason beyond her vanity?" She acted shocked "You are a rare bird."

"Speaking of reasoning, you said the drivers were practicing quick hitching teams. Practicing with what? We only have five horses."

"Last night's raid netted another ten, which brings our total to fifteen. That's seven two horse teams. We're hoping half of them make it back with wagons."

"Where do you want me?" I asked.

"Are you sure you're up to it?"

I shook my head. "I'm not sure of anything at the moment other than I need to eat and we need those supplies. I can solve one and maybe help solve the other. There's nothing else I can do and I'm certainly not sitting here while you and Friss risk your lives without me."

"I don't think I'll be out there," she said, raising her sling in a gesture of frustration. "I'm still too injured to do much good."

Realization dawned and I smiled at her. "That's why you were coming here in the middle of the night. You were hoping Thomas would be awake."

Eagerness burned in her elven eyes. "It's not that I don't love you, Cary, but you can't heal my arm. I hate being forced to sit on the wall like little more than a signalman. These raids are crucial to our survival and I want to be able to do something."

"I'm sorry. Maybe Thomas will awaken soon." I shrugged. "There's no way to tell."

Serena straightened, discipline returning to her face and stance. "I know. Thanks for listening. Now. Let's get you some food and get you to Friss."

I nodded and pulled my riding cloak across my shoulders. The clothes were warm and high quality and they fit perfectly. I hefted my potato and followed Serena out the door, past the cow's head standard.

26.

We wound our way through the city until we found a guarded cook wagon near the northern wall. Serena spoke with the guards before they let us through and the cook laughed when Serena told her who I was. She roasted my potato for me while we waited and added it to a large heaping bowl of beef stew, adding a tall glass of fresh cow's milk.

Serena led me to a building after we ate. Friss stood near a map, laying out the last of his battle plans with his chosen commanders. Lord Diea stood with the others, receiving his orders. I nodded at him and waited. When Friss finished, I stepped to the table. "Where do you need me?"

Friss shook his head with a scowl. "I don't need glory seekers on this mission, Cary."

"That's *exactly* what you need," I said. "Every drive team that brings back a wagon is guaranteed to fill their beds from now till Solstice. You need all the able bodies you can get and that includes me."

"Are you sure you're an able body?"

"I'm fine, Friss."

"Very well. You'll be with Diea's group gathering wagons. The mercenary camps are too far away and too heavily guarded to get at, but the converted wagons and the faire wagons are parked almost within bow shot." He gestured to the map. "There's a circle of supply wagons that are only a half mile from the gate. Get as many of those inside as you can; push them, pull them, drag them. I don't care. Just get them here.

"Once we push the enemy off the wagons," he said, "we'll give two horn calls. The enemy should retreat up the road where the forest closes on it from both sides. We'll hold them there, but we won't be able to keep them occupied for long. You will have to make it quick. The converted we can handle, but the mercenary forces are experienced, better equipped, and they outnumber us. Once they engage it will be only a matter of minutes before we have to fall back to the city."

"Understood."

"And find yourself a shield." He added. "You'll be a perfect target for every archer in range."

Friss turned to address the other people assembled and Lord Diea touched me on the shoulder, motioning me to follow him out. We stepped into the drizzling rain and he grinned at me. "Let's try to get you something some armor," he said.

He led me through the winding streets and into courtyard surrounding the central keep, passing the guards with a casual wave. We turned around the wall toward the rear of the keep and I started to laugh. The rear courtyard was filled with sleeping cattle and armed guards. Lord Diea shrugged. "There have been seven separate attempts to steal cattle in the last two days. I've had to double the guard on them twice since you brought them in."

"When people get hungry, people get desperate."

"Agreed."

We threaded our way through the makeshift cattle pastures and in through a side door of the massive keep. Once inside, Lord Diea led the way through a twisting maze of hallways and corridors packed with people. We passed several rooms serving as nurseries or clinics and I stared into each, trying to count the people crammed into the safety of the keep.

His Lordship led us easily through the throng of people and down a long, winding set of stairs that spiraled deep into the bedrock below the keep. We emerged in a set of long hallways filled with storerooms. The first few dozen rooms scattered through the halls all stood open and empty. Black grime and rot clung to the inside walls, reeking with the stench of old meat. Diea caught my look and gestured as we passed. "Each of these rooms held a month's worth of dried and preserved food until we were betrayed. The same man who had preserved the food ended up destroying it." He shook his head wryly. "Did you know a Mage can preserve food better than any canning or drying process there is? It even still tastes fresh afterward."

I didn't answer.

We stopped in front of a heavy wooden door and Lord Diea produced an old worn key, using it to twist open the heavy lock. The walls of the room behind the door were lined, floor to ceiling, with half empty weapon racks. The weapons were all heavy metal and though they were clearly old, they'd been well taken care of. "Luckily, the Landsmen discovered his treachery before he got this far."

On the far side of the room was a stone arch that led to a second, wider room filled with scattered remnants of armor. Most of the wooden racks and stands were empty. "Most of the travelers carried their own weapons with them," he said. "But almost no one was prepared to need heavy armor." He took a long slow look around the room. "I'm sure we can find something, though."

We scoured the shelves, trunks, and the few piles that remained in the room. I found a thick wooden shield that fit my arm well and a half helm a size too big that fit well enough when I thickened the lining with a few nearby rags.

Lord Diea crossed the room, carrying a small mail shirt glittering with rust and missing the left sleeve. He tested the links with a knife and smiled. "My grandfather had this made for me when I was a boy," he said. "I wore it hunting once. The boar I was after turned at the last minute and tore the arm open. I didn't even know it was still down here, but the links are still strong and it should fit you."

He opened the clasps and helped me struggle into it. It sat tight around my chest and hung to mid-thigh, but I buckled my sword belt into place over the hard metal to keep it in place. It hung tight against me but let me move well after a few minutes practice. Lord Diea watched me a critical eye, walking around me as I moved. "It fits you well enough for now, and we can easily have an armorer see to it later."

I smiled and tugged on a pair of thick leather gloves with plates riveted over the knuckles to protect my hands. "I'll try to return it in good shape."

"Don't bother. Consider it a thank you gift for the cattle."

I shook my head and the helmet teetered to one side. I pulled it off to rearrange the stuffed rags. "I don't need any thanks, my lord. I was just doing my job."

"Job?"

I smiled wryly. "I'm a tavern wench, Lord Diea. I bring you the food you need and if you're a good customer, you leave a nice tip and don't grab my ass when I walk by."

He jerked like I'd slapped him, his jaw hanging limp for a second until the laughter roared out of him. I finished arranging my helmet and buckled it back into place as we walked out of the storage area. Lord Diea was still chuckling when we passed the guard post at the entrance to the keep several minutes later. When he finally paused for breath he said, "Actually, I do have a favor to ask of you."

"Is it grabbing my ass?"

He snorted, threatening to trail off into laughter again, but held in check. "No," he said, considering. "But it's something almost as intimate."

I raised an eyebrow. "I'd like to borrow your horse," he said. "She's the only one not assigned to a wagon detail and I may need to move swiftly during our raid. A horse would be an extreme asset."

My stomach twisted in my belly and I was suddenly very cold. I wasn't sure I could do it. Varya had become so much a part of me. Lord Diea nodded in understanding. "I know how you feel," he said. "I'm a horseman too. I've had to sacrifice my whole stable to this siege and I won't make you do it if you don't want to, but I am skilled in mounted combat and I promise she won't be harmed."

I drew in a deep breath and nodded. "Okay, but please be careful. She's all I have."

"I pledge my life on it."

"Do. The last Lord who mistreated her died with my sword in his chest."

He blanched and then smiled slowly. "I'll keep that in mind. Meet me on the left hand side of the courtyard in front of the north gate in two hours. You'll get your final orders then."

I turned away from him and began walking back toward the temple. I had two hours and I was going to use them. The temple was deserted, the cow standard still standing outside. I walked on silent feet to the only filled cot in the building. I pulled off my chain shirt and belt while I walked, letting them fall on my cot as I passed, also leaving behind my boots, pants and bodice, crawling into Thomas' blankets in nothing more than my shirt. I woke him softly, pulling the blankets over both of us. His tired mind focused quickly and his body responded eagerly. I stopped his mouth with mine; no questions, no words.

27.

I rose from the bed over an hour later, slipping into my shirt in the cool pre-morning air while Thomas lay still, watching me dress. I shrugged into the chainmail and buckled my sword in place as my senses spread out around me. I kissed him gently. "I have to go," I said, "but Serena will be here shortly. Try to heal her arm and eat something before you fall back asleep. We need both of you."

Thomas opened his mouth to speak, but simply nodded instead. I blew him a final kiss and walked away, meeting Serena as I left the temple. Her face held a furtive, determined look. I gave her a crooked smile. "It's okay, Serena. He's awake." I winked at her. "Join me at the north gate when you're ready."

I passed another guarded cook wagon as I moved through the deserted streets. The people of the city rotated what time of day they got their meal and the line for the breakfast shift hadn't yet started forming. I slipped past the guard, telling the cook to send food to the temple for Thomas as soon as possible. She nodded and gave me a glass of cow's milk with a nervous grin.

The courtyard was surrounded by the Lord's militia. Armed and armored men stood in rigid formation, blocking the streets from all sides. They challenged me as I approached. Friss wasn't taking any chances. I told them my name and where I was going, waiting while they sent a runner to Lord Diea directly before letting me pass.

The streets leading into the courtyard were packed with people. Armor and weapons bristled from every doorway and alley. Soldiers clumped into groups, listening to their officers give final instructions. I looked around, watching scared faces peek from behind fierce masks. I nodded to the few I recognized and those who seemed to need a friendly face and kept walking, breathing slowly to calm my nerves.

Nearly a thousand men stood in formation in the courtyard proper, each contingent of militia regulars supplemented by well-armed volunteers. Friss stood in the center of the yard, dispatching last minute orders. I nodded as I moved past, slipping to the left side of the yard to find Lord Diea.

He stood in front of a group of men, readying themselves near an old livery stable. I paused on the side to wait until he finished speaking, but he motioned me forward to stand near him. "We wait for the signal," he said as I approached. "Then we charge and attempt to secure as many wagons as we can. Don't worry about what's in them. Even an empty wagon will be useful. I've given the horse teams specific instructions about which targets to hit, but the rest of you will take any wagon you can. Pull, push or drag, just get as many as you can inside. I'm leaving command of the second wave to Raid Captain Carytas."

He pointed at me and I froze in the middle of pulling one of the thick leather gloves onto my hand. I swallowed hard and yanked the glove the rest of the way into place, desperate to hide my shock.

"You know her as the reason you got to eat today," he said. "She's engaged the enemy on multiple raids and been successful every time. Follow her lead and get those wagons in." His gaze swept his assembled men. "Get ready. Our attack begins in five minutes."

As soon as Lord Diea stopped talking, I pulled him to the side hissing in his ear, "Raid Captain?!? I don't even know what that is."

Lord Diea scowled, pushing me inside the stable and out of the view of his men. "Friss is siege commander," he hissed back at me. "He's in charge. Beneath him are four raid commanders, each of which has one or two raid captains. You're mine. I listen to Friss, you listen to me. The men listen to us both."

"But I barely know what *I'm* doing. How can I lead men into battle?"

His eyes blazed. "Figure it out. You focus on your mission first, your men second, and the siege third. Friss said you can handle it, so handle it."

I scowled and swore under my breath. "Yeah," I said. "I can handle it."

"Good." He said with a smile, leading us out of the stable. "Now, you've got five minutes. I suggest you look over your men." He waved toward a group of scared looking men huddled out of the rain in the lee of a nearby building.

I forced myself calm and strode across the muddy street toward them. They were hungry and scared, most of them probably wondering if volunteering had been a good idea. I swallowed the urge to wonder the same thing. It was too late now. I came to a stop in front of them and removed my helmet, pushing the rags in the lining back into place and meeting every eye turned my way. "You all know your orders and you all know how much we need those supplies. Wait for the signal, stay together, try to protect each other, and do what you can. The living get to eat, but the dead don't go hungry. Get ready."

Friss' main force assembled around us, nearly fifteen hundred strong. They stood in ragged lines and nervously their fingered weapons, waiting and whispering prayers. A horn call cut through the air and the north gates swung open.

The assault force poured through the gates in a single solid mass, splitting into groups on the other side of the wall to charge the mass of screaming converted that thundered toward them. Behind the converted, frantic horn calls rang in the distance as the more disciplined and dangerous mercenary camps hastened to assemble. The crash of our people slamming against the wall of the converted was loud enough to echo off the buildings in the courtyard. Friss stood in the center of the attack, just behind the front wall of men, issuing orders in a calm tone.

I watched the courtyard empty in front of me and turned to face the men behind me. "Get up and spread out. Stretch your muscles and limber up. It's going to be a few minutes before they can clear our way but I want you all ready to go when we hear the call. Break into groups of five. Two groups to a wagon."

A sharp voice snapped across the air from behind me. "You heard the Captain. Move it!"

I turned, trying to hide my confusion. Serena strode across the courtyard toward me, scowling at my men. She wore shimmering mail beneath her great coat and carried her leather bag slung across her chest. Whisper lay cradled in her arms and she'd somehow attached a slender silver blade to the end of the barrel, turning the rifle into a spear. She stopped in front of me and saluted. "Permission to join the regiment, Ma'am?"

My shoulders slumped in relief. I didn't have to face this alone. "Granted."

Serena's lip quirked into the start of a smile, but she spun on her heel and stormed toward the men, pushing them into position with her harshly barked commands and berating them for not moving fast enough. Lord Diea crossed the distance to me. "You've got an effective Sergeant."

"She's another insane volunteer," I said. "At least she has experience. It should make it harder for me to get everyone killed."

Diea nodded. "My men are in position. Friss is going to try to force their troops away from the wagons and into the bottleneck. It's their strongest defensive point and our weakest. They should break for it to recover the moment they get in trouble. It should give us just enough time to grab the wagons. Good luck."

I took his outstretched hand. "You too."

I watched him go, my palms itching with sweat inside my gloves. I fought away the panic. Almost eighty men were waiting for me to tell them what to do. I moved to the stable, taking off my cloak and slinging it over a hitching post before hefting my shield, feeling the weight on my arm. I breathed deep, hesitating for only a second before pulling myself into motion. I could only do what I could do. Everything else was a matter for fate. My senses played around me and I opened my mind, reading every presence and feeling every influence. Even the ground itself opened to let me sense it. I pulled power from the connection and fed myself through it, feeding calm and confidence into the men and women surrounding me as I felt Serena approach. I pulled my senses back in and turned to face her.

She saluted formally, her closed fist striking her chest above her heart. "Captain, sixteen squads of five men each assembled."

I rolled my eyes. "Don't salute me. You're the professional."

She winked. "Sixteen groups means eight wagons. Which ones would you like us to go after?"

I scowled at her enjoyment and strode past her to address my people. If I was going to have to do this, I may as well do a decent job. "When the assault pushes the enemy back, we move through the gates and head straight forward. There's a circle of faire wagons there, grab one and bring it back here as fast as you can. I'll personally see to it that every team that brings in a wagon gets an extra meal." The men whispered together. "Two groups per wagon, understood?"

They stood readied and nodded their assent. I strapped my helm in place and drew my sword, turning to face the gate. Twin horn calls broke the twilight morning air and I looked up, meeting Lord Diea's eyes for a second before he bellowed and lunged Varya forward, followed by his drive teams. I glanced at Serena for strength and shouted, "Move!"

I ran through the gates, fighting for balance as the heavy shield drug at my left arm. My people followed behind, racing along the smoother sections of ground toward the wagons. The air rang with screams. The bodies of the dead and wounded started only a few dozen yards from the gate. I lifted my shield and ran, stray arrows falling around us. Twice, I heard a heavy *Thunk* and felt the shuddering impact of an arrow hitting my shield.

One of my men fell and my feet slowed. I looked over, watching blood drain from his stomach. I wanted to stop but Serena ran past, grabbing my arm and pulling me forward. She spun to look at me, her face hard. "The wagons!"

I yanked my eyes away from the fallen man and ran. Some of the faster volunteers had already reached the wagons, ripping away the ground hitch and swinging the tongue toward the city. Serena barked orders over the sound of the chaos and I waded into the mass of men, pulling several away from the moving wagon and shoving them toward the next.

Another arrow hit my shield as I yelled orders, trying to keep the men organized. Two wagons were on their way to the city. I heard a man's scream cut short as a spear found him. Three wagons. One of the converted broke, screaming, through our lines, charging my people until Whisper stopped him. Four wagons moving. When the fifth wagon shifted toward the city I grabbed one of the people pulling it. "When you get this wagon inside," I shouted, "get our men back out here to collect bodies. The wounded *and* the dead. Ours and theirs, understand?" He nodded, heaving against the weight of the wagon.

The world bent. The sounds of battle faded around me and I spun, searching. A single bright spot of color blossomed behind the enemy formations. I could feel the source clearly. A

Blood Priest, a woman, beautiful and terrible, with her power exceeded only by her vanity. Serena screamed my name down the seemingly growing distance between us, and I ignored her.

I could see the twist of the Blood Priest's spell pulling in power from the world. It gained in strength and ached with the need to be released. I took a step in her direction, dropping my sword and shield to the ground, my empty hands rising. I pushed out forward, pressing against the air in front of me. My awareness raced outward, slicing into the twist and ripping it open like the snarled ties to a bag of onions. I spoke a single word and felt it echo with power through the world around me, "No."

The world burst. Silver fire erupted through the night. It slammed against the stored force of the Blood Priest's spell and burned backward through the enemy. The magic fire consumed sky, ground, and flesh alike. The enemy lines broke. Waves of silver fire cascaded away from the Blood Priest and the converted went wild, screaming in fury and terror. Some of them ran panicking into the night and others launched themselves into our ranks without regard for safety or weapons.

Serena caught me as I staggered, yelling something I couldn't make out. I shook her off, regaining my balance as the silver light began to fade. I could feel my heart pounding, the blood raging through my ears. I turned, grabbing my sword and shield and screaming for my men to keep moving.

Seven wagons creaked toward the city and I ran with Serena to help push the eighth. Friss' men surged forward, devastating the broken lines of the enemy. They slaughtered the converted, but the mercenary forces were gaining speed, charging toward the open gates. I couldn't see any of the horse teams and could only hope they'd gotten through.

Only four people remained to move the last wagon, including me and Serena. We threw ourselves against its weight. Men raced past us toward the city, our lines beginning to break under the mercenary advance. I grunted with effort and felt the wagon jolt as a dozen more bodies threw themselves against it. I looked up. Several of my people had come back through the gates, risking the battle a second time to help grab the final wagon.

The mercenary cavalry slammed into our assault lines and three frantic horn calls split the air. The remainder of our lines broke on command, men and women racing toward the city. Most of them passed us without a second look, but another dozen men under a Raid Captain's command hit the rolling wagon, leaning into the run and sending the wagon thundering across the ground, through the city gates.

Archers on the city wall threw volley after volley of arrows into the mercenary troops that came in range, culling their numbers. A small group of enraged converted ripped through our retreating men, raging into the city in front of us to slam against a readied wall of pikes. The city gates slammed shut, trapping a small group of mercenary horsemen inside with us. Their horses screamed and a dozen arrows found two of the riders before the rest surrendered.

Serena and I slumped exhausted against the wagons while dawn broke over the surrounding hills. The heavy sound of hammers echoed across the courtyard from carpenters and soldiers re-bracing the heavy gate. I looked around. The courtyard was a gathering ground for the dead and dying. My men had followed my orders, dragging bodies into the city without wasting time to check who was alive or dead. Surgeons and surgeon's aids moved among the men, treating the wounded and comforting the helpless.

I climbed to my feet and walked through the ranks of people that had followed my command. I clasped hands, gave praise, thanked many, and saw to my own wounded. Of the eighty who had followed me out, fifty three had returned with all eight wagons. Serena raised a tired eyebrow when I approached. "Why did you have the men drag in the bodies?"

I grunted. "Save the injured, strip the dead, hire the mercenaries." She nodded and rose, moving away to organize several small scavenging units.

The horse teams had fared badly on the outskirts, trying to bring in the more valued wagons. Only four of the teams had returned successful. The other teams had lost four horses, and three men. When I found Lord Diea, he was sitting on the ground in front of the stables while a surgeon cut an arrow from his shoulder. "You did well," he grunted through the pain. "Thank you."

"You're welcome." I smiled. "Maybe."

He snorted a breathy laugh and gestured toward a stable with his uninjured arm. "Your horse is being rubbed down and cared for like the others. Not a scratch."

"Thank you."

His eyes clouded for a moment. I turned to leave, letting the healer tend him. Diea's uninjured arm shot out, grabbing my hand in a surprisingly strong grip. "Cary..." His eyes burned with fever. "I saw what happened out there. I saw what you did."

Before I could respond, a young boy darted past me, sliding to his knees in front of Lord Diea. "My Lord. Siege Commander Friss requests you send your men to support the southwest gate." The boy swallowed. "They're going to hit us hard."

Diea rolled his head to look at me, his face pale. "Go!"

I spun on my heel and ran back into the courtyard. "Serena!" I yelled, spotting her as she moved through the crowd of people. "Get them up!"

The roaring crash of the siege weapons echoed from the south, punctuated by the thunderous sound of stone on stone. The boy beside Diea sputtered. "They have a ram, sir."

My people were already struggling to their feet around the wagons as I bolted toward them. I threw my cloak around my shoulders and cut the shafts from the arrows hanging in my shield. "Get your things. We're needed at the southwestern gate."

The creaking roar of the siege weapons gained in speed, and horn calls echoed from the south. Serena's smile gleamed with battle lust. We ran south while the thunder of the ram tolled through the city like a chapel bell.

28.

We hit the southwestern courtyard almost half an hour later, panting and exhausted. We entered the courtyard on the run and saw the huge gates beginning to splinter. The wood and iron doors rang with the blows of the massive ram, trembling with each crash. The defenders on the wall were too few. They looked to be nearly drowning under the weight of the attacking forces. Two light catapults stood on either side of the courtyard, motionless and empty. Their crews had rushed forward, bracing the gate with whatever spare timber they could find.

I ran without stopping to the wooden braces behind the gate and heaved my weight against the wooden beams as my men flowed in behind me. I yelled orders at the men coming in behind me and a dozen people broke away to grab more bracing timber. The rest threw their weight in with ours, wedging every timber into place as hard as we could and spelling the small catapult crews that were already there. Serena and I threw our shoulders into the last of the wooden beams together. She turned to dig her small feet deeper into the sand and glared at me. "Blast them."

"What?!?"

She made a shoving motion with one hand. "Blast them! Like you did before!"

"I don't know how!" I screamed.

I turned around. A dozen of my people leaned into supports with the other defenders. The rest threw themselves up the scaffolding on either side of the gate, pushing into the enemy on the top of the wall. I yelled at the men around me. "I need two men on each beam. The rest of you, on the Wall!"

I raced up the nearest open ladder and shoved my shield into the belly of the man on top of the wall, knocking him backward to the ground below. The bulk of the enemy was concentrated in two great ramps on either side of the gate. My people flowed around me, spreading across the wall and forming a wall of shields and swords to stem the tide.

The bulk of the enemy vanguard stood patiently out of bow range, waiting for the heavy ram to do its work and the flow of attackers up the heavy ramps slowed against the reinforcements. The men on the great ram hid behind thick boards on either side to protect them from our archers, but the disassembled wagon beds mounted above the ram smoked and burned, the smell of lantern oil thick in the air.

The closest enemy archers launched arrows casually at any open target on the wall, gutting their own people as often as ours. I threw my shield up barely in time to catch an arrow and leapt from the scaffolding, yelling for Serena. "Take half our people." I yelled over the noise as she appeared next to me. "Anyone with a bow or crossbow and spread them outward from the gate. Aim at the men coming up the ramps and the feet of the men under those boards. They can't push a ram if they can't walk. Then get a dozen people without bows and send them to me here." She saluted and ran off to the west, pulling men from the wall as she went, delivering orders to the others.

I ran east doing the same thing, spreading the orders and pulling another dozen people off the wall, running with the last of them to the gathering group. I swiveled until I saw what I was looking for and pointed. "We're going to demolish that house. Grab any tools you can find and get to work. I want it in rubble and I want four piles; one on each side of the gate between the scaffold stairs, and one near each catapult. Carry any long beams into the courtyard for use as gate supports. Work in your armor and keep your weapons near, you may need them on short notice. Now, move!"

They left at a run, jogging toward the house. I snagged a long legged boy of about fifteen and held him back from the others. "You're my new runner. Find Siege Commander Friss. Tell him I've taken command of Lord Diea's men and reinforced the southwest gate. Tell him we're holding. An assault is formed but not advancing. And if you see any more of Lord Diea's raid force bring them back with you. Got all that?"

He nodded. "Captain Cary. Southwest gate. Lord Diea's men. Enemy formed but not attacking."

"Good." I slapped him on the arm. "Go!"

The boy spun and ran toward the heart of the city. At the same moment a small hand grabbed my sleeve. I turned to see an out of breath young girl about thirteen years old with a knife on her belt. She looked up at me. "Are you the one the raiders call Captain Cary?"

I nodded. "Apparently."

The girl stood straighter. "With respect ma'am, Gate Captain Menzick would like a word." I nodded and followed the girl at a run, wincing inwardly for not finding the Gate Captain first.

We ran to a beaten guard house on the side of the courtyard. Inside, a sweat-covered man was barking orders with the same urgency I'd used earlier. The girl ran to the table without stopping. "Captain Menzick, this is Raid Captain Cary. Captain Cary, this is Gate Captain Menzick."

Menzick nodded in my direction and stripped off the heavy bracer covering his left forearm. Blood flowed slowly from a jagged tear across the back of his hand. He was an extremely fit man in his late fifties, balding and missing several teeth, but his powerful arms moved with ease and his heavy chest fit snugly into his breastplate. He grabbed at a roll of bandage, but the girl I'd followed in beat him to it. She stood silently beside him, wrapping the bandage around the wound with calm, practiced fingers.

He watched her for a moment before turning back to me. "Water?"

"Please?" I nodded. "It's going to be a long day."

Menzick filled two cups from a rough clay pitcher. "I wanted to meet the commander of the men who reinforced us. I hadn't been told of your coming."

I drank deeply to gather my thoughts. "I apologize for that, Captain. My reinforcing you was a little spur of the moment. I've got my men in two groups. My archers are on the wall with your men, they're led by my elven Sergeant and I've sent the second group to dismantle a house nearby in order to use the stonework for projectiles."

He nodded. "Most of my people went to this morning's raid and another group went to strengthen the southeast gate. How many men do you have with you?"

"Fifty-three. Maybe a few stragglers on the way."

Captain Menzick gestured with his cup. "Have you seen the enemy force?"

I nod.

"It's almost three thousand strong," he said. "They have heavy equipment, horses, reinforcements, and that damned bloody ram. With your forces we have approximately six hundred men until reinforcements arrive. Any suggestions?"

"Prayer."

Menzick's face soured. "I've been doing that for days. It's left me little more than a splintering gate and a handful of rocks to do battle with a force five times our size."

My eyes widened. "The rocks!" I slapped my cup down to the table. "Menzick, give me all the men you can spare and any tools you can find."

"Why? What are you planning?"

"If we can demolish several of the houses in the area, we can have our men start throwing the pieces over the wall. If the ground outside the gate is strewn with loose rock and nailed boards, the enemy won't be able to reach us at a full charge. They'll have to slow down to approach. It'll give our archers more time."

Menzick turned and barked at a nearby soldier. "Mailin! Tell Sergeants Orf, Secra, and Tinan to have their men gather tools and meet with Captain Cary in the courtyard. Then tell the engineers to leave the gate bracing to the reinforcements and go back to the catapults. Get them firing."

The guard snapped a salute and ran. Menzick raised his glass. "New Gods help us." I emptied my glass in agreement.

I left the guardhouse at a run and found Serena on the wall. I quickly explained my plan. She nodded toward the ram. "We've already forced them to withdraw once to change out their wounded for fresh troops and we're planning on setting it on fire again, but I think they're just trying to keep us busy and draw manpower away from a more serious attack elsewhere. If they were really desperate they'd just hit the wall with more ramps and overwhelm us, but they seem to be content to take their time."

I nodded and moved away to meet the people assembling in the courtyard. A long-legged runner came around the group, almost collapsing at my feet. "Message from Siege Commander Friss to Captain Cary: North gate under heavy assault. Enemy forming to attack southeast gate. Coordinate defense with gate captain, expect enemy to come in waves."

I looked down. "What's your name?"

"Charles, ma'am"

"Okay Charles, well done. Head to the guard house and give the report to Captain Menzick. Then come find me again."

He nodded and turned to go, stopping suddenly. "Ma'am? Another dozen men from Lord Diea's raid group are following. They should be here shortly."

"Have them report to Sergeant Serena on the wall when you see them." He spun and left, jogging to the guard house.

I met the three other sergeants in the courtyard. Each one was leading a full score of men. I explained everything, pointing out nearby houses. The trio moved off swiftly, leading their men to the houses I'd pointed out.

29.

The converted charged the wall at midday. Their mad screams rang through the air. They tripped and stumbled over the shattered rubble of four houses, but they kept coming. They fell by the dozens, but hundreds more swarmed over the shrieking bodies of their comrades to throw themselves at our lines. Behind them, the disciplined mercenary troops advanced slowly, carefully picking their way across the open ground.

Our people filled the air with every missile they could find. Arrows, bolts, sling stones, and hand thrown rocks arced into the racing lines of madness. The screeching creek of our two light catapults echoed in the courtyard, launching hundreds of pounds of jagged rock over the wall.

Power stirred through me at the first sound of the converted screams. I dropped the tools from my hand and turned, yelling orders. The destruction teams dropped their tools where they stood and ran for the wall, grabbing weapons on the way. I slung my sword belt around my hips and buckled my helmet into place, hefting my shield. Some of the men kept working on the houses under Sergeant Orf, carrying large sections of stone wall into the courtyard for the catapults.

My hand caught one of the long-legged runners by the arm and spun him around, sending him into the heart of the city with a message for Friss. After the boy bolted away I turned and hurled myself up the stairs of the scaffolding directly in front of one of the ladders.

As soon as I hit the top of the stairs, I shoved my shield into the belly of one of the converted, knocking her backward over the wall. The woman beside me fell to a knee and my sword flashed, biting deep into the converted above her. He screamed in rage and tumbled off the wall into the courtyard below.

I spared a glance at the fallen woman beside me. She was a hard-bodied woman of middle age who'd pushed wagons beside me this morning. She grunted her thanks and grabbed her spear, stabbing forward as she came to her feet, sweeping the legs from a converted as my sword came down.

We heaved the small wooden ladder away from the wall, watching the men on it fall. It wasn't far enough to do much damage, but it at least slowed them down. More ladders and wagon bed ramps approached. Some of them had make shift hooks on the top to grab the wall and I cursed myself for my stupidity. Too late, I called down to the people loading rocks in the courtyard to bring up tools and pry bars.

The strange roping veins covering the front of the wall waved and danced, catching at legs, arms, and weapons. Many of the converted were pulled from the ladders before they even reached the top of the wall. The bristling, dagger-length, thorns woven through the veins glistened wet in the noon sun and everyone who touched them instantly began screaming in pain.

Raging winds screamed around the outside of the city and lightning slammed out of the clear blue sky far to the north. The earth buckled and shuddered, groaning as it heaved open from the east. Thomas' presence rode the air, echoing with fury.

The converted wedged ramps into place and more of our people leapt atop the wall in front of them. They held back the tide while others worked with pry bars behind them. My sabre and shield wove around me with the combined force of panic and instinct. Men and women died around me, passing their last moments in time with the relentless pounding of the ram. I could feel my strength draining. We were outnumbered almost five to one and we were already exhausted.

I missed a block and the haft of an axe dented my helmet on its back swing, knocking me from the scaffolding. The world spun in my vision and I landed hard. Hands gripped my arms and pulled me away, dragging me backward into the courtyard.

Dirty hands leaned me against a post and pressed a cup of water to my lips. I drank greedily, shaking off the stun from the fall. Charles knelt near me. "Message from the Commander." He yelled over the noise of combat. "Situation dire. Heavy assault on all three gates. Send all wounded to the keep immediately. When the gates fall, sound horns and retreat to the keep walls."

I stood up with his help and shook my head the rest of the way clear. "Report to Gate Captain Menzick."

"Menzick's dead. You're in charge now."

I cursed. "Send all the runners to me. Then tell Sergeant Orf to get his people to the wall." Charles ran off.

When the runners arrived I sent them along the rear of the wall with water, giving drinks to those who could spare a moment to swallow. The injured who couldn't fight supported each other north through the city in pairs.

The battle ground slowly, largely limited to five places. The great ram hammered relentlessly at the splintering gate and four large ramps clung to the walls, anchored heavily by steel spikes. The enemy mercenaries flowed up them, meeting our defenders while the converted raged outward along the wall, searching for openings to hang their ladders. Our people stood on top of the wall, fighting for every inch of ground, dying when they grew slow, tired, or unlucky.

The mercenary troops on the wall were patient and well-trained. They fought in pairs on top of the ramps with dozens more behind them. As each front pair fell or was injured more appeared. If the troops in front tired they'd step backward, falling off the ramp to the ground below while fresh troops surged ever upward from behind.

I ran between the fights, lending a sword where I could and pulling wounded out of the way. The air outside the city was failing, the mercenary banners snapping loosely in the breeze while the raging veins on the wall grew still. I cut across the courtyard, racing toward a weak point on the wall when a young girl I didn't recognize ran to me. "Message for Captain Cary."

I turned away from the fighting and nodded at her, already fearful. "Siege Commander says be ready. City walls and gates now completely undefended by magic."

My senses flew into the air, searching for Thomas' presence. I found nothing. "Understood."

Cold fire burned in my belly and I turned toward the wall, my eyes narrowing. The enemy was everywhere, surging up the ramps while they waited for the gate to shatter. I took a step forward, wanting to throw myself over the wall to drown in their blood. My eyes swept the wall and I stopped moving.

On the ground in front of me lay the discarded body of the woman I'd first stood beside on the wall. Her side was rent open and her eyes were vacant in death. The fire within me twisted and power ran through my veins. It wasn't just me. We had all been hurt, we were all angry. My awareness slipped outward, joining the defenders, uniting them as I had the cattle. If the enemy wanted a war, we'd give them one together. Rage burned through me and I let go, giving myself to the greater whole.

Reckless emotions pounded through our combined essence: panic, rage, pain, excitement, revenge. We collected them and poured them back through each part of us, burning them like lantern fuel to keep the fires alive. A wall of opposing presences pressed against us, but we reached out, taking them one at a time. We crushed their minds with our will and drained strength and endurance from them, overwhelming them, feeding from them like fruit from a ripe orchard.

We pulled their strength into our failing muscles and their confidence into our minds. They fought both against our draining will and against our swords, but the tide had turned. No single mind could match our unity and we took them one at a time.

I stood in the center of the courtyard, a construct of controlled rage, holding the unity together. I watched the battle with two hundred and forty seven sets of eyes, fought with all of their arms, heard with their ears. Each member of my army knew the battle in its entirety, not simply from a single view point. Shields raised in defense of attacks aimed at a person's neighbor. Swords struck out blindly to slide perfectly beneath the guard of an attacker, exploiting a weakness the sword wielder didn't see but one of us in the distance had. With every passing moment more of the enemy weakened and fell; their strength passing into us.

The mercenary soldiers beneath the armor of the great ram screamed in madness and turned on each other. The tore at themselves and the heavy ram with every weapon they had. The main force of the advance slowed, sensing the change in the fight.

Time slipped past, measured in the screams of the wounded and dying until desperate horn calls reached us: first from the north, and only seconds later from the east. Both gates had been breached.

My men collapsed away from the wall and into the courtyard, streaming into the city toward the keep. Every person that passed within range of the catapults struck out once in passing, obeying my last unspoken order. The rigging and beams splintered and the last man to pass each catapult cut free the rope holding the basket down. The sudden release of tension caused each machine to shatter, spraying splinters and wood shards in all directions. I let the unity collapse and we ran, each person choosing their own path to the keep. The enemy swarmed over the wall behind us and tore the bracing away from the gate.

I paused in my run, ducking behind a building as arrows fired from the courtyard hissed down the street. Serena slipped in behind me, grinning. She ducked into the street, Whisper thundering from her shoulder. "They'll come slowly," she said, ducking back. "Looking for any traps we may have set."

"Too bad we didn't set any."

She shrugged. "It wouldn't matter anyway. We didn't have the man power to do a good job and they'll still waste the time looking."

We moved, cutting through a house and heading for the back yard. I paused in the kitchen. Serena stopped and looked back at me. "What is it?"

"Fire. If we set fire to some of these buildings it should have time to grow before they get this far."

Serena grinned. "We'll need to start several."

We struck torches to life and ran through the streets of the city, setting fire to anything we thought would burn. The enemy troops crawled along the city streets behind us, fearful of traps while the fires began to rage.

We reached the area around the keep near sundown. The mercenaries to the south hadn't chased us very far beyond a few routine patrols, choosing instead to fortify the gate areas before moving inside the city. The fires we'd started were beginning to roar behind us, lighting the evening sky as we hailed the gate from concealment. The area around the wall was open park land and archers lined the high keep wall, watching us carefully as we stepped into view. The soldiers who recognized us threw long ropes down to us over the edge of the wall.

We crawled onto the top of the keep wall, hoisted like sacks of potatoes, and surveyed the keep defenses from above. The great wall circled the keep. It was at least thirty feet high and massively thick. The main gate was the sole apparent entrance with the keep proper located in the center of the courtyard. Hundreds of cows milled below, mixed with the scattered remnants of city defenders and the innocents who had sheltered here.

Word of our arrival had already spread, and a runner waited patiently nearby. He snapped a salute. "Siege Commander Friss would like to see the both of you immediately."

We followed him around the curve of the wall, through one guardhouse and into another, southern facing one. The runner led us up a small set of stairs and into a large circular room. Inside, Friss and two Siege Captains stood around a large central table. Exhaustion dominated the features of everyone in the room. One of the Captains was covered in minor wounds he seemed largely to ignore. On the side of the room was a smaller table holding food and a wash basin. The runner turned and left.

I stumbled toward the side table, scrubbing the grime from my face in the wash basin while the Captains discussed the situation. The fighting had been bad at all three gates, but heaviest from the north. The city's side wall had also been overrun, breached while most of our forces had held the gates. Out of nearly fifteen thousand people to inhabit the city at the start of the siege, the keep now housed less than five thousand. Many of whom were infirm, elderly, or children who had been there since the beginning.

I caught Friss' eye as the room fell silent. "What happened to Thomas?"

"You can see him when we're done," he said. "We need to hear from you first. Your gate was the least manned and the last to fall. We need to understand why."

Serena swallowed a hunk of cheese and jerked her chin in my direction. "Ask Cary. She's the reason our defenses held."

Friss turned to study me. "Were you also the source of the SpellFire we saw on our raid this morning?"

"I was." I said, wiping my hands.

"You hit them pretty hard," he said. "You broke their lines with a single spell, and our information says you almost the crippled the Blood Priest you attacked."

Serena responded before I could say anything. "This was different, Friss. I've been on both sides of every kind of pitched battle you can imagine and I've never felt anything like it. Even elven high magic wouldn't do it. Her spell seemed to hit all of us at once. Suddenly, I could have told you what shape a defender was in ten ranks down from me. I knew everything that everyone else knew and could act on it like I'd noticed it myself. After a few minutes, strength began to re-grow in my muscles and no matter how hard I fought I felt stronger and more revived with every passing moment." She shook her head. "I'm a fifty year veteran of elven forces and it was the most effective combat spell I've ever experienced."

The captain stared at me, but I kept my eyes lowered and refused to look at anything except my food. Friss broke the silence, "Cary?"

I shook my head like I was being scolded. "I don't know, Friss." I raised my eyes to look at him. "I don't know what I'm doing. That SpellFire, or whatever you call it, this morning just happened. I acted on instinct and the sky erupted in flames. The unity thing Serena's talking about has only happened once before and I didn't know it could work on people. I've only done it with cattle. This power is half the reason I need to see Thomas."

He nodded and rang a small bell. A runner appeared at the top of the stairs and he gestured. "Take Captain Cary to the temple to see Master Thomas."

I stood and turned, grabbing my things. "Cary." Friss' voice stopped me short of the stairs. "Can you do it again if you have to?"

"I think so. Yes."

Friss nodded, and I turned away, following the runner.

30.

We moved quickly into the keep and down several flights of stairs into the basement area. The runner leading me moved quickly, picking up on my anxiety until skidding to a stop at a large ornate door deep below the keep. "This is the temple of Earth," the boy whispered. "Master Thomas is inside."

I dismissed him with a wave of my hand and opened the temple door. Candles burned inside, filling the room with a soft glow. Near the center of the room a very low stone altar was being tended by priests. Thomas' body lay on top of it. I started to rush forward, but one of the priests rose to block my path. My voice was a harsh whisper. "What's happened to him?"

The priest shook his head. "It is in the New Gods' hands now. There is nothing that can be done."

My slap knocked him to the floor. I stepped over his fallen body and crossed the remaining distance to look at Thomas. His shifted and rippled in my vision, twisting with the power cascading over and around him. His skin was yellow-green and slick with sweat and he moaned slowly through labored breaths. The older priest who sat at Thomas' head rose angrily. "Why have you attacked our brother?"

"He didn't answer my question," I said. "I need to know what's happening."

The older priest sighed in irritation. "His soul is being attacked directly by the combined power of twin spell casters. We do not have the power to stop it. We know only that Brother Thomas may not be strong enough to fight them both." He spread his hands. "So, now you see the young brother is correct. There is nothing to be done. We cannot fight his battles for him."

I sank to my knees beside the altar. "You may not be able to fight for him, but by the Gods, I'll fight *with* him."

I closed my eyes and took hold of Thomas' arm, reaching into him and joining him in the spell. Pain filled me instantly. My mind went numb from the agony and tears filled my eyes. I grit my teeth to keep from screaming and mustered my will against the spell, pulling it away from Thomas and into me. I could feel the twist of the two spells merging inside Thomas' essence. They danced together, fueled by anger and fear. He had held the armies and powers of three Blood Priests at bay single-handedly. Now one of them was dead and the other wounded. I stiffened my resolve ad reached past the spell, melting my awareness directly into Thomas' essence.

Power thundered through us, raging against the attacking spell. We shifted, twisting away from the pain to wrap around the attack, hammering relentlessly. Decades of studying magic merged with a well of raw power, peeling away the layers of the spell.

The Blood Priests fought back. Their powers roared forward, burning through our bodies. The rush of power burned like an enraged flame. We wound around it, capturing it in our unity and twisting it backward unto itself, welding its rage and strength into our oneness. The strands of the spell striking at us began to splinter, ripping open as we hammered spikes of fury into the spell. The spell shattered and our adversaries tore themselves away. I collapsed to the floor, pulling myself out of unity, carrying a final imprint from Thomas' mind: *Sorcerer.*

I slumped into the arms of a priest as exhaustion swept over me. The acolyte I had slapped earlier took my arms and helped me rise to my feet. He bowed his head at me and whispered softly. "I am sorry for my assumption, sister. I did not know you could help."

I stumbled and he caught me, wrapping one of my arms around his shoulders to support me as I walked toward the temple door, shaking my head slowly. "I shouldn't have slapped you. I was scared for my friend."

We walked in silence. I leaned heavily against him and he led me up the stairs to the main level of the keep. I gestured weakly toward the main doors. I was hoping the cool air would clear my head, but as we neared the entrance a strange wailing filled the air outside the keep. A sound like hundreds or thousands of wild animals all screaming at once.

I stepped away from the support of the priest and looked around in alarm, feeling a wall of rage and panic pressing against the keep. The priest stepped down from the doorway and spoke quickly to a passing guard before returning to my side. "What did he say?"

The priest's face was dark. "The Converted have gone berserk."

31.

It was still pre-dawn when I woke, but the converted had at least stopped screaming. The priest had helped me find an empty cot in a side room and agreed to carry word of Thomas' state to Friss before returning to his duties. I rose to my feet and strapped my sword into place, stumbling through the crowded hallways to find a kitchen.

The guard at the door checked a roster when I gave him my name and his eyes widened. "You're on the list for food when needed, ma'am. They don't have much ready but you can take anything you find."

"Food when needed?"

"Yes, Ma'am. As much food as you wish, as often as you wish." He swallowed. "The only people with that level of access are Lord Diea, Master Thomas, Siege Commander Friss, and you ma'am."

I snorted at his look. "You don't have to worry about me, soldier. I'm not anyone important. I'm just the one who brought the food."

The guard blanched, his mouth dropping open. "*That was you!?*"

I laughed and pushed past him, ignoring the sleepy looking faces that peered at me from the surrounding doors and passages. The cook on duty placed me at a table and muttered like a mother hen, setting a large bowl of stew in front of me. He bustled away, leaving me to eat in peace while he fetched a pitcher of fresh cow's milk.

After eating I left through the rear door of the kitchen and walked outside into the cool morning air. It was not quite dawn, but the cows were awake and moving, the milking mothers lining up to be seen by the few farmhands we had and all the children old enough to be taught how to milk.

Lord Deia's horse paddock was nearby and I walked across the open lawns until I was close enough to see Varya's sleeping form. I smiled and thanked the New Gods she was alright. From there, I walked around the keep, following the inside of the circular wall, passing dozens of active guard stations and hundreds of people sleeping near wagons and other out buildings. I found a set of stairs and climbed to the top, crossing to the outer side of the wall and surveying the enemy positions.

Camp fires and guard torches dotted the ground below me, illuminating hundreds of separate camps. Dozens of mercenary banners flapped slowly in the twilight breeze, standing just short of the double crescent standard of the queen. At the base of the wall, hundreds of bodies lay scattered and broken, shot from behind or dead by their own hands. They hadn't even tried to control the converted after they'd gone berserk. They'd just slaughtered them where they stood.

I studied the dead with a mixture of relief and sorrow. The trapped minds and souls of the people those bodies belonged to were free now, at least. Thomas and I had torn away too much of the Blood Priest's control, draining them of their power beyond the point where they could keep control. I prayed they would find peace.

I walked along the great circle of the wall and studied the enemy positions and banners. I climbed the stairs inside the northernmost guard tower, reaching the windowed room at the top. Outside, the stars began to fade and dawn threatened. A lone figure stood at one of the windows, her silver hair shimmering softly where it escaped her strange hat. She turned slightly as I entered, before silently casting her eyes outward again. I slipped softly over to stand beside her, joining her vigil at the window.

After a few minutes, Serena sighed. "Cary, we haven't had much of a chance to speak, but I need to say 'Thank you'."

"I haven't done anything."

"You have, though you may not know it. Remember yesterday morning before the raid, when you saw me walking toward the temple?"

I nodded.

"I was on my way to wake Thomas and ask him to heal my arm," she said. "Friss had left the strictest orders that no one should wake him and just as strict orders that no one would bother him for healing unless Thomas chose to do it." She turned back toward the window. "I was on my way to break those orders. I wanted to fight. I needed to fight. I would have sacrificed everything. I know you don't know what it means to be an elf but our society is based upon honor. If a rifleman loses her honor she is nothing.

"I was on my way to disobey direct orders. To exchange my life and my honor for a chance to fight, to show everyone what it means to fight with an elf." Her glowing eyes turned back toward me. "You saved me from that. Your actions stopped me from disobeying orders. Whether you meant it or not, I still have my honor because of you and I won't forget that Cary, I can't. Everything that I am from that moment forward I owe to you." She turned to kneel, holding Whisper out to me, her head bowed. "My Rifle, My Service, and My Soul are yours to command when you need them. They wavered once. I swear to you they will not do so again."

She stayed there patiently, on her knees, waiting for my response. I reached out slowly, knowing instinctively that if I made any sign of rejection she'd be crushed. I touched Whisper gently. "Serena, I... Thank you, now please get up."

A smile spread swiftly across her features as she bounded to her feet, wrapping me in a hug. I hugged her in turn, pulling her tight as we smiled. We pulled apart, still smiling. A thought struck me. "Serena, did you mean what you told Friss?"

She nodded smiling. "It was the most impressive spell for combat I've ever seen. I don't know how you did it, but it worked. I felt like I knew everything. I could see every angle. The strength returning to my limbs was a godsend." She hesitated. "And it felt like I was part of something. I know that's strange. But I felt like I was where I belonged, like I was part of something bigger than myself, more important. If an outcast elf can feel that way among Human volunteers, the thought of what you could do with a real regiment is inspiring."

I flushed in embarrassment. "No." I laughed. "I meant have you really been in the army for fifty years?"

Serena looked stunned until her harsh, barking laugh echoed into the night. "Yes. I have served my clan, my family, and my nation for almost fifty two years now. I'm a decorated soldier and veteran of dozens of conflicts."

I gaped at her, studying her face and frame. "Serena, how old are *you*?"

"Last month was my seventy first birthday. I earned the right to my rifle when I was seventeen, three years before my final coming of age."

"Seventy one?"

Serena shrugged. "We grow to adulthood a little slower than you humans. But once there we don't age. It's the magic of my people."

I smiled, shaking my head. "At least now I understand what omen freakishly long ears portend."

She laughed. "And does a crooked nose make you a spell caster? If it does, I could hit you again and increase your power."

Our laughter was cut short by the sound of running feet on the stairs. I slipped a hand to my sword hilt and Serena tightened her grip on the spear pointed Whisper as a young girl rounded the corner into the room, skittering to a stop. "Message, Ma'am."

Serena and I both nodded together. The messenger faced Serena and spoke crisply. "Siege Captain Serena, Commander Friss reminds you that your watch wanes with the dawn. You are hereby directly ordered to report before sleep." The young girl turned to face me. "Captain Cary, your presence is requested by the priest Thomas at his breakfast in the temple."

I eyed Serena. "Siege Captain?"

"Friss promoted me last night. No more sergeant's pay for me."

We both laughed and followed the young girl out, splitting up on the wall as the sun rose. Serena went to report her watch to Friss and I followed the stairs back down, returning to the temple to meet Thomas.

32.

The very walls of the temple rang with power as I approached. Thomas' deep voice rose in song, echoing through the long corridors to the temple. I slowed my pace, wanting to hear his languid voice without interrupting it. I knew the hymn, it was a morning prayer to the New Gods, but I had never heard it sung with so much passion before. In the temples of religion I was definitely a stranger.

I waited outside until the service ended and the temple emptied of people before entering. Thomas stood at the front of the temple, speaking softly with several people. His face was lit in a way I'd never seen. Faith and passion radiated from him and I watched in silence as he extended blessings to some of the people present before they left. When the temple was empty, Thomas turned again and knelt before the altar, whispering silently in prayer before rising and turning to me. The glow in his face softened as he came closer, his smile widening.

His voice was soft and warm. "I owe you my life."

"Yes, you do. It's too bad I'll never be able to collect." Thomas looked confused until I continued. "Though they may form relationships, the Priests of the New Gods are forbidden to marry."

Thomas' smile faltered, but I took pity on him before he could respond. "But for now, I'll take breakfast."

He smiled and grabbed a small cloth bundle from behind the stone altar and slung it over a shoulder. We left the temple together and Thomas led the way through the basement levels of the keep. At the end of each corridor Thomas would pause and either close a door behind us or mutter a soft spell. I tried to ask what he was doing, but he only motioned me to silence, leading me further into the deeper reaches of the keep. Finally, we reached a large closed wooden door with a pair of alert guards standing on either side. Thomas nodded to the guards and produced a key from inside his vest. We stepped inside and Thomas locked the door behind us, whispering yet another spell.

I gaped. Soft, pale blue light emanated from the walls around us, bathing the area. We stood in a large circular room with a great open circle in the center of the floor. Strange symbols were engraved around the circle, each glowing softly. Stationed around the great circle were four swinging arms, each holding a long winded rope and bucket.

Thomas smiled. "This is the Keep's deep well. It's the most secure and private room there is. The spells I left behind us will warn me if anyone tries to follow and the one on the door will stop anyone from overhearing."

I tugged at the buckle on my sword belt. "Did you have something special in mind?"

He laughed, leading the way to the far side of the room, carrying the bundle with him. "Breakfast. And I think we should have a conversation."

I laughed, pulling my hair free from its braid. "If you insist."

Thomas spread the bundle on the floor on the far side of the room. The thick heavy blanket rolled easily outward, freeing several small wrapped packages of food. I snatched hungrily at an apple and sat, pulling off my boots. I spent a few minutes watching him move, his muscles and bones almost visible through his thin skin. "Okay, what's a Sorcerer?"

He spun on his heel and I laughed. "The word echoed through your mind last night when we joined. Is that what I am?"

He eased himself onto the blanket, grabbing something to eat. "Yes. Yes, I think it is."

"I guess you were right about me after all."

"Maybe, but I don't think I would ever have guessed this."

"Is it something rare? Like some sort of Magician? I don't think I've even heard of one before."

"No, you're not a Magician. Do you remember when I told you how magic works?"

I nodded and mumbled around my mouthful of apple, "The pull."

"Exactly. A simple explanation, but accurate for most people. What I didn't tell you is that's only one kind of spell caster, the most common one. Anyone can learn to harness the pull within themselves, but technically people who work like that are Adepts or Priests, like me. There are other kinds of casters too, like Magicians. There is no real pull for them. They're able to work with magic on a pure level, the raw substance of the world. They can take one thing and turn it into another or twist the magic that runs through something and put it to a different use.

"A Magician could make stone so strong it can't be broken and have it light as a feather at the same time. Lord Diea's personal magician betrayed this city by turning the food supply into a poisonous rot."

I paused to look closely at my apple before swallowing. "How did he attack the gate? He didn't turn it into anything. There was no magic for him to twist."

"He used the torch he was holding somehow. I'm not entirely sure how, but that's my best guess."

"But if he could do that how was I able to kill him so easily?"

Thomas smirked. "I admire your definition of easy. Charging a mounted spell caster in the middle of an army sounds difficult to me."

"You know what I mean. He could have ripped me apart, how did he fall to a sword?"

"Spell casters are just people Cary. Some of them can do impressive things, but without preparation they die just as easily as anyone else. That includes you and me."

I shook my head, trying to get back on topic. "Okay, that's a Magician and you're a Priest. What does that make me? What's a Sorcerer?"

Thomas shook his head. "I don't actually know."

I stared at him, open-mouthed, until he shrugged. "I'm sorry, Cary. I really am, but there's just not much I can tell you. Sorcerers are the rarest form of magic user there is. In all the stories and histories they're only mentioned a handful of times.

"The last known Sorcerer died fifty years ago when he was murdered by his own apprentice. And, before you ask, the apprentice was hanged for the murder a week later."

I closed my mouth. "Then how in the world do you know I'm a Sorcerer? If there are none left how can you be sure?"

"Because there are stories about what a Sorcerer can do. They bring things together and tear things apart. The stories say a sorcerer could form a bunch of sticks into a solid wall of wood. Or combine the minds of people to share a single point of view. One story tells of a sorcerer who could tell the life story of a man he'd never met simply by sensing him. I don't know what sensing means, or how you sense someone you've never met, but I can see from your eyes that you do." Thomas shook his head. "Cary, last night, when you helped me fight that spell... You shouldn't have been able to do that. No one could. That kind of power doesn't exist anywhere. It was like nothing I'd ever felt. I wasn't myself anymore. I had stopped being me and I became..."

He threw up his hands, searching for a way to express, but I knew what he wanted to say. It was the same thing Serena had been trying to say. "Part of us."

"Exactly. Nothing else can do that. I don't know how it works, but now that I've experienced it, there is no doubt about what it is and I also know that you need to be careful."

My mind flashed back to Marcus and I shuddered. "My power has already struck out once when I didn't want it to. It nearly killed a man."

"That's a terrible thing, but it's not what I meant." Thomas drew in a deep breath. "I trust you, Cary. I trust you with my life and the lives of those around me, but I'm also on your side. If I found out about your abilities and you were with the enemy, I would do everything in my power to either turn you to my side, or kill you in your sleep." I blanched, but he kept talking. "That's why we're hiding in the well room with spells on every third door. The fewer people who know the better."

I smiled slyly. "Is that the only reason we're hiding behind locked doors?"

"We wouldn't need all the spell work otherwise," he said, matter of fact. "We want to keep all this quiet so we can keep you safe. Sorcerer's are so rare you could be in danger from inside the kingdom as well as outside."

"So, what do I do? Hide?"

"No, you've got to learn as much as you can. You're going to need to develop your strengths and your friendships until you can be safe. There may even be a way for you to learn from another sorcerer."

"But, you said they were all dead."

"I did. And he is, but he kept a diary. It's confusing, difficult to understand, but you might be able to make sense of it. It's in the royal magician's personal library in the capital city."

"The capital city is almost a thousand miles away. That really doesn't do us much good right now."

"No. Not now, but it might help you someday. Until then, I can help you with some of the basics. The SpellFire you channeled, for instance. The basics of spell work. Maybe by working together we can give you an idea of what you're working with."

"Okay," I sighed. "Where do we start?"

"Tell me everything you've been through so far."

I nodded, starting at the swamp and working my way forward. I told him about working with Travis, about the feeling of unity, and what it felt like when I was near other magic. "Wait," he said, stopping me. "What do you mean you see the spells take shape? You mean you felt it?"

"No. Every time I've been near someone who's casting I can see it. Both times with the Blood Priests and even with you. It's like the world bends around the power. I... What's wrong?"

His jaw hung slack, his face blank. "That's incredible," he said, shaking himself out of it. "Do you know how rare it is to actually *see* a spell being cast?"

"I thought everyone could do it." I stared at him. "You mean you can't?"

He chuckled and pulled me into a hug. "You're one of the most gifted people I've ever met, little wench. I just wish you didn't have to learn like this."

He laughed again and waved at me to keep talking. When I was done, he began to teach, going over the basics of spellwork, the pull, the formation, and the release. I didn't understand everything he said, but I was able to put a lot of things together.

Thomas took a breath. "There are dangers associated with magic," he said. "More than just those terrifying moments where you might lose all you have and all you could ever become. Magic doesn't just change the world, it changes us as well. If you live long enough and use magic too much, you'll change. It's inevitable. You won't even notice, but one day you'll stop even being human. The only way to stop it is to find something to balance you. I fought my way into air powers to balance the earth within me. I don't know what will balance a Sorcerer but you should find something."

"I'll be careful."

He started to speak again, but I interrupted. "Tell me what SpellFire is."

"SpellFire is a weapon that can only be used by one spell caster against another. It's your magic directly opposing their magic. The clash is so strong it rips open the world around it, burning away the magic of both spells. If you fight another spell caster with magic, SpellFire will result until one of you becomes exhausted or gets caught by surprise and can't control it."

"So what do I do?"

"When SpellFire erupts, it strikes backward against the source of the power, which is usually the caster. When that happens, you have to try to protect yourself, either by dodging, blocking, or absorbing it. Eventually, one of you won't be able to protect yourself enough." Thomas shook his head. "The pain is unlike anything you've ever felt. Your own magic catches fire and tries to burn its way out of your body."

Thomas made a point of meeting my eyes. "Using SpellFire against another caster is a declaration of war. It shows your intent to kill without hesitation. Once released, both people will hunt each other down until their opponent lies dead. The two casters clash on a level so deep that there's nothing you can do. Your magics will always know each other and they will hunt each other. That Blood Priest will know your magic for the rest of time as though it was her own and she will know it's you even if your body is unrecognizable. You will never be able to hide from her."

"You mean she'll always know where I am?"

"Only when you cast near her, but she will know *every time* you cast near. She'll be able to sense you miles away and you'll sense her. SpellFire feuds can be the stuff of legends. People have hunted each other for decades, while others try to avoid the fight, but no one ever forgets the pain."

I nodded, exhaling softly. "I'll be careful. At least-"

"Someone is coming," Thomas said, sitting bolt upright, "and they're moving quickly."

I growled and reached for my boots, but Thomas grabbed my wrist, spinning me into his arms. Our mouths closed against each other and I melted into him until the metal key jammed loudly into the lock. The door flung open and Thomas and I jerked apart to look at the door. The guards had admitted a young, pale faced, messenger gasping for breath. He fell to one knee inside the door. "Forgive the intrusion, but I bear an urgent message from Commander Friss. Master Thomas and Captain Cary are to report to the wall at once."

Thomas nodded and instantly began cleaning up our blanket while I slipped into my boots. Thomas rose into a jog, and I slung my sword belt around my hips jogging after his retreating form and attempting to dress as I went.

33.

I buckled my sword belt as we crossed the courtyard. The final two shoulder clips of my armor hung open. The walls were heavily manned, the portcullis raised, and a large armed force stood in front of the gate, but I heard no sounds of fighting.

Friss and Serena met us at the guard tower next to the gate. Serena had brushed the soot from her great cloak and hat. Friss had donned clean clothes and looked like he'd bathed. They both shared a forced look of calm. Friss looked us both over. "They wish to parlay."

I swapped glances with Thomas and started straightening my clothes while Serena attacked my hair with a brush. When she finished I swept my hair forward, hanging it over my shoulder to hide the rust on my armor. Serena looked me over and nodded while Friss helped Thomas change into a new doublet. Once finished, we turned and followed Friss toward the small man door located on one side of the great gate.

Serena whispered to me as we walked. "Say nothing. Answer only direct questions and volunteer nothing. If someone attacks you may defend yourself, but don't strike first. And if anyone challenges you to a duel, kill them quickly."

I gaped at her, but she had looked away. I shook off my anxiety and fell into step next to her, wondering if duels were common place or if they were strictly elven diplomacy. We reached the central guards and found Lord Diea waiting for us. He was immaculate in polished armor and oiled hair, his shoulder wound completely hidden or healed. He smiled at us like a man going for a morning hunt rather than a besieged city lord. He nodded at me, still smiling before addressing Friss. "They're still waiting patiently. They've put up a pavilion with a table as agreed."

Friss nodded and looked us each over again. "Alright, let's hear their terms."

We stepped through the man door in the gate and exited the safety of the keep to stand face to face with our enemy. A large pavilion had been raised to bathe the area in shade without blocking sight of the interaction from troops on the ground. A table had been placed in the center of the pavilion and loaded with food and drink. Three people stood behind the table, waiting calmly.

A man in thick black banded armor wore the double crescent crest on his chest and carried a wickedly curved axe. The man in the middle of the group made my blood run cold. He was tall, lanky, and stunningly beautiful. His well-manicured hand brushed imagined lint from his sleeve as we approached and my eyes narrowed. He was the Blood Priest that had crucified my village and converted its people. His eyes widened slightly when he saw me. I smiled coldly, reading the recognition on his features.

I turned to look at the third person and froze. The only woman in their party was tall and lithe, flowing honey colored hair cascaded down her back. She had blood red lips and her arms were crossed around her narrow waist, drawing attention to her ample bosom and thighs, but my eyes never left her face.

The left side of her face and neck burned crimson with angry scars. She wore a patch over her left eye while her right eye burned with the fury of recognition. I knew her instantly as well. She was the Blood Priest I had struck with SpellFire. I gripped my scabbard and bent my knees slightly, unbidden rage rising within me, readying me to strike. I could feel her power rise within her and saw her fists clench. Something blocked my vision and I stepped back, prepared to strike, my vision refocusing slowly. Thomas stood calmly in front of me, looking concerned. I felt the rage subside, my urge to kill fading with it.

I straightened and released my sword, forcing my mind to clear and nodding at Thomas. He smiled softly and turned back toward the table. This time when my eyes fell on the woman I was ready for the fury. I forced myself to breathe, holding back the rage. I could feel her restraint as she did the same. We both knew that one of us had to die. We also knew it couldn't happen now.

I turned my attention away, focusing on Friss and the Blood Priest in the middle. They had shaken hands and Friss had introduced each of us. The Blood Priest bowed to each of us in turn and introduced his comrades. "This is General Roln, Queen's commander of mercenary forces." He indicated the armored man. He gestured to the woman next. "And some of you appear to already be acquainted with my twin sister, the Lady Elsbeth. I am the Blood Priest, Lord Garren." Garren gestured toward the food and drink. "Please."

Friss glanced at Thomas who nodded briefly. The food was clean. He took a glass and sipped politely while the rest of us were served by an old man wearing little more than a loincloth. Once we all held drinks, he scuttled out of the way as quickly as he appeared and Garren raised his glass ceremonially. "To Bravery."

We each muttered a reply and slipped softly from our cups as Friss stepped forward, smiling. "General Roln. It is good to see you well. After I defeated you at the battle of Watchmen's Falls I feared for your health." The general simply sneered.

Garren laughed easily. "I see many of us are acquainted. Excellent. Adversaries should know each other as well as friends, if not better. But come, we shall be quick about this. We are here to discuss terms for your surrender. Will you hear them?"

Friss nodded. "We will."

Garren bowed again. "The Queen requires your city, not your lives. These are the terms I am commanded to offer. If you surrender within the next three days you will all be allowed to live. You may leave this city with your arms and all the food you can carry. Further, you will be given two days of travel without harassment. Should you surrender *after* the three days then your children will be allowed to leave unharmed. The officers will be killed, every third man will be blinded, and every fourth woman will be taken as payment to the mercenaries. If you force us to capture the city, there will be no leniency for anyone."

Friss looked about to reply when a commotion broke in the ranks of the men waiting behind the pavilion. I felt something familiar for a split second before a high pitched wailing scream cut through the air and everyone turned to watch. My hand slipped to the hilt of my sword as a man broke from the ranks of the mercenaries, screaming wildly as he ran toward us, one sleeve of his tunic flapping emptily. "Witch!" he screamed running forward.

My hand fell from my hilt, my eyes widening. "Marcus!" I hissed.

"Wiiiitch!" Marcus screamed again racing toward me.

Garren raised his hand and Marcus screamed in pain, tumbling to the ground and crawling the last several feet to kneel beside the Blood Priest's boot. "Witch," he whined, pointing at me.

I snarled, starting to draw my sword. Serena found my arm first. I snapped my head to the side with a glare. She shook her head slowly, her gaze riddled with meaning. I looked forward. General Roln and the two Blood Priests stood ready, waiting for violence. I dropped my hand and Garren smiled, looking at me thoughtfully. "It seems you're well acquainted with many of my people, Captain...Cary, Yes? Captain Cary."

"Witch!" Marcus screamed again, lunging forward.

Lord Diea's voice snapped. "Control that Man!"

Garren smiled, reaching a hand down toward Marcus. "Man? This is no man. He's just a pet, a stray dog I found wandering through the forest." Marcus stretched as high as his knees would allow, covering Garren's hand in kisses as the Blood Priest smiled. "But perhaps there *is* something to his madness, after all."

Friss straightened, scowling. "Thank you. We've heard the Queen's terms. We will consider them." He turned his head to the side and snapped, "Back."

We slid backward to the man door, stepping through one at a time as Garren softly muttered, "Please do."

The moment Friss stepped back behind the wall the man door was slammed shut and rebraced heavily. I walked to a stack of bracing timbers and slumped, taking several slow deep breaths. Friss spoke softly to each of the others before walking over to me. His question was a single word. "Marcus?"

"I shattered him, Friss. I thought I was in danger and my powers acted out of reflex. Then later, I finished the job when I tried to stop him and his friends from betraying us to the Blood Priests. He knows about Travis contacting the garrison at Narissa. He knows about me. He knows about the ranchers. He knows about everything." I shook my head. "I never expected him to survive his arm wound. I'm sorry, I should have finished him."

"Some people don't die easily, Cary. If you're lucky you'll be one of them. Is there enough left of his mind to tell them everything?"

I shrugged. "Maybe not about the ranch camp, but I'm sure he could tell the Blood Priest enough about me to make things difficult."

"Things are already difficult, but what's done is done. Take ten minutes to clear your head and join us in the keep tower. All of the officers will be there to discuss our options. I want you there."

I nodded at his retreating back, thinking about how bad things could get. The keep walls were strong, but our defensive force was almost half children and people who'd never held a weapon. Every time I used my abilities I would be screaming my location to the Blood Priests and probably wouldn't be long before they pieced together enough clues to discover what I was. Not that I was entirely certain what would happen if they did know.

I listened to the soft sound of cattle in the background and the noise of thousands of people milling through a small space and sighed, turning to walk into the center of the keep.

34.

The keep central tower stood in the exact center of the great circle formed by the wall. It rose nearly a hundred feet high and gave excellent visibility of the city and the countryside beyond. Seven of us stood gathered in the large circular room at the tower's top: Friss, Serena and the two other Siege Captains whose names I didn't know, Lord Diea, Thomas, and myself. A large table dominated the center of the room, the top of it painted with a map of the city and surroundings. We stood silently around the table while Friss related the given surrender terms. When he finished, silence reigned in the room until Lord Diea spoke. "Do we even know if they'll honor these terms?"

Friss shrugged. "Mercenaries get paid either way. The question is; do we have a choice?" He turned to face the woman siege captain. "Morina, how are we set for supplies?"

The woman shook her head. "Not well. We managed to save most of the supplies we had, but that still doesn't leave us with much. We have less than five hundred arrows. We have two hundred crossbow bolts, but we only have eight crossbows. We have twelve functioning wagons and eleven standing horses. The light siege weapons atop the wall are well kept and ready. Murder holes, pit traps, oil cauldrons and all other siege defenses have all been armed, but half our people are still fighting with bent swords, rusty armor, and cracked shields."

Friss nodded, turning to the second captain. "Gregor, how's the food situation?"

The scarred man smiled grimly, revealing missing teeth. "About as bad. We're down to our last hundred pounds of flour and our last ten pounds of salt. The vegetables are completely gone." He nodded in my direction, "Thanks to Captain Cary we have beef. We use approximately twelve cattle a day and we have two hundred and three cows left, with twenty three more earmarked for milking. We can stretch it a little more than we are but I'm afraid it won't matter. As of tomorrow morning, we will have absolutely nothing to *feed* two hundred and thirty cows. The milkers will go dry first, but as long as we can bring up enough water from the deep well, it will take the heard between fifteen and thirty days before the last of them die of starvation."

Friss turned again. "Serena, our people?"

The elf stood straighter and spoke without reserve. "Dire. In the entire keep, there are approximately six hundred people with actual training and we have almost a thousand able-bodied amateurs manning the walls with everything from hereditary halberds to kitchen cutlery. Sick and wounded: three hundred thirty. Dying: fifty seven. Non-combatants including children, the elderly, caretakers, courtiers, priests, and various others: Eight hundred ninety three. In total we have a few thousand people crammed into the limited space of the keep and the situation is getting bad. Twelve rapes have been reported in the past eight hours and fights are breaking out over everything from blankets to space to spread them."

"Thomas, what can we expect?"

"With this many people this close together plague and disease will spread like wildfire. I've got an ambitious platoon of young boys killing every rat they find, but it's only a matter of time. People have already begun moving into the abandoned store rooms on the lower level but even I don't know what will happen if they expose themselves to the Mage's rot for too long."

"Diea?" Friss asked.

Lord Diea cleared his throat. "Five hidden tunnels leave the main keep for various points throughout the city and another tunnel leaves the city and exits into the surrounding forest. All five in city tunnels have been accounted for as secure and stable, but my men are still checking the forest tunnel. Before dawn this morning Larson used one of the exits to infiltrate the city and we sealed it behind him. We are to open it for precisely ten minutes at midnight and again at dawn. If he hasn't been captured, he'll make it to one of the two openings."

We stood silently together, each of us pondering the situation before Friss spoke again. "We know a LampLighter was sent to Narissa to rouse the garrison to our defense. What we don't know is how long that will take or if he even made it. Larson assures me the dispatched LampLighter should have made the garrison by now, but if they're coming they won't make it for weeks. So the question is: do we surrender or do we hold?"

Gregor spoke, his deep voice rumbling. "If we surrender, we do it now. I will not wait to be butchered before hundreds of innocent people are blinded and raped."

I cleared my throat, stepping to the table as all eyes turned toward me. "Travis, the LampLighter who went for the garrison, had a way with birds. He could speak to them. If he sends help, or finds it lacking, he'll send word. If we don't hear soon, we'll know he didn't make it."

The others nodded in understanding and Friss faced me. "Cary, Serena has told us of the effectiveness of your combat spells. What can you do to help?"

I shook my head. "Not much, I'm afraid. If it comes to a fight I can help, but I don't know if there's much I can do from here. I'm still new at this. After what happened on the raid yesterday, if my power so much as blinks, that bitch Elsbeth will know and will come running straight for me."

Friss looked over the room, briefly meeting every eye. "Very well," he said, "Everyone return to your watches. Cary, you're with Thomas. We'll meet again later tonight after Larson comes through and we'll hear from him before we make our final decision."

The meeting broke solemnly, each officer moving in separate directions, lost in their own thoughts. I found myself walking next to Serena. She stood erect. Her head was held high and her eyes gleaming. "How are you not upset like the rest of us?" I asked.

She smiled wryly. "I'm an elven rifleman in troubled times, war is part of who I am. From a very young age we are raised with the knowledge that serving the cause of honor is our greatest destiny. Often smaller battles must be lost if the greater battle is to be won. It is how these things go." She shook her head. "If it helps, I would prefer the news were better."

I watched her walk away and Thomas laid a hand on my shoulder. "Don't look sad," he whispered. "Let the people see you in a good mood. It will help them face their troubles."

I forced myself to relax and put on my best tavern air; the one I usually saved for the worst nights. We walked through the keep, sometimes wading through people and children. Once, I paused at a window and looked down into the courtyard. People were packed everywhere. I'd thought the earlier crowd had assembled in response to the parlay, but now it looked like they were constantly there. I looked up. The sun had slipped behind a heavy blanket of clouds. It would rain again soon and I didn't want to think what would happen to those people once the rain started.

Thomas led me through the keep and I watched from the side while he worked in the infirmary. He tended the sick and wounded with the help of the surgeons and blessed and prayed for the dying whose wounds or illness were too severe even for magic to help.

After several hours, we wound our way back to the monk cell he was using alongside the earth temple. His face was haggard and pale and exhaustion echoed from his hollow voice. "I need a moment to rest, but if there's time I'll teach you more about magic."

I pushed him to the wall, stopping his mouth with mine. His tired body twitched with need, pulling my armor off almost faster than I had unbuckled my sword. Together we fell into his narrow bed and into each other's arms.

We lay together afterward and basked in each other's warmth. Occasionally, the rumble of thunder would reach us through the keep walls. I snuggled against his bare chest, feeling his warmth flood through me as my mind drifted. I thought of the people outside, wishing we could help until my mind moved past them, slowly circling outward from the city. I was looking for Travis, but it was no use. Every time I came close, my vision would slide off like water on glass. I sighed and slipped away, shifting back toward the city. Suddenly I saw them; a long column of men, horses and equipment, thousands strong and headed our way. Along one side of the great train of men was a milling pile of wagons and cattle. My heart rejoiced. The garrison was on its way.

The dream faded like broken clouds and I smiled wistfully, breathing Thomas' scent deeply and sighing. The dream had been so real. "Welcome back." Thomas whispered.

"Hmm?" I said sleepily, looking up at him. "I must have dozed off."

Thomas gently brushed the hair from my face. "What did you see?"

"The garrison from Narissa is on its way. Probably about two weeks out." I sighed softly again. "If only it were that easy."

"You weren't dreaming."

"Hmmm?" I said again.

"You weren't sleeping, Cary. I was. I woke when I felt your power blossom next to me. I think you were projecting. It's the same thing you did when you spoke with Serena."

I sat up. "Are you saying that was real?!?"

Thomas slid from under me and quickly scribbled a note, stepping to the door and catching a passing priest. "Take this to

Commander Friss immediately," he ordered. The priest nodded and hustled away. Thomas spun around. "Two weeks," he said fiercely. "We could hold for two weeks."

I shook my head in fear. "Thomas, No. Even if it wasn't just a dream, I can't be sure of the time. You can't send word to Friss based on little more than a hunch."

Thomas danced naked through the monk's cell. "I know you weren't just dreaming. I could feel that. And being exact as far as the distance goes isn't that important. Friss knows these things are never certain." He stepped over, lightly taking my chin in his hand and raising my eyes to his. "I trust your powers even if you don't yet and, unless you object, I'll put them to good use when I can."

I laughed and kissed his hand, releasing my hold on the blanket to let it cascade to the floor. "Is that the only thing you'll find a use for?"

35.

Thomas and I came out of his cell hours later and climbed through the bowels of the keep, finding a kitchen nearing the end of the evening meal. We waited in line for one small bowl of stew each and ate slowly, savoring each other's company until Thomas left to check on his patients.

With him gone, I wandered through the keep until I found the room where I'd slept the night before. A family of nine was crammed inside the small room, but they passed me my cloak and shield without hesitation when I assured them they could stay.

I slipped into the cloak and out of the keep, striding into the mud covered courtyard. A light rain fell from a cold gray sky and people huddled everywhere that held the vaguest promise of warmth and shelter. Children gathered beneath wagons while their parents tried to sit out of the wind. Dozens of people were pressed together in the cattle pens, huddling with the cows for warmth.

I moved past them all without comment, making my way around to the backside of the keep where the large forge fires blazed. People sat or stood around the outside of the forges, working hard to patch armor, mend shields, or sharpen swords. Many of the people working had the look of conscripted apprentices, people who'd sold their backs for warmth, shelter, and a reason not to fight.

I stepped out of the rain as my turn in line came and slid out of my armor, handing it to the smith. I explained that it needed to be resized. He grunted and nodded like he'd heard it all before, but took my measurements and ticked them off on a piece of slate he had near. "With luck," he said. "It'll be ready tomarra." I nodded and left, praying I wouldn't need it before then.

My shield also needed mending. It was splintered from impact and one arrowhead was still deeply imbedded in the wood where I hadn't been able to pull it free, but without my armor I decided it could wait.

I left the warmth of the smith's forges and cut through and around the masses of people huddled against the keep wall in the hope of cutting the biting wind. I fought my way around to the front of the keep until I finally found the only open area large enough to suit my needs. The space directly behind the front gate was open and empty. People on either side of the courtyard huddled near shelter and seemed to shy away, like they were afraid the massive gate might open.

I stretched and worked the tension from my legs and arms with a few of the warm up exercises Jason had shown me as we marched out of my village. It seemed so long ago. My joints popped and cracked. I used the sensation to help empty my mind, focusing only on my body's movements. My sword leapt into my hand and cut through the air, carving out strikes, thrusts, blocks, and counters. The world faded away as I slipped through the motions again and again.

Swords slid from their sheaths around me and people stepped forward, scared and armed. I whirled at the sensation, sword raised. A dozen people stood behind me. Their swords held awkwardly in untrained fingers. A couple of them had already started trying to imitate my moves. I let out a deep breath and nodded, turning back around and going through the movements again, slow and steady.

The numbers of scared and shaking amateurs behind and beside me grew. Each of them had been pressed into service and most of them were probably praying they wouldn't need what they were learning, but we practiced together for more than an hour before Friss joined us, adding his masterful strokes to ours.

He moved through the line, offering suggestions, correcting mistakes, and fielding questions before coming to a stop beside me, scowling as he watched. He barked at my every swing, correcting my every movement. He'd stop me mid-strike to adjust the direction my elbow was pointed, or how my feet turned. Most of the people drilling with me came and went, practicing at their own speed while Friss grilled me.

I didn't stop practicing, and Friss didn't stop scowling, until the light failed completely. My arms hung limp at my sides and I could barely slide my sword back into its scabbard. The rain and cold were getting worse, sapping away strength faster than the sword practice. Friss grunted and gestured, leading me into one of the guard towers.

We stepped inside and the heat from the fire enveloped me, assaulting my numbed senses. The three guards present rose instantly and vanished from the room at Friss' gesture. I slumped into a vacant chair and warmed myself by the fire until the smell of boiling coffee tickled my nose. "Your form still needs work," Friss said, handing me a steaming mug, "but it's good to see you've been practicing."

"Practicing makes me feel safe even if I'm not."

"Tell me about the garrison."

I sipped my coffee slowly, reveling in the warmth while I related the vision. When I finished, Friss asked, "You're certain this was real?"

"I'm not certain of anything, but Thomas is. I've done things like this in the past. I've been able to talk to Serena and see what she was seeing. This was similar to that."

Friss leaned forward. "Could you talk to anyone in the garrison like you did with Serena?"

"I...I don't think so. I know Serena, that's the only way I was able to get close enough to her. I don't know anyone in the garrison."

"Two or three weeks..."

"Friss, I know that's what I saw and I guess I trust it, but something's wrong. I know Travis well enough to know that he'd send word. If the garrison is only two weeks away then we should have heard by now. And *how* are they two weeks away? They would have practically had to leave before Travis even got to Narissa." I shook my head again. "It has me worried."

Friss barked a cold laugh. "Now you're talking like a soldier. Every bush is a trap and all good news comes too late." He shook his head. "I've been through too many campaigns and more than one siege. I'm not going to start getting anxious now. The decision to surrender will depend largely on Larson's report." He heaved a sigh. "Still, it's good to know." He eyed me, thoughtfully. "Any chance you could find Jason and Tara?"

I blinked. "I'm not sure. I can try, but I don't know if I'll be able to speak with them."

Friss nodded once, rising. "I'd consider it a favor if you did. Give me a report tonight when we hear from Larson." He turned and strode from the room, leaving me to consider my coffee.

I sat in the warmth of the fire until the guards came back in from the rain. None of them said anything to me directly. They all seemed to accept my presence without question since Friss had let me in. They served themselves coffee and moved through the front room on the way to other places, leaving me alone to think.

I leaned my chair back, propping my feet on the worn wooden table. I shrugged, though there was no one there to see it. Now was as good a time as any. I sipped at my coffee and let my mind drift. The sound of the rain and wind roiling outside lulled me into relaxation and I thought of Jason, wondering where he could be and trying to picture him. I felt my power stir, my awareness drifting away a few seconds before I fell to the floor, my world erupting in pain.

Fire exploded everywhere, burning through the stone walls of the tower, ripping into my skin. I rolled into a ball, screaming in pain. My power tore outward, pushing the fire into a wall. Laughter echoed through the air around me and I could feel Elsbeth standing nearby, waiting on the other side of the keep wall. My screams rang from pain and rage and I thrust outward, pouring my being into the SpellFire, feeling her laughter turn to screams.

I crawled across the room and pressed my hands against the stone wall while the fire danced around me. I could feel Elsbeth pressing against my will. Her power raged against mine. My body screamed in pain. My flesh burned. I gasped in a breath of screaming hot air and focused my mind, pushing away the pain to find a place of calm. I reached past the raging heat, past Elsbeth's hatred and twisted the fire around me, forcing it to obey *my* commands. Elsbeth's power swirled against mine, raging against my attempt to control it.

My world narrowed. I blocked out everything except the fire and feigned a moment of weakness, letting my shield crack. The SpellFire exploded through the crack, flooding the room around me. Elsbeth poured her being behind the force of the flames, funneling the full strength of her power and rage. My mind screamed with the effort and I let the SpellFire slide past me, reaching out to grab hold of Elsbeth's presence and dragging her into unity with mine.

Her screams echoed above the roar of the flames as the fire turned silver around me. The heat melted the great stone walls of the tower. I twisted the unity around us and slammed the SpellFire against Elsbeth's presence, funneling the raging magic through me to tear into her being. My vision blurred with flame. My world was being consumed with the roar of heat. The unity tore away and I collapsed to the ground, wrapping the torn ends of my power around me like a blanket, desperately trying to shield myself.

The flames died around me in seconds, but the glowing stone still dripped in molten rivers down the wall. I could hear people shouting and the sound of something massive beating against the sides of the tower. The door finally splintered open and guards rushed into the room. They wrapped me in a blanket and lifted me into the air, pulling me into the freezing rain. I heard Thomas' voice giving orders and felt myself lowered face first to the ground.

The blanket was ripped away, exposing my body to the cold rain. Most of my clothing was gone and the frigid water hit my skin, sending shockwaves of pain through me. Thomas' soft hands probed the still burning flesh of my back and side and I groaned in pain, whimpering through clenched teeth. He wrapped me in the cold, mud covered blanket again and lifted me into a stretcher, placing me face down to expose my burns to the rain so the freezing water could steal the heat from the wounds.

In the infirmary, Thomas squeezed ointments onto my skin while several guards held me pinned in place. I choked down a cold bitter tea and tried to force my body to stay still. My limbs trembled and shuddered. Massive spasms shook through me every few seconds and Thomas cursed my every move. After an eternity of pain, the tremors finally started to slow and the world darkened around me as I finally collapsed.

36.

I rolled in my sleep and pain seared through me. I gasped awake, coughing and gagging on the pain. My every movement sent splinters of pain running down my spine. The room tilted and spun. I felt like I was going to vomit. I grit my teeth and collapsed in a heap on my cot until the agony began to fade. I gathered the blanket around my bare shoulders and pulled in several deep breaths before trying to move again.

At the foot of the cot was another set of clothes: loose black wool pants and a heavy gray linen shirt. The smooth fabric of the linen was coated in ointment and I slipped into it slowly, letting the heavy fabric ease into place against my burned skin. A young woman in a bloody apron hustled toward my cot with a steaming mug of foul tea. I scowled at the mug, but the tremors of pain shaking through me made me reach for it.

I quaffed the mug of foul-smelling liquid before I could taste it and prayed it would work fast. Every movement of my arms pulled my skin tight over my injuries and sent lancets of pain through me. I threw my senses outward and away from my aching body, searching for Elsbeth. She was alive, but seriously injured. Her presence was barely a glimmer. I stood swaying on shaking feet and slowly buckled my sword into place. The belt leather was singed and blackened, but everything else seemed undamaged.

The nurse scowled. "Where do you think you're going?"

"Is it still raining outside? I could use some air."

"I'm afraid I can't let you leave. Master Thomas has left strict orders."

I swept the room with a gesture. Dozens of people lay crumpled on the floor near the walls. "They need the bed more than I do." I met her eyes. "And I hate hospitals."

The nurse gave a tired sigh and shrugged. "Fine. Don't do what you're told. We probably won't live long enough for it to make a difference anyway." She drew in a long breath. "You'll need a new cloak. Yours was burned from your body."

I nodded, remembering. "How bad was the fire?"

"The entire guard tower burst into silver flame. Two men were killed and six more seriously wounded, not counting yourself. It was bad. Near the end, the fire tore away from the tower to burn into the enemy camp, but no one knows how bad it hit them."

I staggered, thinking about the guards who had shared their coffee and their warmth. A wave of dizziness swept over me. The nurse reached out to take my arm. "Let's get you back in bed. SpellFire heals faster than normal wounds, but you still need more time."

I straightened and shook her off. "No, I'm fine. I just need some air." I fished around for a change of subject. "Do you know where I can get a new cloak?"

She jerked her chin toward a side door. "In a pile through there: the cloaks, clothes, and boots of all those who're never leaving this place."

I crossed the room to the door she'd pointed at, using every ounce of will to keep from staggering until I was through and the door shut behind me. As soon as the nurse was out of sight I reeled, gasping for breath. Piles of clothes lay in separated heaps around the room. They smelled of sweat and fear, but nothing seemed bloody. I didn't linger in the room. I grabbed a long gray cloak that looked like it would fit and staggered out the room's only other door.

It was still a few hours before dawn when I stepped outside. The rain had tapered to a slow drizzle and left the air cold and wet. I shrugged the cloak off my shoulders and let the cold air sink into my skin. I pulled my sword from the scabbard and closely inspected the blade in the light of the door lamps. The thick enamel on the pommel showed a few more cracks, but the blade seemed to be undamaged. I took a few practice swings, letting the weight of the heavy sabre gently stretch the muscles and joints.

My right side was ridged in burnt flesh from the top of my shoulder to my hip and much of my back was tight with scarring flesh. After several minutes of careful movement, the rain and cold had managed to leach the pain and the feeling of burning skin from my body. I resheathed my sword and walked across the courtyard to the flame ruined guard tower.

The strong stone tower still stood, but it was heat streaked and warped. Much of the stone had melted together, running like water down the outside of the tower while some of the great stones on the wall nearby had cracked from the heat. I moved along the inside of the wall, climbing the stairs to the top. The effort left me weak and hurting, but I pushed it away, moving to the outside edge of the wall to look over the enemy, standing straight despite the pain.

The trail of scorched ground stretched away from the base of the tower, burrowing deep into the nearest enemy camp. I shivered at the memory of the fight and felt someone approaching. I smiled at the feeling and turned, watching her approach.

Serena moved easily along the top of the wall, carrying Whisper casually in her small hands. Her long silver hair was trapped beneath her heavy coat and she looked tired. I smiled at her and ran my fingers through my own shortened hair, remembering the smell of it burning. Someone had cut it while I slept.

I turned back to watch the city and Serena leaned easily against the wall beside me. "You're supposed to be in bed."

I nodded. "That's what I was told."

"But you're not."

"Can't keep you fooled."

Serena snorted and shook her head. "I saw what happened, Cary. I saw your burns. SpellFire only heals with time. You need to rest."

"I can't."

"I know it's tough to rest in the middle of a fight, but you have to focus on the bigger picture."

I rounded on her. "No, Dammit! All I can think about it revenge. Every other memory is pain, rage, or shame. I-" I bit off my anger and shook my head. "Give me something else to think about. Please. Tell me what Larson found."

"I can't."

I counted out several slow breaths, forcing myself calm. "Why not?" I asked, my voice cold. "Is this like the drugged tea last night. Something for my own good?"

"I've never drugged your tea, Cary. I can't tell you because I don't know. Larson hasn't returned yet."

I stopped and stared. "He's been captured?"

Serena shrugged. "We don't know anything. If he failed to make the tunnel by midnight he has one more chance. In the pre-dawn, a short while from now. If he doesn't make that, then we seal the tunnel permanently and consider him lost."

I turned back to the city, scowling down at the enemy camp as Serena stepped closer, sliding her arm around my waist. "Hatred only makes you weak. Larson knew the risks."

I shook my head. "It's not Larson. He's one of the best there is. He'll be fine."

"Then what is it?"

I pulled free and turned away. "She snuck up on me. She took me by surprise and nearly killed me. My actions cost two men their lives and I let it happen because I was warm, out of the rain, and too lazy to check if she was nearby."

Serena moved closer. "There are easier ways to punish yourself."

"Like what?"

She slapped the palm of her hand hard against my burned back. I gasped in pain and stumbled to a knee. Serena smiled at my shocked look. "Yes, you screwed up, but you will never make that mistake again. Nothing teaches so well as the pain of surviving our mistakes and *everyone* makes mistakes. You choose what happens afterward. Does she win, or do you?" She turned and walked away.

I scowled at her retreating back while my flesh burned. The pain was almost overwhelming. I knelt where I was and let the cold rain ease into my body. After a while I stood, sweeping off my cloak as the rain picked up speed. I laid the heavy wool on the wall beside me and rested against the outer wall.

My senses ranged through the darkness around the city. I was searching for Larson even though I knew it was useless. The old man's presence hadn't made a single ripple in my awareness even when he was near.

A spark of awareness flickered in my awareness and I turned, feeling Elsebeth waken. I moved slowly around the top of the wall until I was directly opposite her presence. She was too far away to be a threat, but I stared toward her, sensing her presence and feeling it grow slowly stronger as she summoned strength. I could hear the sounds of livestock and people milling as the camps slowly woke around the city and somewhere in the distance the Blood Priest waited.

Serena's words ran through my mind and I turned away, moving down the nearest stairs and wandering through the waking courtyard. If Larson was to make it through he'd do so now. My woolen cloak absorbed most of the wet, leaving only a soft chill against my back. I settled onto a pile of unused stone, enjoying the cold as I let my mind drift. Elsbeth was too far away to do anything this time.

The world faded around me as I dozed and Jason's simple face appeared in my mind. His hair was longer but his cheeks were clean shaven. He was asleep in a large, rich bed. His left arm was bandaged heavily, bound around his chest to prevent it from moving. The scar on his side stood out starkly. There was a slow rustle of movement next to him and a woman's slender arm slid lovingly across his bare waist. Jason snuggled into the embrace, smiling in his sleep as Tara stretched toward him, placing her head on his bare chest, her flame red curls cascading across her naked shoulders.

I snapped out of the vision and flushed. *At least they're both safe.* I thought, smiling despite the rain. Friss deep voice echoed from across the courtyard. I rose and moved in that direction.

Friss met me half way, coming to meet me as soon as he saw me. "I was about to send word," he said. "Larson has returned."

I let out a slow breath. "Thank the New Gods. Is he alright?"

Friss nodded and turned to walk toward the keep. "He'll meet us in the central tower when he's ready."

I nodded and forced myself to match Friss' stride. "I found Jason."

Friss spun to face me. "And?"

I flushed softly. "He's fine. He was sleeping when I found him and one of his arms is bandaged pretty heavily, but he looks okay."

"Where was he sleeping?"

"I don't know. It was a large bed, that's all I could see."

He nodded and we fell back in step toward the keep. "Thanks Cary."

The seven of us stood waiting in the central tower for Larson to arrive. Thomas stood next to me, watching the sun rise through the eastern window and smiling hesitantly at me. I rolled my eyes and gave his forearm a quick squeeze to let him know I wasn't angry. The others milled about the room, restless, waiting to hear the news. Serena's questioning eyes found mine and I nodded, thanking her for earlier.

Friss rapped on the center table, gathering everyone's attention. "It's now day two. Larson is on his way up, but before he gets here does anyone have anything to report?"

Thomas stepped forward. "I've kept the weather cold and bleak for most of the past few weeks. It's better for us and will bog down the enemy, but I won't be able to keep it up for much longer. The longer you try to hold the weather a certain way, the harder it gets and if it starts to flood the keep, our potential problems with disease are going to triple."

I followed Thomas up to the table. "The King's messenger and her escort are both alive and well. I was able to find them this morning. Unfortunately, I couldn't get more than that. I don't know where they are."

"The guard tower that was attacked yesterday was completely gutted by the flames." Lord Diea added. "All wooden material was destroyed: doors, floors, shutters. Much of the stone fixtures are now too brittle to be of use and repairs could take days or even weeks. Until it is repaired it represents a blind spot in our defenses."

Larson's voice spoke from the door. "And it has not gone unnoticed."

The circle of Captains turned toward the door to see Larson standing at the top of the stairs. He looked exhausted, but he strode to the table with ease. "But the pillar of flame that cut through their ranks and struck one of their leaders was well noticed too."

"How badly was she hurt?" I blurted before I could stop myself.

"Bad. The rumors say she's near death, but I'm afraid the problem is bigger than her physical pain."

Friss raised an eyebrow. "What do you mean?"

"She was near the wall when she first launched her attack, hidden from us, but in full view of almost all her people. When the fight turned and the fire rebounded against her, everyone heard her screams and everyone saw her start to run. She was shamed in front of her entire army and she'll want revenge."

All eyes focused on me, but I stared straight ahead, not wanting to know the expressions on their faces. Friss broke the silence. "What else did you learn?"

"They haven't bothered to start constructing siege weapons yet. Talk around the camps is that they're just going to wait us out. They know our food supplies are low. They have plenty and are expecting more. The mercenaries are all under campaign long contracts. They're Queen's men now until the end of the war and it's going to be a long war. After they take our city, they're going to head south, not north. They have allies to the south and they plan on taking the entire southern section of the kingdom." He shook his head. "And there's not much that can stop them.

"They have several different corrals of horses and cattle, yet there are at least two separate corrals that no one is feeding. They're letting the horses and cows starve to death and no one knows why, but it's being done on the Blood Priest's orders, which no one questions.

"Since the SpellFire the woman Blood Priest has been secluded in a tent, butchering cattle. I'm not sure how or why, but the cattle are being led in and carried out afterward. She's doing all the butchering for the entire army."

"Blood Priests traditionally get their power from killing other living things." Thomas said. "They absorb their life essence and put it to work."

Larson nodded. "That may explain it. Everyone expects us to take the three day surrender deal, but they won't uphold all of it. The mercenary companies have already assigned pursuit parties to hunt the escaping refugees. We may not have many valuables to loot, but they're hoping for women and young girls."

Lord Diea spat on the floor and Larson reached slowly into his coat. "Everyone in this room has a price on their head." He said, stretching a long parchment onto the table. "The Queen has issued bounties on all officers of any resistance against her and General Roln has added a special price for your head, Friss, but the real prize winning head belongs to Captain Cary."

I blinked and looked up, confused. My name wasn't on the notice. Larson was looking directly at me, unfolding another sheet of parchment. He laid it open on the table. The notice contained a description of me, along with my name and enough of a bounty to make a rich man drool. I picked up the paper and studied it carefully, aware of the eyes watching me. "Apparently, Elsbeth has no sense of humor," I said. No one laughed.

Larson shook his head. "She wants you dead. Any surrender offer from now on will include your head as a sale term."

I let a breath out slowly into the silence, but no one seemed to notice. Friss began talking, asking Larson to detail the enemy's numbers and placement but I had stopped listening. I could only stare at the notice in front of me. It was an official notice, signed by the Queen and giving everyone in the world a reason to kill me. I read it and re-read it. The description was vague but I didn't think that would save me. I couldn't quite believe it, my head on a platter. My death as part of the surrender terms? "What about Marcus?" I blurted out, interrupting the discussion that had been taking place.

Larson looked at me confused. "Who?"

"Marcus. The crazy man with one arm that ran into the parlay."

"Oh, aye. They call him a pet. He's insane. He screams and mutters endlessly about the witch who came out of the darkness to take his arm, kill his lover, and steal his soul. Garren keeps him around to use as an amusement, but the Blood Priests got real interested in him after the parlay."

I nodded and collected the notice, folding it carefully before stowing it in my belt.

37.

Our discussion lasted until mid-morning. No one wanted to surrender, but Larson's information gave us a lot of details we didn't have before. We talked about traps and magic and decided on courses of punishment for people caught breaking the rules. Theft of food was to be considered on the same level as murder. Which, if we had to hold much longer, it would be. When the conference ended, all of the Captain's drifted from the tower. Each of us considering everything we'd heard and everything we'd decided. The reality of the situation was beginning to weigh me down.

Thomas caught up to me after the meeting and led me to a private space for another lecture on magic and spells. He talked and I pretended to listen. My thoughts kept straying toward the folded notice tucked into my belt. Someone wanted me dead and they were willing to pay a lot of money to get it. The soldiers outside had wanted me dead before, but only because I was fighting against them. There was a strange kind of comfort in that anonymity. Now, it was focused, directed. I could almost feel the rage and greed waiting behind a wall of swords and arrows. When Thomas finally started his shift in the infirmary I crawled into the cold darkness of his cell and cried myself to sleep.

I leapt awake in the frigid darkness of Thomas' cell, my sword ringing as I yanked it free. My heart pounded in my chest. My blood roared in my ears. I was alone. The cell was empty. I drew a shuddering breath into my lungs and focused. A presence flared in my awareness, hostile and hunting, circling the wall and looking for a way in; Lula. I laughed and threw my sword belt around my hips, running through the keep and tucking my wild hair down the back of my shirt.

I paused on the main staircase and stretched my senses outward again. She was in the central tower with Friss and Larson. I threw myself up the stairs, bursting into the room at the top of the tower. Friss jerked toward the banging door. His twin silver swords leaped into his hands, but I ignored him. My eyes were locked on Larson and the wet bird clinging to his arm.

I bounded across the room, beaming as I clapped Larson on the shoulder. Lula chirped in recognition and I stroked her chest, wishing I had a barrel of fish for her. "I knew he'd send word!" I said, turning to smile at Friss. "What did she say? How close are they?"

Friss' face was grim. "Yes, he sent word. The garrison is on its way here and they're close."

His voice sent shivers down my spine. "What's wrong?"

Friss turned and flattened the small note that had been tied to Lula's leg onto the table in front of me. I read it quickly, blinking uncomprehendingly at it for several long moments while my mind recoiled:

Fly!

The Garrison has turned to The Queen.

I read the message repeatedly, hoping for some sign that it wasn't true. "It's a lie," I said flatly, "a forgery."

Larson shook his head. "It's written in his hand and attached to his bird. There's no forgery here."

Raising my eyes to meet Friss' level gaze I asked, "What happens now?"

"Now we surrender."

I nodded. "If they do ask for my head," I said. "I'll give it if it saves everyone else."

"I'm not going to give them that option. I've already sent for Lord Diea. He'll show you the passage out of the city. You'll escape tonight."

I blinked at him. "I...I can't just leave. What about you, and Thomas, and Serena? We've all got a price on our heads."

"Yes," Friss agreed, "but none so large. I'm ordering Serena to go with you. She'd die before surrendering anyway. Thomas will stay to help the wounded and I'm officer in command. I'm not going anywhere."

"But I..."

"No, Cary." Friss' gaze pierced me, holding me in place. "If you don't go they will kill you. Your head will either be added to the price of surrender or Elsbeth will strike you down the instant you step in range. We all know that they're probably not going to honor the surrender terms anyway. I'm not going to sell your life for false hope.

"You also have to take Serena out of here. If she doesn't leave, then when the surrender order is given she will disassemble and destroy her rifle before burying her dagger hilt-deep into her own heart. Riflemen don't surrender. If you leave now we all get a chance to live."

I trembled with frustration, staring at the note and thinking of the bounty notice in my belt. I couldn't see any other way out. "We'll go."

"Meet Lord Diea at the rear keep doors at midnight."

I nodded and turned away. I wanted to fight, to scream and rage, but it was no use. Friss had a point. If I didn't leave I was dead. Then Serena would be dead and Thomas perhaps not long after. Staying wouldn't solve anything. It would just cause more pain. I walked through the keep, watching people mill about, cowering in fear or standing openly under the freezing drizzle in the courtyard. Even the cattle complained, lowing hollowly from their pasture near the rear of the yard.

People watched me pass, gazing at me with eyes that were hungry, shock-filled, or simply empty. I shook the rain from my head and walked to the smith to collect my armor.

The dark metal chain was almost unrecognizable. "Once I realized how good o' quality your chain was, miss," the smith said. "I did all the work maself, rather than 'aving a prentice do it."

I looked at the softly gleaming links and smiled. "It's beautiful. Thank you."

His smile broadened. "I was also able to take the extra off the bottom and use it to resize the rest so's not to lower the quality."

The dark links glowed with reflected firelight. I ran my fingers over the smooth metal links of the mail. The fit was perfect. The chain shirt hung to mid-thigh, and sat snuggly everywhere without bunching from my movements or making it difficult to breathe.

I slid my sword belt across the counter toward him. "Can I ask you to see to these as well? I'll need them before midnight."

The smith nodded. "You'll have 'em."

I thanked him again and left, carrying the heavy mail in my arms and walking into the keep to search for Thomas. I threw my senses outward and checked for Elsbeth before searching for Thomas and following his presence back to the infirmary.

He froze in mid movement when I stepped into view and his face tightened with emotion. He finished tending to the injured man in front of him and turned to speak with the nurse nearby, before walking away and beckoning me to follow. I followed him through the levels of the keep, slipping into the dark priest's cell behind him. He bolted the door behind us and muttered a spell to seal us away from prying eyes. I threw myself into his arms and we said our goodbyes with our hands and bodies. After, as we lay together exhausted, Thomas turned to me. "I have a gift for you."

I looked up into his eyes and he pointed toward a corner of the room. Sitting on the floor was my backpack. The one I had left behind so long ago when sneaking up on the Blood Priest's camp. I laughed and pressed myself against him, snuggling into his warmth. "Where have you been hiding that?"

"Friss had it. He brought it here just in case."

We held each other for as long as we dared before he rose, signaling the end of our goodbye. I sighed and followed, dressing well and tightly braiding my hair for traveling. I slipped into my armor and Thomas smiled, ogling me. "What is it?" I laughed.

Instead of answering he turned, muttering softly and running his hands over the face of the wall. The stone softened and ran, smoothing out and growing as shining and reflective as the finest mirror. My eyes widened at the display of power and then locked on the image within. The dark gleaming metal of my chain shirt hugged the curves of my body, accentuating my hips and bust. I snorted and turned away, shaking my head and kneeling next to my pack. I took a thorough inventory before re-packing everything. Thomas' voice interrupted me. "I'm sorry, Cary."

I looked up. His face was full of pain. "I feel like we've dragged you into this," he said. "Our little tavern wench become Sorcerer."

I rose and kissed him gently. "You didn't drag me into anything. The army of the Blood Priest ended my old life and fate made me a Sorcerer. You, Friss and the others gave me everything else. I'm alive because of you and because of you I have a fighting chance to *stay* alive. Don't feel sorry for me. I'm not a victim in this. I started out that way, like all those people hiding in the keep. Since then I could've walked away any number of times and I haven't. I'm not a Landsmen. I'm not in the army or conscripted to service and no obligation holds me anywhere. I'm here because I chose to be."

Thomas opened his mouth to speak, but stopped before saying anything. He closed his eyes, heaving a sigh. "Okay, Cary," he said. "Do you need anything?"

"Do you have any more of that burn lotion?"

He turned and unsealed the door. "I'll go get some."

I finished re-packing my bag and left it in Thomas' cell as I made my way toward the kitchens. I sat at a table, eating several heaping plates of steaming meat covered in soupy gravy. Word must have made it to the kitchens that food conservation wasn't an issue anymore.

Thomas met me half way through my third helping and sat next to me, waiting for his food to cool. "I added some medical supplies to your pack: herbs, bandages, and a wound poultice. Plus a small jar of burn cream."

I gave him a weak smile around a mouthful of food and went back to eating. We finished the meal in silence. Anything we needed to say had already been said. We left the kitchen and slipped around the huddled masses of people sleeping in the keep's crowded hallways. The wind cut through the courtyard but the freezing drizzle had stopped for now. I collected my knife and sword from the smith. Their edges gleamed with reflected firelight. I buckled my sword belt around my hips and tossed the smith several coins for his work, hoping he'd live long enough to spend them.

We turned away and walked through the courtyard toward the rear of the keep. I gripped Thomas hand tightly. "What about Varya? I can't leave her behind."

"You won't have to," he said. "The tunnel you're taking is large enough to lead horses through. The farrier is tending to Varya now and Serena picked out a horse of her own."

Varya stood on three legs behind the farrier's wagon while the tradesman tended the fourth leg. She was clean and well-brushed and I ran to her side, gently wrapping my arms about her neck and kissing her softly. She nickered in response and leaned into me. My saddle, bags, and all of the supplies I'd brought to the city lay nearby.

Lord Diea stood alongside the other horse, holding it steady. He smiled. "This is everything you brought with you, save for the crossbows. I'm afraid they have been put to use."

I gathered my saddle and bags to one side, adding a long coil of rope, a bottle of brandy and some other odds and ends. I motioned to the rest. "Let Serena take anything she wants and give whatever's left to someone who needs it." I stooped and gathered Travis' tent and lantern, delivering them to Larson on my way back through the keep.

Thomas and I held each other in silence for the last hour before I had to leave, sharing the warmth of his body and his cell, listening to the late night chants echo from the temple of Earth near us.

When it was time, I rose slowly and re-inventoried everything in my pack before slinging it across my shoulders with ease. Thomas kissed me once, pulling me tightly into his arms before leading the way through the keep to where Lord Diea was waiting. I nodded to Serena and Friss and checked over Varya, making certain everything was properly secured and well packed. I added my pack to her bundle and spread the weight evenly across her back, covering everything with an oil tarp. I finished and turned to, checking Serena's horse the same way I had mine. The elf smiled and stepped to Varya's side, rechecking my work as well.

Lord Diea led us around the back of the cattle corral and over near the vacant hog pens. The long heavy poles of several of the pens had been pulled from the ground and a pair of open trap doors led onto a wide, down-sloping, ramp. Diea turned to face us. "The tunnel slopes downward for several dozen paces before it opens into a natural cave system. We'll close and reseal the tunnel behind you to make it harder to trace you. Always keep a wall on your right and you'll make it to the exit. It empties into the forest a few miles west of the city.

"Parts of the tunnel are extremely cramped, so you may have to unpack the horses before you squeeze them through, but if you take it slow you'll make it. I've added a large bag of food to each saddle. It's all jerked and salted beef, but it's at least food. We don't have any feed for the horses and they haven't been eating well, so you'll have to let them graze as soon as you can."

Friss held out two large black cloths. "Blindfold your horses and keep your voices low. The sound will echo through the caverns for miles. Thomas is bringing a storm in to cover the sound of hooves on stone, but you can't be too careful. Once you're out, head north. Serena has a map and small oil lamp in her saddle bags."

I nodded and stepped aside, pulling Thomas close a final time while Serena said her goodbyes. He kissed me softly, squeezing me tight. "Keep your powers bottled up if you can. Don't use them at all until you're well out of range of Elsbeth."

I nodded and turned away, saying my goodbye to the others while Serena blindfolded the horses. I let out a long slow breath and took Varya's lead rope in hand, moving to the edge of the tunnel. Serena met my glance and nodded, slipping her horse in behind mine as I led the way down the ramp. As soon as we were clear, the twin trapdoors boomed shut behind us, locking us into darkness.

End Book 1.

A Note from the Author

Thank you all for reading <u>Fortune's Hand,</u> Book 1 of the Sorcerer's Diary series. Now that you've finished, I would like to invite you all to leave feedback for this book. You can leave it at any of the places you bought and if you didn't purchase it and are either borrowing it from a library or stole it from a friend/stranger, then I'd like to invite you to leave feedback on my personal author's website at: <u>tyviner.wordpress.com</u>. I love hearing from readers. I want to hear from you whether you loved it or hated it. Feedback helps me improve as an author and helps other people find my book. So, please, if you have the time, let me know what you thought.

I know a lot of authors that like to describe their books as a work of art or an exercise in creative energies. Maybe they've been doing this longer than I have. Maybe they're better at it. Or maybe they are just better at expressing some things than I am. For me, this book has been a hodgepodge of: love, anxiety, panic, stress, and way more procrastination than I'd care to admit. When I first started this story, it was a throw away project to keep me from being bored at work. It kept my stress levels down and kept me from falling asleep all at the same time. That grew into an incredible desire to keep writing. I had to know what happened next. I had to keep reading. I needed to finish the story and the only way to do that was to finish writing the story.

There are, at least, a couple more books coming out after this one; books that won't let me rest until I finish them and deliver them to everyone else. After that, I don't know. I've got the bug now. I enjoy this. I truly hope that you've enjoyed this book and I hope you'll enjoy the others, but I'll keep writing them regardless. I'll write until I no longer have to know how the story ends.

Which means I'll probably never stop.

Acknowledgements

I would like to take this opportunity to say thank you to a few people who helped make this story everything that it has become and everything that it is evolving into. First on the list of people to thank, and apologize to, are my beta readers: Echo Viner, Orrin Viner, Maureen Cahill, and Shanna Avery. My god guys... How the heck did you put up with it? Those first few drafts were so bad, but somehow you all managed to force yourself through it and you all even gave honest criticism in the end. Thank you. Seriously. And I'm sorry.

I need to say thank you to my, Copy editor and friend Helen Gerth: She gave me the 'friends and family' discount and a much needed course on grammar and punctuation.

To my beloved wife, Corinne: Thank you for withholding your opinion and for knowing when to push and when to back off. Perhaps now that the book is published, you'll actually tell me what you think of it?

Finally, I need to say thank you to my Line editor and best friend, Stephanie Siler: You stuck with me when you probably shouldn't have and kept me sane when I was fairly sure it was impossible. You were always the first to read and the first to comment and it means more to me than I can truly say. Thanks, Stephi. You're the best.